SEAL TEAM SIX: HUNT THE DRAGON

ALSO BY DON MANN AND RALPH PEZZULLO

SEAL Team Six: Hunt the Wolf

SEAL Team Six: Hunt the Scorpion

SEAL Team Six: Hunt the Falcon

SEAL Team Six: Hunt the Jackal

SEAL Team Six: Hunt the Fox

Inside SEAL Team Six: My Life and Missions with America's Elite Warriors

SEAL
TEAM SIX

HUNT THE DRAGON

DON MANN
AND
RALPH PEZZULLO

MULHOLLAND
BOOKS
HODDER

First published in Great Britain in 2016 by Mulholland Books
An imprint of Hodder & Stoughton
An Hachette UK company

First published in paperback in 2017

1

A CIP catalogue record for this title is available from the British Library

Paperback ISBN 978 1 473 60319 6
eBook ISBN 978 1 473 60317 2

Printed and bound by Clays Ltd, St. Ives plc

Hodder & Stoughton policy is to use papers that are natural,
renewable and recyclable products and made from wood grown in sustainable
forests. The logging and manufacturing processes are expected to conform
to the environmental regulations of the country of origin.

Hodder & Stoughton
Carmelite House
50 Victoria Embankment
London EC4Y 0DZ

www.hodder.co.uk

"The world needs anger. The world often continues to allow evil because it isn't angry enough."

— Father Bede Jarrett

In tribute, honor, and with great respect to those who serve and have served our country. Let us never forget the sacrifices they make in securing our freedom.

SEAL TEAM SIX: HUNT THE DRAGON

CHAPTER ONE

Perfection is a road, not a destination.
—Burk Hudson

IT WAS supposed to be a quick snatch-and-grab. Raid the old farmhouse ten klicks east of the Donetsk airport, take Igor Fradkov, leader of the Russian rebels, and turn him over to Ukrainian authorities. According to Jim Anders of CIA's Special Activities Branch, Fradkov's real name was Sergei Sokolov and he was deputy director of Zaslon—a special operation (Spetsnaz) unit of Directorate S of Russia's foreign intelligence service, SVR. Anders claimed the Russians were currently more active in opposing and infiltrating the West than they were during the Cold War.

That seemed obvious to Crocker, leader of Black Cell—a special deep-cover unit attached to SEAL Team Six/DEVGRU. The Russians under President Putin had already bitten a chunk out of independent Ukraine, seizing Crimea after the ouster of Ukrainian president Viktor Yanukovych. Several months ago pro-Russian "insurgents" shot down a Malaysia Airlines Boeing 777-200ER, killing all 283 passengers and fifteen crew members, using a Russian-built Buk missile system. Now they were launching attacks on cities in eastern Ukraine.

Recent developments had brought him here, kneeling on the ground behind a clump of bushes, the half-moon glowing beyond his right shoulder, clutching the stock of his specially modified AK-47. His goal: impeccable execution, which had become more difficult due to the number of vehicles parked outside—four, to be exact, two UAZ-452 jeeps, a newer GAZ Tigr, and a UAZ Hunter (a Russian-made version of a Land Rover) that supposedly belonged to Fradkov. Anders had told them to expect two, max.

They were told this would be a weekend getaway with Fradkov and his exotic-dancer girlfriend. He might have a personal bodyguard with him. But this was something else. What it was wasn't clear right now.

All Crocker had observed so far were the four stationary vehicles and a lone armed guard wearing blue camouflage—which made him look like a cartoon character—sitting beside by the front door drinking from a bottle of vodka. So security sucked, which ruled out the likelihood of an important operational meeting.

What's going on?

Crocker in his many deployments in the past ten years had asked that question many times. Realities on the ground were often different than those described in intelligence briefs. Part of what made him successful was his ability to take unexpected contingencies in stride. Simple might be better, but it wasn't the norm in his line of work.

His right-hand man Mancini (alias Big Wolf) had deployed behind a stone well fifty feet left and close to the gravel path that formed an S leading to the farmhouse. The third member of the four-man team, Akil (Romeo), was out of view, having just slipped around the right corner of the rectangular structure. Suarez (Padre) hid behind a tree on the rear right, covering Akil with his AK.

They hadn't brought microphones and surveillance equipment, which weren't the usual tools of their trade anyway. They left those tasks to the Activity—the surveillance arm of U.S. Special Operations also known as the Intelligence Support Activity. They were tip-of-the-spear surveillance operatives who had helped track down drug kingpin Pablo Escobar in Colombia in 1993 and locate Bin Laden in Abbottabad, Pakistan. The Activity guys weren't going to help them this time.

Through his head mike Crocker asked, "Romeo, you read me?"

"Deadwood, loud and clear. Over."

"What have you got in terms of visuals?"

"A half-naked chick dancing on a table. Out of her mind on coke and vodka, probably."

Interesting, and typical Akil, distracted by a pretty girl. Correction: any female between the ages of seventeen and eighty. Interesting for another reason, too. It confirmed that this wasn't an operational meeting. It appeared that Fradkov, their target, was "entertaining," if he was there at all.

"Romeo, Fradkov, our target. Have you located him? Over."

"Negative."

Is he even inside?

Some guys liked to spend their downtime with their feet up, drinking a beer and watching a football game on TV. Others preferred naked girls and orgies.

"Padre, Deadwood. You read me? What do you see?"

"Roger what Romeo said. Over."

"Our target has close-cropped salt-and-pepper hair. Burly. Five-foot-ten. Deep-set blue eyes. Stop staring at her tits, and focus. Is he in the house or not?"

They had been told to expect Fradkov and his Ukrainian girlfriend—a tall ash-blonde named Katrina, like the hurricane. Maybe she was the one dancing on the table.

Something always went whack on every op. Crocker secretly liked it that way—the chaos, the rush of the unexpected challenge. The only easy day was yesterday. Haha, boom. Bring it on! Plans always changed the second the first round was fired.

Like a coiled snake ready to spring, he waited. Checked his watch. Five-point-five MOTs (minutes on target). Their PLO (patrol leader's order) had allotted ten.

In his head he was trying to figure out how to create a diversion, snatch Fradkov, if he was there, without engaging the other soldiers and women inside, and get back to their vehicles, a 2002 Chinese-made ZAZ Forza sedan, and two Royal Enfield Bullet Electra motorcycles parked on the main road, three hundred feet past the ridge at Crocker's back.

Only this morning the Russian "rebels" had attacked the airport and seized the eastern suburbs. Putin's PR people put out a press release that described them as Ukrainian separatists, which was complete BS. These guys were Zaslon operatives dressed in hunting gear, armed with tanks, surface-to-air missiles, and automatic weapons. Cheeky bastards were now celebrating in the house.

The opening chords of "Start Me Up" ripped across the landscape and hit his ears. It was one of Crocker's favorite tunes.

"Deadwood, Wolf. Sounds like someone invited the Stones."

"Very funny. Has anyone established visuals on Fradkov?"

He and his estranged wife, Holly, had danced to it at their wedding. He pictured her for a second throwing her head back, her eyes filled with joy and even ecstasy. What was she doing now? He couldn't be distracted into thinking of Holly but couldn't help scratching that itch. All the mental discipline he had acquired frayed when it came to her.

She'd left two months ago and was living with a female friend in DC, Lana was her name—an athletic blonde beauty who had sworn off men after a series of bad relationships. What her sexual ambivalence meant in terms of Holly, he didn't know. Tried not to speculate.

Some wise guy on Team 2 had made a remark shortly after the Leap Frogs—the Navy SEAL jump team—landed before the Ravens' season opener about Holly turning lesbian. Crocker kept his cool until he left the stadium and followed the big dude into the parking lot. Pulled him out of his pickup and kicked his ass in front of fans with cell phones. Bad move.

He was called on the carpet. Agreed to pay medical expenses, damage to the vehicle, attend anger management sessions with the team shrink, and make a personal apology.

His CO, Captain Sutter, remarked, "I know you've got some issues with your personal life, but you've got to stay in control."

"Yes, sir."

Less than a year ago he'd broken into the apartment of a young woman who had been taking money from his father, and in the process assaulted a Fairfax County policeman who he'd caught smoking meth with her. Charges were still pending. He tended to take matters into his own hands, single-minded as he was, driven by a wild primitive energy. At least he knew that about himself.

Now he was here, peering through his NVGs, growing restless. The house and landscape all appeared in eerie shades of green. Light spilled out of the window, white. Everything like a weird, still dream, except for the young woman's surprised scream ripping through the night air like a knife.

He heard his alias through the earbuds. "Deadwood?"

"Yo. Why's the girl screaming? Pain or pleasure?"

"Unclear. Romeo's at one o'clock."

"See him. Thanks. Over."

They'd gone in zero footprint. Canadian tourists from Toronto on a fly-fishing expedition to the Lyutyanka River. Nothing to identify them as Americans, including the gear they carried.

Akil arrived by his side and knelt there, followed by Suarez, the former smiling, wearing a black hoodie over his head, his hand holding a Glock, finger above the trigger guard, barrel down. Tall, square-jawed, muscular. Not what you'd expect when you imagined an Egyptian American. This one was into judo, Metallica, Mexican food, and off-road vehicles. Weekends he liked to take his tricked-out 2002 Toyota 4Runner and jostle his insides over Virginia trails with names like Rocky Run and Dictum Ridge.

"What'd you see?" Crocker asked him.

"Lots of female flesh and bottles of vodka. Man, those Russians know how to party."

"Forget the party. You see Fradkov?"

"Rear left bedroom, getting his knob polished."

"You sure about that?"

"Which part?"

"Fradkov. Our target. Burly dude, five ten—"

"I know what he looks like. He's in the back bedroom with some brunette."

"Brunette? Not a blonde?"

"What the fuck does that matter?"

"The bedroom have a window?" Crocker asked.

"Yeah, two. One facing back, one looks right."

Crocker nodded. "All right, here's what we're going to do." He looked up at Suarez, the breacher on the team, and asked, "You got something to light up their rides?"

"Brought an RPG-7. It's hidden in the trees beside Mancini. Got a couple strips of C 4, too."

"The RPG should do the trick."

Suarez made a very quick sign of the cross with his right hand, kissed his fingers, and looked up as though checking with God.

Crocker continued, "Akil and I are going to circle around back. When I give the signal, you're going to launch the seven at the vehicles."

Then into his mike, "Manny, wipe the boogers out of your eyes, because you're gonna cover the front. Make sure the guard goes down."

Crocker heard Mancini's response through his earbuds. "Boogers in my eyes? Is that the best you can do? I got him."

"Soon as you take him out, I want you to run up to the road, start the Forza, and get ready to bug out."

"Roger that."

"Suarez, you cover the front. Engage the enemy if you have to and pull back. We'll meet you on the road."

"God is good."

"We need to move fast. We all clear about that?" Crocker asked.

A chorus came back. "All clear, boss. Pedal to the metal, yeah."

Crocker slapped Akil on the shoulder and pointed. He ran

in a crouch, AK chambered and ready, his teammate following. Skirted some bushy pine-type trees, and picked up the sound of women laughing that sent a jagged chill up his spine. Reminded him of nights alone with Holly, having fun. Silly tickle games, messing around under the covers naked like a couple of kids.

His right foot hit a branch, causing it to snap. The laughing from inside stopped. He wanted to scold himself but couldn't afford another distraction. *Dumbass!*

He needed to focus. *Spirit lives in the doing and the perfection of the task.*

He and Akil froze behind some trees. Somebody inside poked his big head out. Crocker noted long ears and freckles. The man muttered something in Russian and two female hands reached out and covered his eyes. He grunted and pulled his head back, laughing.

More fun and games. The SEALs continued. Behind the house they saw a broken patio with a warped Ping-Pong table, lounge chairs with missing plastic lattice, and a large birdcage—unoccupied.

To the right of the rear window stood a weathered blue door, which Akil had failed to mention. Crocker hugged the back wall and tried the knob. Locked. He removed the laminated card he kept in his pocket and slid the long end into the doorframe just above the bolt, then firmly pulled the card toward him while turning the handle. It opened.

Sweet.

Turning to Akil, he signaled with his hands: Move the table under the window, get on it, stand ready to crash through.

Then he whispered into his head mike. "Go! Go now!"

Crocker waited several seconds for the distinctive whoosh of the 93mm PG-7VL rocket, and pushed in moments before its impact. KA-BLAM!!!

The farmhouse jumped, shook, and settled. Dust, debris, and pieces of the vehicles flew everywhere. Screams resounded from the front rooms. He heard feet scurrying, shots, all in a flash. He was already in the bedroom. Through the dust quickly IDed Fradkov on the bed by his gray hair and eyes, pulled the woman off him, tossed her aside like a toy, jumped on his bare chest, put him in a headlock, and pulled so tight the Russian couldn't speak.

The girl backed up against the wall and covered her mouth. Naked except for a pair of heels; her little breasts shaking. Akil crashed through the window and pushed her into the corner, Glock to her forehead, left hand over her mouth. Quickly slapped some tape over it. Tie-tied her wrists behind her back and pushed her to her knees.

Bursts of automatic gunfire and strains of "Torn and Frayed" accompanied Crocker out the door with Fradkov, holding him with his left arm, dragging the Russian, semiaware his captive wasn't wearing pants and had a funny black belt around his belly. AK ready, heart pounding, Crocker was so charged with adrenaline he pulled Fradkov up the embankment like a rag doll. He lived for moments of pure excitement like this, better than anything, with the possible exception of sex.

Heard an urgent voice through his earbuds, "Deadwood, contact. Enemy right!"

Soon as he hit the ground and turned, he heard a burp of automatic fire. Rounds tore up the branches and dirt around him. One ripped into Fradkov's right thigh four inches above the knee. Blood splattered. Crocker's hand muffled the Russian's scream.

Simultaneously, dirt in his mouth, he fired back, trying to locate the target through the dense brush.

More rounds came zinging past, burning through the night air, then a muffled burst from a distance, and a groan.

"Got him, Deadwood. Over!" Mancini's voice through the headset.

Manny was solid. He'd depended on him all these years in scrapes all over the globe, like his right arm and leg.

Crocker pulled Fradkov to his feet. His eyes had become slits of fear, self-loathing, and pain. The Russian had pissed himself. Blood and urine ran down his leg to his foot. No time to attend to the wound now.

"You'll live."

He hoisted him into a fireman's carry, up the embankment that grew even steeper over loose and loamy ground, through shrubs and ground cover, sweating profusely, breathing hard. The firing below let up, replaced by the sound of crackling flames and a woman calling out in Russian. The heavy smell of burning rubber, metal, and gasoline filled his nostrils.

One last burst of energy and he emerged from the trees to the road with Fradkov on his back. His heart thumped fast. Looked left, then right. Familiar-shaped bodies approached out of the shadows. He flashed his Maglite twice, then heard something hit the ground near his feet.

He looked down and saw the black polyester belt Fradkov had been wearing around his stomach. Bent down and retrieved it with the Russian still on his back.

"Boss, you okay?" Suarez asked.

"Fine. Get him in the car."

"Fucker is covered with piss and shit."

"Doesn't matter."

Mancini leaned into the wheel, driving at full speed, head-lights out. Suarez in the passenger seat looked back to see if they were being followed. Akil on one of the 345cc four-stroke Bullet Electras zoomed up behind them, on their right rear bumper.

On the backseat Crocker brightened at the growl of the single-cylinder engine as he set the Russian's injured leg. Reminded him of his own bikes over the years and the feeling of freedom, wind in your face, tearing down country roads.

He watched the rise and fall of Fradkov's chest and on his thigh saw a splotch of dark red reflected in the moonlight. Reaching for his med bag on the floor, he opened it with his right hand and ripped the plastic off a blowout patch with his teeth.

"Romeo, anyone following?" he asked into his head mike.

"Nothing but road, Deadwood. All fucking clear."

"Watch your language."

"Fuck, fuck, fuck."

He smiled, fixed the patch over the wound to Fradkov's thigh, and saw the sneaky look in the Russian's eyes. He was reaching for the belt, which Crocker had tossed on the floor.

"Mine," the Russian groaned.

"Not anymore." Crocker snatched it away from him and un-zipped one of the pockets, which was stuffed with money. Brand spanking new hundred-dollar bills.

"Give me!" the Russian grunted.

Crocker pushed his hand away. "Keep quiet."

CHAPTER TWO

It is not easy to find happiness in ourselves, and it is not possible to find it elsewhere.

—Agnes Repplier

IT WAS already 1013 and Crocker was running late, which he didn't like. But the DC Beltway was jammed and the 395 not much better, and he was in a lousy mood despite the fact that "Tumbling Dice" by the Stones was pouring out of the stereo.

For the past several days he hadn't been able to stop thinking about next week's pretrial hearing on the breaking-and-entering and aggravated-assault charges that had been filed against him in Fairfax County, Virginia. Like the court was tossing the ivories with his fate.

Epic BS.

He assumed the meeting he was now rushing to concerned that. News of it had been texted to him last night by an aide at ST-6 headquarters. Simply: "Presence required. 1711 17th Street. 1030hrs." Since returning from the Ukraine, he'd been feeling anxious, trying to settle into his new apartment and get his life together.

It didn't help his current state of mind that his wife had left him after his previous very difficult deployment to Syria and Turkey.

The sky hung milky gray over the glass-and-steel towers along the K Street corridor—very un-April-like for DC. Crazy city had been built over a swamp—actually "wetland with trees," according to a recent article in the *Washington Post*.

As he turned up 17th Street, he told himself that there was no way he would serve time in jail if convicted and he would appeal if he received something even as light as a three-month sentence. In his head he was already planning his escape to Patagonia or New Zealand—two raw, sparsely populated locales where he imagined an individual could still carve out his own destiny without interference from corrupt cops and narrow-minded public officials.

Not that he really wanted to. He loved the United States and what it stood for.

Crocker gripped the steering wheel so hard the muscles in his back and neck tensed. He was getting himself worked up, just like ST-6 psychiatrist Dr. Petrovian had warned him not to do. According to the doc, repeated trauma had produced symptoms of PTSD, including erosion of his faith in God, justice, and predictability. His psyche needed time to process and integrate some of the shocking shit he'd experienced. Some of it haunted him day and night—the human degradation and destruction in Syria, the surprise attack on his teammates, the Dear John letter from Holly when he returned home.

The only people he trusted these days were his Black Cell teammates, who had suffered through some of the same shit he had, minus the rejection from his spouse. But they weren't here now and couldn't help him with this—a personal, judicial matter. An unjust stupidity.

Pigeons looped in front of the windshield as he spotted the address on a brick office building on his left and turned his pickup into the entrance to the underground parking lot. Screeched to a stop at the barrier, maybe a little too abruptly, so that a second later an armed African American man emerged from the booth looking alarmed.

"ID, sir?" the guard barked.

Crocker lowered the stereo and understood why the big dude in the blue blazer might be concerned. Based on his appearance— the beat-up fifteen-year-old pickup, his head-to-toe casual black attire (jeans, tee, pullover, boots), and unshaved face—he could easily be mistaken for some angry wacko with a beef against the federal government. DC was full of them—anti–gay marriage protestors on Capitol Hill, antiabortion advocates across from the White House, free speech activists in front of the Supreme Court, angry veterans demanding better and more timely medical attention.

He showed the guy his Virginia license, and the guard frowned.

"Sir, this is a federal building. Do you have an appointment?" he asked, placing his right hand on the holstered pistol at his side.

"Yeah, but I don't know who with. Maybe an attorney."

"Which agency?"

"Excuse me?"

"Sir, this is a government facility. Entry requires a government ID or prior appointment. If you don't have one of them, I'm going to have to ask you to leave."

Crocker reached into his wallet and produced the laminated

card that identified him as a Tier One U.S. military operator with a TS (top secret) SCI (sensitive compartmented information) Rainbow 9 clearance.

The guard nodded. "That's better, sir. Thank you."

He felt unprepared as the guard scanned a list attached to a clipboard.

What the hell am I gonna say? That I didn't know I was breaking the law when I broke into that lady's window?

"Sir, proceed to Level B. Park anywhere you find an empty space, then take elevator one to the fourth floor."

"Thanks."

He descended into the dark garage, still not knowing what this meeting was about. Thinking ahead to the pretrial hearing, he decided he couldn't trust his attorney—a sharply dressed recent grad from Georgetown Law School. Nice kid, but maybe a tad too sure of himself. He had tried to convince Crocker that the charges would be reduced to a misdemeanor and he would escape with a slap on the wrist.

What if he was wrong? Overconfidence didn't sit too well with Crocker. Besides, the circumstances of the case were so absurd he shouldn't have been charged in the first place. Sure, it had been wrong to break into a woman's apartment, but how could the court ignore the fact that she had been ripping off his seventy-six-year-old father, and that Crocker had caught her smoking crystal meth with a Fairfax County cop—the same one who had filed the charges?

His blood pressure rising, he stood near the back wall of the elevator, staring at the perfectly pressed uniforms of the two officers—one female, one male and Hispanic—standing in front of him whispering to each other about the long-term value of investment property on the Eastern Shore. He had a vacation house there as well, which he had used so many times with Holly. It had been their refuge. She had been his safe place. His harbor in the storm.

People, even military officials with desk jobs like the two riding with him now, didn't understand the perils the United States faced around the globe, and the stakes. He didn't blame them: How could they be expected to if they hadn't seen the horror, violence, and human misery he had? How could they appreciate the razor-thin line between civilization and chaos, good and evil, free society and forced obedience that men like him fought to protect?

Dr. Petrovian had warned him not to let his mind spin wildly like this. He tried to catch himself as he exited the elevator and stepped into the over-air-conditioned lobby. But how could you trust a justice system in which pampered superstars like O.J. Simpson got away with murder and poor people were shot for driving with a broken brake light—a story he'd just seen reported on CNN?

The male clerk behind the desk dressed in civvies examined his ID again, then asked him to sign a ledger and follow him down a gray hallway lined with photos of former secretaries of the Treasury.

Where the hell am I?

No signs on the walls or plaques beside the doors.

The clerk punched a code into a keypad at the end of the hall, pushed open a wooden door, and stepped aside. Crocker's eyes darted, registering as much as he could see in the dark room in two or three seconds—a dozen men and women seated around a rectangular table, all relatively young, all in civilian clothes, facing the wall to Crocker's right where something was projected onto a screen.

Another symptom of PTSD was hyperawareness. His mind raced as he blinked twice and tried to focus on the image—a blowup of something that resembled a president's face. Benjamin Franklin.

I'm in the wrong place.

He was about to excuse himself and leave when a voice from the other side of the table interrupted him. "Crocker, glad you could make it. Have a seat."

The woman had said it like she was singing, which stood out in this bland, cold place. As he pulled back a chair and sat, he traveled back into his memory bank, to a town in the Caribbean. Palm trees, colonial buildings golden in the sun.

Jeri Blackwell?

Seconds later, he located her wide dark face near the head of the table on the opposite side. One of the first African American women to join the Secret Service. She and Crocker had accompanied President and Mrs. Clinton on a trip to Ghana, Uganda, Rwanda, South Africa, Botswana, and Senegal in '98, when elements of ST-6 provided backup and support. Previous to that they had met in Cartagena, Colombia, while President Clinton was attending a regional drug summit.

"Hi, Jeri," he said. "Long time."

"Sure has been, honey. Good to see you again. Pour yourself a cup of coffee. We're looking at those bills you brought back from Russia."

"Oh." Suddenly the pieces snapped into place. The captured money, the fact that the Secret Service was the government agency that investigated financial crimes, including the counterfeiting of U.S. currency, and his presence.

"Something I can help you with?" Crocker asked. "They were part of a stash we found on a Russian official in the Ukraine."

"I stand corrected. Watch."

She gestured to the projected image on the screen to his right: a blowup of a hundred-dollar bill. A thin young guy in a tight gray suit and gelled hair directed a laser marker at the collar of Franklin's jacket. In a slightly nasal voice he said, "The overall quality is exceptional in terms of paper, ink, watermark, et cetera. But if you look closely along the left lapel you might be able to make out a slight anomaly."

Crocker's mind drifted back to the house in Chincoteague—the view of the ocean, the long walks he and Holly had taken along the beach, making love in front of the living room fireplace, the sweet delicate scent of her body.

The young man continued, "Missing is the microprinting near the collar. It's a small detail, but highly significant. All the new Treasury bills have it. These don't. Here's a genuine Franklin for comparison."

The room went dark for an instant and a new slide appeared on the screen. The young man said, "If you look closely, you can make out the words 'United States of America' along the lapel."

He missed her at least forty times a day, which Dr. Petrovian said was natural. In time she would fade from his memory. He wasn't sure he wanted that to happen.

Jeri caught his eye and smiled at him. He glanced back at the screen and tried to focus. Benjamin Franklin stared at him from the hundred-dollar bill with a weary, slightly disapproving expression.

Outside in the hallway, she told him that she would be continuing the probe into the counterfeit hundreds in Las Vegas. "Okay if I ask your CO for permission for you to join me?" she asked.

"Okay. Sure," Crocker answered. "What's up?"

She put her hand on his shoulder and whispered, "Surveillance. You'll be there to back me up in case you're needed. Chances are nothing's going to happen. You can sit by the pool for a couple days, sip margaritas, and relax."

"Thanks, Jeri. I think I'd like that."

"You look like you can use some personal time."

CHAPTER THREE

*I wouldn't know how to handle serenity if somebody
handed it to me on a plate.*
—Dusty Springfield

JAMES RYAN Dawkins wasn't as alert to danger or as physically
fit as Crocker. At forty-seven, he had a soft belly and a round
face, thinning hair, and owlish eyes. A naturally shy man, he had
a yen for performance from his days as an amateur opera singer,
which he satisfied by speaking in public—a skill he had per-
fected through many hours of practice. He now stood at a lectern
in the ballroom of the Swissotel Metropole in Geneva, Switzerland, and began his address about the restoration of the ozone
layer, which he kicked off with a humorous remark.

Holding up a can of aerosol Velveeta, he said, "I want to begin
by taking a poll. How many of you think cheese in a spray can is
more important than the continuance of life on earth?"

A half-dozen people in the audience of three hundred raised
their hands. Many more chuckled and laughed.

Dawkins, showing his satisfaction with the response with a shy
grin, signaled the technician to dim the lights and project the first

slide—a shot from a NASA satellite of the earth's ozone layer in 1979. It showed a small patch of dark blue over the South Pole.

Dawkins explained in a deep resonant voice that this was the first time scientists had noticed a significant hole in the ozone layer. In subsequent pictures taken at five-year intervals the dark blue grew dramatically larger, until 2006, when it practically covered the entire continent and extended to the tip of Tierra del Fuego.

That was the bad news, Dawkins explained. The thin shield of ozone helped deflect harmful UV rays—the cause of skin cancer, cataracts, and immune system deficiencies in humans. The good news was that the disruption of the ozone layer had slowed since 2006, due primarily to the worldwide ban on chlorofluorocarbons and bromofluorocarbons. But there was still a lot of work to do.

The speech he was about to deliver, he said, proposed a relatively easy and inexpensive way to restore the ozone layer by injecting oxygen under high pressure into the stratosphere.

Members of the International Society for Ecological Economics (ISEE) and their guests listened for the next thirty-five minutes as Dawkins, using slides showing chemical formulas and wavelength equations, explained the science behind his thesis. He ended with a quotation from former U.S. Secretary of Energy John S. Herrington: "There are no dreams too large, no innovation unimaginable and no frontiers beyond our reach."

As the assemblage applauded, Dawkins exclaimed into the mike, "I really believe that! All of us should."

It was the perfect coda to a succinct and thought-provoking presentation.

Afterward dozens of audience members came forward to

thank him and ask questions. Standing at the back of the group was an older man with a beautiful head of white hair, wearing an immaculate gray suit, and an attractive blonde in dark blue and white. They waited patiently for well-wishers to disperse, then stepped forward.

"Mr. Dawkins, Darius Milani of Raytheon," the man said with a slight foreign accent, extending a hand. "This is a colleague of mine, Dr. Naomi Nikasa, professor of physics at St. Andrews University."

"An inspiring speech, Mr. Dawkins," she said, extending her hand. She seemed young to be a professor, with high cheekbones, smooth amber skin, and a sweet dimpled smile.

"Thank you," he responded, feeling a bit overwhelmed.

Mr. Milani spoke quickly, his words skimming off the surface of Dawkins's consciousness like stones across a lake. He said that he represented an exclusive group of scientists and wealthy men and women named AVAN, derived from the ancient Greek word for "solution." He and Dr. Nikasa were members of the acquisitions committee, and were interested in funding practical solutions to global problems exactly like the one Dawkins had outlined in his speech.

Dawkins had never heard of AVAN, but his attention was pulled away from the smooth arc of Dr. Nikasa's neck, the gentle indentation where her collarbones met at the top of her chest. He had immediately made an association with Puccini's *Madame Butterfly* and the beautiful love aria *"Un bel dì, vedremo."*

Milani said, "I know this is somewhat off the cuff, but if you're free, Dr. Nikasa and I would like to invite you to dinner and introduce you to some of our colleagues."

Dawkins was remembering the time he'd heard that aria sung by Renata Scotto at Wolf Trap, where he sat on a blanket with his then girlfriend, Nan. The memory of the ripe, heartbreaking humanity of it under the stars, and how it had touched him then, brought a tear to his eye.

"Dinner? Uh...the three of us?" He inhaled heavily and glanced at his watch. It was 6:34 local time. Nan, now his wife, was expecting him to call at around seven, which corresponded to 1 p.m. in DC, where she worked at the National Archives as a curator of historical documents. He was going to tell her about his presentation and remind her that his SwissAir Flight tomorrow was scheduled to arrive at Dulles at 5:45 p.m. Since it would be Friday and Nan was Catholic, she'd likely be preparing fish for dinner. Afterward, after he put their adopted eight-year-old daughter to bed, he imagined they'd watch the new season of *House of Cards* on Netflix. Then she'd undress in the bathroom, slip into her side of the bed, and read. Dawkins thought he might suggest his interest in physical intimacy with a mild remark like, "You want us to hold each other?" Usually he wasn't confident enough or sexually compelled to take action on his own, but this time he thought he would.

It emboldened him that Dr. Nikasa smiled at him and let her arm brush his elbow. There were no accidents. Even if the gesture wasn't premeditated, it hadn't happened by chance. Not in Dawkins's mind.

Inhaling the floral aroma of Dr. Nikasa's French perfume, he stammered, "Uh...Well...I—I don't have time for dinner, but maybe a drink."

"Delighted. Of course," Milani offered, "we'll keep it brief, so as not to waste your time."

Dawkins smiled at that, thinking to himself, *If they only knew how pedestrian my life is.*

Clutching his briefcase, he took long strides to the elevator with Dr. Nikasa by his side asking about his scientific background. Milani punched the button to the penthouse.

"Actually, I'm not formally trained in atmospheric chemistry, physics, or even climatology," he explained to her. "My field is aerospace engineering, specifically as an inertial navigation engineer for UTC Aerospace Systems. Do you know it?"

"No."

"Why would you? Stupid question," he muttered under his breath, his head cast down.

"That makes you a true scientist," Dr. Nikasa remarked. "Someone who crosses disciplines in search of practical solutions."

Said so generously and gracefully, he thought. He imagined he saw a sparkle in her eyes. "I like to think so, yes."

Milani led them down a beige, teal-green, and sepia-patterned hallway. The thick carpet hugged the soles of Dawkins's Florsheims. For a moment he felt underdressed and ill-groomed, things he normally didn't care about. But the occasion seemed auspicious. AVAN sounded important.

Milani ushered them into the Da Vinci Suite. A large imitation of the great artist's *Leda and the Swan* hung on the entrance wall. Her glowing nude figure stopped Dawkins in his tracks. Female nudity had had a powerful effect on him since he'd first glanced at pictures in *Playboy*. Furthermore, he knew the lurid mythology behind the painting, which had fueled his fantasies. He froze and lowered his head in embarrassment.

His condition grew more acute when Dr. Nikasa touched his

shoulder. His whole body trembled as she pointed to two men sitting in the recessed dining area. They rose together and turned to greet him, an Asian man and another who looked elegant and European, and sported a salt-and-pepper goatee.

He carefully descended the three steps as Milani made the introductions. "Dr. Dawkins, this is David Lee of the South Korea Ministry of Technology, and Dr. Luigi Zucarella, a member of our board of directors. Another one of our directors, Elon Musk, CEO of SpaceX, has been delayed and will join us shortly."

The name Elon Musk pulled him out of himself and into the moment. Instinctively, he reached for his iPhone, which he usually kept in his back pocket. His intention was to text his wife to tell her who he was about to meet. But he didn't have his cell with him, because he'd never purchased the international data feature that would have allowed him to text from Geneva.

Dr. Nikasa touched his arm. "Please have a seat."

"Oh. Of course."

The sofa was covered with light-blue-and-purple silk. He was imagining Dr. Nikasa standing in front of him in a kimono when a tall, fit-looking waiter asked him what he would like to drink.

"Iced tea with lemon, please."

As he oriented himself to his surroundings, Milani told the two other men about the brilliance of his idea for restoring the ozone layer and the skill with which he had delivered his speech. The two men nodded and kneaded their brows as they listened. They sat opposite him on a blue-and-purple brocade sofa identical to the one he now shared with Dr. Nikasa. A glass coffee table with a vase of white orchids occupied the space between them. Milani sat in an armchair to his right.

When the drinks arrived, David Lee asked Dawkins about his interest in atmospheric chemistry, but Dr. Nikasa's proximity continued to distract him. An awkward silence followed. The men seemed to look at him more intently.

As Dawkins opened his mouth to answer, an aide in a dark suit interrupted with the news that Musk had just called from Geneva Airport. "He apologizes for being late, and will be here in ten minutes."

"Thank you," Milani said. "Before we ask Mr. Dawkins any more questions, maybe we should tell him a little about AVAN and our mission."

"Of course," said Lee.

Dawkins nodded, eased back into the sofa, sipped the tart drink, and concentrated hard on what Lee was saying, in an effort to ignore the effect Dr. Nikasa was having on him. AVAN had been created to address global problems—problems so large and complicated that they taxed the capacities of individual governments and bureaucracies.

"Time is our most precious commodity," Lee explained. "When we look at things like the scarcity of natural resources and global warming, we have to admit that we're running out of it."

Dawkins nodded and realized that his head felt heavy. His eyes wanted to shut. He reminded himself that he was jet-lagged and hadn't slept well since arriving in Switzerland. But when he forced his eyes open, he couldn't focus, and saw only a swirl of light and color.

That's when it occurred to him that he might be experiencing the symptoms of an incipient stroke or heart attack. Starting to panic, he grabbed his chest and fell forward. He couldn't stop.

The communication between his brain and muscles had been compromised somehow.

Without saying anything, Dr. Nikasa caught his head in her hands and guided it into her lap. He felt the fine wool against his cheek and her hard thighs under the skirt. He wanted to put his arms around her and hold her but lost consciousness first.

CHAPTER FOUR

*If you do not change direction, you may end up where
you are heading.*

—Lao-Tzu

CROCKER LAY on a lounge chair by the Caesars Palace swimming pool in the ninety-degree Las Vegas heat, his skin turning reddish brown from the Nevada sun, obscuring the navy anchor on his forearm, a snake wrapped around a dagger bearing the legend "Too Tough to Die."

The place he thought he really should be was the Ukraine, but his CO, Captain Sutter, had sent Mancini with him to back up Jeri Blackwell. Crocker suspected it was really an excuse to give him time to get his head together. Everyone on the team knew he was suffering from anxiety and the aftereffects of a string of difficult missions.

Despite the sumptuous surroundings and the nearly naked bodies, his mind drifted back to his recent phone call with Holly. She was happy, she said, with her new life. She had told him in no uncertain terms that their marriage was over. All he could do was pour out his heart to her, as well as he could. No sap; no squishy sentiment. He simply told her, "I love you with all my heart and have always operated under the assumption that we would spend the rest of our lives together. I don't want to be with anyone else."

She had responded coolly, "I appreciate how you feel, Tom, but that's not a possibility anymore."

Bam! Door slammed in his face. A whole bucketful of hurt.

Part of it, he knew, was his responsibility, part of it hers. The fact was that while focusing on his work with Black Cell, his marriage had unraveled. He was fully aware that he and Holly had problems. Both of them had been suffering from different forms of PTSD—Crocker from his various deployments, Holly after she had witnessed the execution of a colleague in Tripoli.

But how can you know what's going on in someone else's head?

He had given her space, which is what she said she wanted. They had both sought therapy and supported each other. They both took pride in their physical and mental toughness. They worked things out. The bond between them had seemed rock solid. But it wasn't. Okay, yes, he had gone on another deployment when she'd wanted him to stay home. But this is what he did for a living. It was his calling, his mission. Didn't she understand that?

Maybe she did. Maybe that was the problem. Whenever it was a choice between his teams and her, he always chose the teams. But not in his heart! He carried her and Jenny there always. Thinking of them got him through the tough spots.

He had no interest in fighting with her. He wanted Holly to be happy. He promised her half of everything, but…how could you love someone and do something like this? How could you build so much together and throw it away? Maybe the marriage had never meant as much to her as it had to him. Obviously, she had been imagining a future without him for some time. But it didn't matter. Neither did the beach house, the cars, or their other possessions. Neither did the money he was still sending her every week to cover expenses.

But he still wanted his old life back. Even his eighteen-year-old daughter, Jenny, had moved out and into her own Virginia Beach apartment, where she was living with a friend while she worked three days a week at a clothing store and attended community college.

He wouldn't feel sorry for himself. That wasn't in his DNA. He still had his health, the job he loved, his daughter, brother, sister, father, and teammates.

He turned to Mancini soaking up the sun beside him. The two of them had spent the past several days at the nearby Nellis Air Force Base firing range and kill house. Endless rounds of 5.56mm and 9mm ammo fired at paper targets. Endless repetition of cover tactics, fire angles, engagement points. They had been sent to train SEALs fresh out of BUD/S in desert tactics and close quarters combat (CQC).

By 4 p.m. it had been a long hot day, but Crocker's mind and body still wouldn't settle down.

Maybe I should take a run in the desert, or swim laps in the pool.

Then he remembered he couldn't. He was about to meet a young woman that an ST-6 teammate named Storm had set him up with. All the guys had been looking out for him, which meant a lot.

"You hear from anything from Jeri?" he asked, wondering again if their current assignment wasn't really an excuse to get him some R&R.

"She told us to hang tight," Mancini replied out of the side of his mouth. Much of his face was covered with thick dark stubble. "She'll call us if she needs us."

"Yeah."

"Where's the babe you're supposed to meet?"

He glanced at his Suunto watch—the one Holly had given him. "I don't know if she's a babe," he responded, "but she's a performer. A gymnast and dancer, according to Storm."

"I bet."

The introduction had come after Storm heard that Crocker was going to Nellis. He said, "You two might hit it off. Cyndi's a fun girl—kind and smart. When you're out there, you should look her up."

Over the past several days he and Cyndi had exchanged e-mails. He learned that she had a five-year-old daughter and had moved to Vegas from Spokane a year ago. She was currently part of the Cirque du Soleil troop performing its show *O* at the Bellagio—described as an aquatic masterpiece of surrealism and theatrical romance. He had a ticket to see it tomorrow night and was nervous about meeting her. Felt awkward and unprepared.

"You stoked?" Mancini asked over the top of the magazine he was reading—his arms, neck, and torso covered with tattoos and scars; his longish dark hair masking the place on his head where he'd been grazed by a terrorist's bullet in a Paris hotel elevator.

"Kind of. Yeah. What're you reading?"

"An article about fractals. Images of dynamic systems found in nature—like trees, rivers, coastlines, clouds, even a young lady's eyeballs. They derive from the principle of recursion but scale differently than other geometric figures."

"You're a fucking freak, you know that?"

"Thanks, and back atcha. Who got up this morning at six a.m. for a fifteen-mile run in the desert?"

Crocker smiled. He still had a sense of humor about himself. You performed to the limit of your abilities and hoped for the best. The fact that all individuals were islands held apart by ignorance, distrust, and fear wasn't his problem to solve. His job was to protect the sheep from the wolves. To help, protect, rescue, and heal people when he could.

Right now he was trying to relax and quiet the stream of second-guessing about the hearing next week. It seemed as though the entire population of Caesars Palace's four towers had come to cool off in six pools that made up the Garden of the Gods Pool Oasis. Male and female conventioneers, tourists from Asia, vacationers, professional gamblers, high-end hookers, young partiers, confidence men, honeymooners, weekend revelers from L.A. fresh off Route 15. All seemed contained in their private bubbles, barely aware of one another and their surroundings.

When Crocker looked closely he saw that the statues were molded of plaster and resin, and many of the human bodies had been sculpted, tucked, and smoothed by surgeons.

"That her?" Mancini asked, pointing to an approaching tall, dark-haired woman in a leopard-print bikini and large designer sunglasses, her back straight, her chest and chin thrust forward as though she were a movie star attending a premiere.

"I hope not," Crocker said.

The polished and buffed woman, projecting attitude and entitlement, stopped in front of them and pointed at the empty lounge chair beside Crocker. In a low voice she asked, "This taken?"

"Yes it is, ma'am." The breasts seemed fake, the lips cosmetically plumped, the skin around her eyes and cheekbones pulled too taut.

"Well, it's mine now." She set her bag on it, turned her back to him, and lowered her skinny ass down.

He was going to say that the chair was reserved for someone else but was too polite. If Holly were present she'd have scolded him, saying that off the battlefield he let people push him around. And he'd have responded, "No, baby, I respect people. Besides, some things aren't worth fighting over."

As the imaginary argument with Holly continued in his head, Cyndi stepped onto the patio wearing a white baseball hat and a light-blue wrap-type dress, spotted him, and approached.

Her shadow falling over him, she asked, "Tom Crocker?"

He looked up into her sunlit face. An impression formed in his head—friendly, unpretentious, pretty. He stood quickly, smiled, and offered his hand.

"Cyndi? Uh…thanks for coming. It's really nice to meet you." He suddenly felt like a teenager on a first date.

"Mind if I join you?" she asked.

"Of course. Yes, of course." He stood up, turned, and offered her his chair.

Without the least bit of modesty or hesitation, she set down her tote, untied the sash around her dress, removed it, folded it, removed her hat, and shook out her shoulder-length blond hair. Her torso, legs, and arms were strong and toned.

Crocker couldn't help but stare and admire her near-perfect proportions and the radiance of her skin. Now he looked away awkwardly. Behind the magazine, Mancini shot him a pirate's grin.

"Come with me," Cyndi said, offering her hand. "Let's cool off." So easy and natural, like they'd known each other for years.

He followed into the waist-high water in the circular pool built around a colonnade with a golden statue of Julius Caesar at the center. She reminded him of someone, one of the many girls he had dated in high school.

He was trying to remember the girl's name as he offered, "It's really nice to meet you." Then realized he'd said that already.

"Thanks."

"So...uh...how do you know Storm?"

"He and my brother went to high school together."

"Oh, nice."

She bounced up and down in the water and pushed back her hair.

"You're in great shape," she said.

"So are you."

"Thanks. You coming to the show tonight?" she asked sweetly, shielding her blue eyes with her hand.

"No, tomorrow. I'd like to meet you after, for a drink, if you want."

"That would be nice."

She was younger than he had imagined from the photo she had sent of her with her daughter, and slightly taller.

Off to the right, glancing off the water, and over "Summertime" by the Zombies playing over the PA system, he heard a man raise his voice. Even in an intimate moment like this, a part of Crocker remained alert to his surroundings. He noticed a large muscular guy standing before two men sitting on the other side of the pool.

"This your first visit to Vegas?" Cyndi asked, lowering her

head into the water, then coming up so that it washed down the front of her pink bikini top.

"No, sixth or seventh. I've lost count. I mean, I like it, but it's really not my kind of place."

"That's what everybody says, and they keep coming back."

"Yeah, you're right about that."

The muscular guy seemed to be complaining that the two other men had been taking pictures of his girlfriend. One of the men—who looked Asian—held a camera with a telephoto lens. That appeared to be the problem. The muscular guy in the bathing suit was demanding to see the camera so he could delete the photos. The second man—tall and stocky with short brown hair—gestured to him to go away.

"Something the matter?" Cyndi asked, leaning into him.

"No, no. Not at all."

"Storm told me a lot about you."

He blushed like a ten-year-old boy. "Really? What?"

"I'll tell you later." She turned, wrapped her legs around his waist, and leaned back in the water. "This helps stretch my back."

Playful and pretty, just like Storm had said. His gaze traveled up her smooth thighs, past her pelvis, into her waiting eyes. In his head they were already in his room upstairs, making love.

He glanced over her right shoulder past the columns for an instant and saw the two men standing and facing the muscular man and a security guard in a maroon blazer. The one with the camera wore an old-fashioned blue bathing suit and leather sandals. The taller man had on plaid pants, a white polo, and loafers. They both looked out of place.

Foreigners? Crocker wondered. *Pervs. Snapping photos of topless women sunning themselves?*

Lying back in the water, Cyndi pulled nearer until their crotches were close. He was thinking that it would be so easy to enter her in the pool. All he had to do was lower her legs below the waterline, pull the hem of her bikini bottom aside, and lower his trunks.

He slammed the brakes on that train of thought. He barely knew her. There were hundreds of people in the vicinity. Things were happening too fast.

Before he could say anything, he heard men grunting and looked up to see the muscular guy trying to wrestle the camera away from the Asian man. The guy with the camera kneed him in the crotch, then wheeled and kicked him in the chest, causing the muscular guy to stumble backward and hit the tile deck back first. When the security guard tried to intervene, the tall foreigner shoved him so hard he lost his balance and fell into the pool. The men turned and ran toward the casino just as an old woman stepped onto the patio.

Crocker waded forcefully to the side of the pool and shouted, "Lady, look out!"

She seemed momentarily confused by the sound of his voice and blinded by the sun, so she didn't step aside when the first man bolted toward her. He was looking over his shoulder as he ran and crashed into her full force, throwing her off her feet and into the planter behind her.

Others nearby were slow to notice, but not Crocker. He turned to Cyndi, muttered "Just a minute," hopped out of the pool, and gave chase.

Barefoot and wearing only a bathing suit, Crocker ran across the marble floor, trying not to slip or crash into anyone, past the line waiting to get into the Bacchanal Buffet, and veered left onto a long carpeted hallway decorated with large photos of Ancient Rome. The two fleeing men a hundred feet ahead turned right at a sign that read AUGUSTUS TOWER.

Why he was doing this, and why he had left Cyndi waiting in the pool, hadn't crossed his mind. He had reacted instinctively. Now he pushed hard the 150 feet to catch up. A uniformed guard saw Crocker running toward him and raised his arms to block Crocker's access to the elevators.

"Sir, easy. Slow down! What seems to be the problem?"

Crocker stopped, chest heaving. Fellow hotel guests of various nationalities stared at the scars covering his torso and arms.

He blurted out, "Those two men who just passed…they assaulted one of your security guards and a guest. They need to be stopped!"

"Oh…Okay, sir," the guard said. "Yes, I saw them just now. I'll notify security."

"No, I'm sorry. That's not good enough…I need you to let me pass."

Just then he heard his name being called behind him and turned to see Mancini catching up, the veins standing out on his tattooed neck. He was holding a cell phone, which he pushed toward Crocker. "Boss, it's Jeri! She wants to speak to you!"

"Now?"

"Yeah, now."

"You tell her about the incident at the pool?"

"I did, yeah."

Ten minutes later, amid a cacophony of bells and jingling, the two SEALs negotiated banks of pinball machines and gaming tables, and arrived at Jeri's office. She stood at a desk with a wall of video monitors behind her, talking on the phone. Jim Walker, the assistant director of hotel security, wearing a maroon blazer and sporting a Burt Reynolds mustache, stood beside her.

"Yes, Mr. Leong. That's right, Mr. Leong. Carl Wong and Jon Petroc. I know. They claim to be part of a Chinese diplomatic delegation from your Ministry of Industry. Thanks for checking. Yes, please, as soon as you can. Thanks for your time."

She hung up, muttered "Douchebag," sipped from a cardboard cup of coffee on her desk, and sighed. "Hi, Crocker. That was the Chinese consul. I asked him to check the validity of their passports, and he asks me to comp him and his family for dinner for six at your most expensive restaurant. Can you believe that BS?"

"Hi, Jeri."

"Thanks for coming."

"We just saw two guys wrestle with your security guards and run off."

"Yeah, I know. Carl Wong and John Petroc. Those are the guys I'm talking about."

She turned to Walker, who had the glazed look of someone who'd seen it all.

Walker asked, "Which restaurant does the Chinese consul want to go to?"

"The Guy Savoy."

"Of course. Call François. You got his number?"

Crocker stood in his black jeans and T-shirt that he had changed into, looking confused. "You talking about the guys we saw by the pool?"

"Yeah," Jeri nodded. "Wong and Petroc. They're holed up in

their room and refuse to come out and talk. Claim to be holding diplomatic passports and working for the Chinese government."

"They didn't look like diplomats," Crocker said.

"Didn't act like them, either," added Mancini.

She held up her hand to Crocker and Mancini, and picked up the phone again. "Just a sec…François, it's Jeri. Yeah, Jeri Blackwell from the Secret Service. *Comment tallez vouz,* honey? I need a table for six, eight o'clock. Cram 'em in the toilet if you have to, but make it happen. Thanks."

She hung up and pointed to the monitors on the far right behind her. "They're in there. The Titus Suite in the Augustus Tower. That's where they ran to when you were chasing them just now. See? Completely dark. What kind of diplomats know how to find and disable the monitors in their hotel suite?"

"Shady ones," Crocker answered, trying to grasp what was going on.

"They've got something that's interfering with our electronics, too."

"You really believe they're working for the Chinese?" Crocker asked. "Why are they here in the first place?"

"Trouble. What else? I want to show you something." Jeri picked up the phone again and said, "Lester, come into my office for a minute and bring the strongbox."

Two minutes later a man in a blue-and-black teller's uniform entered—gray hair, gray mustache, late fifties. He carried a metal box, which he set on the desk.

"Lester, these two studs are friends of mine. Show 'em what you found."

Lester turned to Walker, who nodded. Then he used one of the keys on a chain attached to his belt to open the metal case. Inside were stacks of new hundred-dollar bills. He pulled one out and handed it to Crocker.

"Thanks," Crocker asked.

"It's counterfeit," Lester said. "So are all the others. We've taken in almost a hundred thousand dollars' worth in the past two days."

"Who's we?"

"Caesars Palace."

Turning to Jeri, Crocker said, "These match the ones we grabbed in the Ukraine?"

"You're smart, honey," she replied, nodding toward the teller. "Check 'em out."

Lester removed a jeweler's loupe from his pocket and held it to his right eye. "If you look closely, they all have the same anomaly along the lapel of Franklin's jacket."

He handed the loupe to Crocker and used a pencil to point to the fine lines in question. "Missing is the microprinting near the collar. It's a small detail, but significant. All the new Treasury bills have it. These don't. Here's a genuine Franklin for comparison."

Crocker checked the real one and barely made out the words "United States of America" along the collar.

"Same as the ones we seized in Ukraine."

"Yup," said Jeri.

He passed the bills and loupe to Mancini. "What do you want us to do?"

Jeri said, "Nothing yet." Flipping through the papers on her desk, she found a report and passed it to Crocker.

"We did a high-resolution scan of one of the bills and sent a report to headquarters. They told us it was part of set of counterfeits, known as 2HK1, that have started to find their way into circulation in Hong Kong, Thailand, Hawaii, and Russia over the past month and half."

"How much?"

"Millions of dollars' worth. This is the first time they've appeared in the U.S. And here are the guys we think have been passing them."

She handed him a set of stills taken by surveillance cameras. They showed individuals of different nationalities standing at casino cashier windows and blackjack tables, handing cashiers and dealers hundred-dollar bills. The time signatures in the right-hand corners indicated the pictures had been taken over the past thirty-six hours. None of the faces in the pictures matched those of Wong or Petroc.

Crocker shrugged. "I don't get it."

"We call the guys in the photos storks. If Wong and Petroc are doing what I think they are, they're the suppliers," explained Jeri. "They're selling the fake stuff at fifty to sixty percent face value to storks, who quickly cash it in and split town. We haven't caught a one of them, but we're looking."

"When did Wong and Petroc arrive?" Crocker asked.

"Two days ago, shortly before this bullshit started. These counterfeits have been showing up at casinos all over town. I figure they've spread about two mil worth already."

"Why don't you just arrest them?" Crocker asked.

Jeri thanked Lester, who left with the locked box and counterfeit hundreds, then continued. "The fact that they're carrying diplomatic passports poses a major obstacle. I figure we need two things to happen before we can grab them. One, the Chinese consul general establishes that the passports are fakes. And two, we get clearance from the State Department."

Mancini said, "By the time that happens those two characters will be long gone."

"I like this guy, Crocker."

Crocker asked, "How can we help?"

Jeri rubbed her hands together. "We've got ourselves a cat-and-mouse-type situation. I've got guys all over town chasing down the fakes, and I know Treasury's not going to commit more officers until clearances have been given to make arrests."

"Bureaucratic nonsense."

"No, it's China. They're big crybabies. Unfortunately, our economy depends on the cheap shit they sell us. So our government is afraid of even watching them carefully. Nobody wants to upset the Chinese."

"How do you know it's the Chinese?"

"Don't know for sure, honey. Maybe they ain't really Chinese. It's Nevada. They could be from anywhere. All I can do in my position is station my guys outside their suite. But if Wong and Petroc pay their bill and leave, which I expect they will, I can't detain 'em."

"Even after the incident at the pool?"

"Caesars' management will let that go."

Walker, who was sitting behind the desk quietly going through paperwork, nodded. "We're cooperating with Treasury, but management strongly discourages any kind of commotion at the hotel. It's bad for business. Any kind of violence keeps people away."

"Got it."

"That's where I'm thinking you come in," Jeri said. "One of those assholes slammed into your eighty-year-old aunt and didn't apologize. As far as you know, you don't know anything about them holding diplomatic passports. So you confront 'em outside the public areas, like, say, the parking lot. A fight breaks out. You get some shots in, then I call Las Vegas PD and have them arrested. LVPD cops don't know shit about diplomatic immunity. They end up holding those guys for a couple hours at least, while we go through their suitcases and see if we can find more counterfeit bills. Not exactly legal, but it's the best we can do."

"Sounds sweet to me," said Crocker.

"You think you can extend your stay past the weekend if we need to?"

"That's up to Captain Sutter."

"I'll call him. My money says Wong and Petroc will be moving soon. I'll have my guys keep an eye on them and let you know. Just don't kick their asses in a public place, like the hotel or casino. Okay?"

"Ten-four."

"Yeah, guys," Walker added. "Please be discreet. No blood on the carpets or YouTube moments. Management will lose their shit."

CHAPTER FIVE

Never give up, for that is just the place and time that the
tide will turn.
—Harriet Beecher Stowe

IT WAS 8 p.m. EST, or 2 a.m. the next morning in Geneva, and Nan Dawkins was starting to worry. It wasn't like her husband to not call. She had phoned his room three times, left messages twice, and spoken to a clerk at the front desk at the Swissotel Metropole, who established that James wasn't in his room. Now, after putting their adopted Chinese daughter, Karen, to bed, she called the room again. Still no answer.

So she contacted the concierge, who told her that the ISEE conference had broken up at 8 p.m. local time. Since it was past 2, all hotel restaurants were closed for the night. Armed with James's description, the concierge searched the lobby, the Mirror Bar, and the rooftop bar. James wasn't there, nor had either bartender seen anyone matching his description. After some prodding Nan was given the name and room number of the ISEE representative. She promised not to call her before 9 a.m. Geneva time.

At 3 a.m. EST sharp she called Joanna Siegel, the event organizer. Ms. Siegel said that she had last seen Mrs. Dawkins's husband yesterday evening, shortly after he delivered his speech and she went up to thank him. She had no idea where he had gone after that but suggested that many of the conventioneers went to dinner in groups, and maybe her husband had joined one of them. Nan didn't quite understand how that explained his disappearance, but she thanked her and hung up. The ominous feeling that had started at dinner deepened and grew stronger.

She wasn't one to put much stock in feelings, but she couldn't come up with a logical explanation for her husband's silence. After fifteen years of marriage, she knew he wasn't the kind of man to act irresponsibly or make a rash decision. Sometimes he could be absentminded, but he usually wanted her to know where he was and what he was doing. James wasn't a gambler or a drinker, but modest, careful, and dependable. The kind of man who enjoyed puttering in his home office after dinner. He fussed sometimes about how Nan spent money but otherwise never complained. Their sex life was infrequent but healthy. He doted over their daughter and loved his work. The prospect of him suddenly running off with another woman didn't seem likely, nor could she imagine him going off to party at a strip club with a group of men without calling her with some excuse.

So where had he gone? Nan racked her brain for an answer. The only ones it came up with involved some kind accident, sudden illness, or violence.

Six thirty a.m. After waking Karen to get ready for school, she called James at the Metropole again. Still no answer. So she contacted the front desk and asked them to send someone up to the room to check it.

A half hour later, the clerk called back. "Mrs. Dawkins, your husband isn't in his room. The bed doesn't appear as though it was slept in last night. But his suitcase and clothes are still there. Does he have a cell phone with him?"

"Yes, but since he's only staying a few days he didn't purchase the international plan. It won't work until he returns to the U.S."

"I understand that he's scheduled to check out this morning," the clerk pointed out.

"Yes, that's correct. He's leaving on an 11 a.m. flight."

"I'll tell him to call you when we see him. Hopefully that will happen soon."

"Thank you."

She dropped off Karen at Hunters Woods Elementary School and arranged with her neighbor Leslie to pick her up and drive her home.

Unsettled and not knowing what to do with herself, she drove to Dulles airport and waited. From the International Arrivals terminal she called the Metropole again, only to learn that James hadn't checked out. Nor did he arrive four hours later on his scheduled flight.

So she called James's best friend and colleague, Kevin Willis. When she told him James was missing, Kevin became as alarmed as she was and suggested she contact the State Department and file a missing-person report.

She spent the rest of the evening calling hospitals in Geneva. None reported admitting her husband or anyone matching his description. Next she tried the U.S. consulate. A junior officer there checked with Metropole security and local police stations. No one had seen her husband. Nan, who prided herself in being a strong-minded woman, was starting to grow desperate. As her anxiety grew, she got angry, very angry, and poured herself a glass of wine. Then another. Then another.

She was slightly inebriated by the time two officers from Homeland Security—one male, one female—rang the front doorbell. *The Late Show with Stephen Colbert* was ending. She turned off the TV, let them in, offered them coffee (which they declined), and proceeded to answer their questions.

"When is the last time you heard from your husband?" the female officer asked.

"It was a little after 4 p.m. in Geneva. He was on his way to the conference to give his speech."

"Did you argue?"

"No. We talked about plans for our daughter's birthday."

"How old is your daughter?"

"Eight. Turns nine on Tuesday."

"Your husband and she are close?"

"He adores her; she adores him."

"Has he recently learned about any problems involving his health?"

"No."

"Have you been experiencing financial problems?"

"No."

"Do you suspect that he has any investments or bank accounts you might not know about?"

"I doubt it."

"Relationship issues?"

"None."

"Does he gamble, drink, take drugs?"

"None of the above."

"Has he recently made any new friends?"

"No. Not that I know of."

"Has any new name or person come up in conversation?"

"No. Why?"

"No particular reason. These are the questions we ask in cases like this."

As Nan watched the male officer record her answers on a yellow form, she started to weep. She couldn't control herself. The female officer sat beside her on the couch and took her hand. In a sympathetic tone of voice, she said, "The only reason we're here is that your husband has a top-secret Department of Defense clearance, but you shouldn't read too much into that. In ninety percent of these cases, the spouse shows up a day or so later with a reasonable explanation."

"And in the other ten percent?"

"Try not to think about that. We'll continue to monitor all local Geneva police and immigration reports and call you in the morning."

"Thank you," she muttered with her face in her hands.

"Is there someone in the area, a close friend or relative, who you can call and ask to stay with you until this is over?" the officer asked.

"No. My daughter's here. I'll be fine."

At 1136 hours PST Friday night, Crocker sat across from Cyndi watching her devour a grilled sirloin at Todd English's Olives restaurant overlooking the Bellagio fountains.

Before he had met her at the *O* stage door, he'd received a call from Ukrainian Special Forces commander Colonel Marko Hubenko asking him for additional help. The Donetsk airport was under attack by Russian proxies and in danger of being overrun. Hubenko's troops lacked operational expertise and leadership.

Crocker told Hubenko he would be happy to help but could only do so under orders from his CO, who he promised to call. This he did ASAP, relaying Hubenko's request to Captain Sutter back at ST-6 HQ in Virginia Beach.

Sutter said in his western Kentucky accent, "More damn crises in the world than we have spec ops to handle 'em. Frankly I don't know if Ukraine is a priority."

He told Crocker he would pass Colonel Hubenko's request up the chain of command, and that Crocker and Mancini should assist Ms. Blackwell over the weekend and report back to Nellis AFB at 0630 Monday morning.

"Yes, sir."

Why training recruits how to survive in the desert was more important than defending Ukraine from Putin's insurgents was something Crocker didn't ask. DC politics and military policy and order of priorities weren't in his purview or part of his skill set. Right now he was on his first date with a woman (besides his soon-to-be ex-wife) in over eight years, and he was enjoying it.

He and Cyndi had watched the fountain water dance and soar to Sinatra's "Good Life" and shared a bottle of her favorite Chardonnay—Beckett's Flat Five Stones. Now they were both feeling warm and mellow, aided by the romantic setting—subtle overhead lighting, the warm tones of the furniture, Mendelssohn's sublime Violin Concerto in E minor, Opus 64, playing over the stereo.

The pretty woman across from him with the sparkling blue eyes started to tell him about her life. Her mother had become pregnant with her in high school. She barely knew her father, and had been raised primarily by her grandparents on her mother's side. No bitterness, no blame, which he admired.

She had her first serious boyfriend at fifteen, and was following her mother's trajectory when she was arrested at a party for selling ecstasy. She did community service and tried to turn her life around.

Sex and boys had always been an issue. She loved it and them, and they loved her back. After graduating from college she drifted from one relationship to another, then discovered ballet, modern dance, and gymnastics. They became her passion. For years she made a good living dancing in gentlemen's clubs. After the birth of her daughter she took a hard look at herself in the mirror, asked herself what she really wanted to do with her life, and decided she wanted to be a legitimate dancer.

She worked hard, auditioned, and got parts dancing in the touring shows of several Broadway musicals, including revivals of *Oklahoma!* and *Pippin.* When she wasn't touring, she performed with a local circus. During a Christmas Eve performance she was discovered by a scout from Cirque du Soleil and was invited to Montreal.

Crocker was fascinated, but as she talked about herself, he started to think about his own history and all the details he'd have to fill in and things she'd have to accept about him before they could really be comfortable with each other. It seemed like a lot.

If he thought his life was complicated, hers was a snarl of difficulties and attachments that included her ex-husband, who had been a drummer in a rock band before a serious accident destroyed his hand. Cyndi was now helping pay for his physical therapy. The daughter they had together had a rare blood disease called Diamond-Blackfan anemia that had to be treated with steroids and bimonthly blood transfusions. She had recently put her mother—who was still struggling with alcohol and drug abuse—back into rehab.

The fact that she remained so upbeat and energetic through all this difficulty inspired him. He told her that.

She responded by saying, "I'm boring you. I'm sorry. When I get excited, I can't stop talking."

"No, it's interesting. Go ahead."

He was already thinking about how their lives could fit together. It would be extremely challenging. She had her career; he had his. She lived in Las Vegas; his home was in Virginia. The only times they could meet were when he was on leave. He'd get to know her daughter. He'd done the same with Holly's son.

Cyndi reached across the table and again placed her hand on his. "Tom?"

Warmth spread up his arm. "Yeah?"

"Is something wrong?"

"No. No, not at all."

"Tell me about yourself."

"I think you know the basics already. I'm a Navy SEAL. Have been for the last seventeen years."

"I want to know about your life."

He gave her a quick summary. His wild, gang-member teenage years; how he had been drifting into a life of crime before becoming interested in long-distance running and endurance racing. After dropping out of college, he joined the navy and passed BUD/S (Basic Underwater Demolition School). One of the proudest moments in his life was receiving the gold trident that made him a Navy SEAL. He talked about some of his deployments, injuries, the times he was captured by the enemy and escaped, his daughter and marriages.

He stopped there. Cyndi looked deep into his eyes asked, "Have you had to kill people?"

It was something he didn't like to think about. "Yes, I have."

"Was that hard?"

"Yes and no. You do it because you have to, but those things...linger."

"I would think so. I'm sorry. You do what have to in defense of our country. You see and do things that most people can't face."

"Yeah, that's right. Some of it leaves scars...on your soul."

It was a big admission to someone he'd just met. He looked away, embarrassed, wondering where she was going with this.

Cyndi sighed. "I admire you, Tom. I do. And I want to get to know you better, even though I'm kind of scared."

"Why?"

"Why?" she asked back. "Because you're a serious dude. That's both frightening and exciting."

He reached across the table, took both of her hands, and looked into her eyes—warm and bright. They started to open something inside him. He wanted to go further, but he wasn't sure he was ready.

He said, "I want to get to know you better, too. But let's keep it simple...for now."

She smiled and nodded. "Sure, Tom. I agree. Simple and straightforward is better."

When he excused himself to go to the men's room, he stopped to pull her close and kiss her on the lips. She felt delicate in his arms.

He was feeling light-headed from the sudden intimacy and

was two-thirds of the way to the men's room when the lights in the restaurant went out. A current of panic passed through the room. A waiter dropped a glass that shattered. The maître d' hurried to the middle of the dining room and announced, "Sorry for the temporary inconvenience. Our waitstaff will provide candles. Until power is restored there will be a delay in the kitchen, but we have an unlimited supply of wine and dessert."

Crocker was in the men's room, using the light from his phone to find the toilet, when Jeri called.

"Crocker, you there?"

"Yeah, Jeri. What's going on?"

"All the electrical power just went out throughout the city. My money says the guys upstairs will use this opportunity to bust out. Where are you?"

"Olives restaurant at the Bellagio, having dinner."

"Oh…Hold on." She came back thirty seconds later. "You think you can find your way back?"

"Now?"

"Yeah. Chop-chop. Meet me in the office."

"See you in ten."

CHAPTER SIX

Everything is dangerous, my dear fellow. If it wasn't so,
life wouldn't be worth living.
—Oscar Wilde

NAN DAWKINS tossed and turned in the bedroom of their town house in Reston, Virginia, dreaming intermittently of riding in a car with James at the wheel. She had a vague sense that they were headed toward the beach, windows open, wind carrying the scent of orange blossoms swirling around their faces. She thought in that moment that they were as close as two people could possibly be. He turned to her with such openness and clarity that they seemed to be reading each other's thoughts. The intimacy frightened her, so she looked away.

The next moment she was awake, staring at the face of the clock and trying to comprehend what it meant. It read 5:32. The trees outside the window were still. The half-moon she had noticed earlier was no longer visible. A lone bird perched on a branch, asleep.

Seeing the empty place beside her on the king-sized bed, she remembered the situation, looked at the clock again, and reached for her cell phone. Still no message from James.

The feeling of dread she had experienced earlier that night returned, worming its way down her neck into her shoulders, arms, and chest, as though it had been waiting and gathering strength. She wanted to look in on their daughter, thinking the sight of her would be reassuring.

She turned on the light by her bed, pulled on the teal silk robe James had bought her for her birthday. Despite his awkwardness, he was always good at picking gifts.

She noticed her laptop recharging on the top of her dresser and stopped. Opening it, she logged in her password and waited for her e-mails to load. Among the various offers of discounts and services, she saw one from jp227@gmail.com—James's personal e-mail account. No subject.

Holding her breath, Nan opened it and read:

Dear Nancy:

I need some time to myself, so I will be away for a period of time. Don't expect to hear from me. I'm safe and I don't want you to worry. I'll return home when I'm finished.

Love,
James

Her hands trembling, she read it again, and then a third time. The message struck her as oddly formal and didn't sound like James at all. For one thing, he almost never called her Nancy. It was always Nan, or in an intimate moment his pet name for her, Bird.

Second, there was no mention of Karen. Third, what did he mean by "when I'm finished"? Didn't that imply that he was working on something?

She read it again. There seemed to be a disconnect between the phrases "I need some time to myself" and "when I'm finished." As a detail person, she noticed things like that. The sequence of logical thinking was important. Why would James need time to himself, when he always carved out plenty of that in his life and Nan was almost always willing to give it to him? She wasn't a nagging, needy wife.

The only possible explanation could be his job. He was a senior engineer at UTC Aerospace Systems, which worked almost exclusively on highly sensitive contracts for the U.S. government agency DARPA (Defense Advanced Research Projects Agency), a branch of the Department of Defense.

That's the reason the two Homeland Security officers had visited her earlier. James rarely talked about his work, except in general terms. The idea that his research into guidance systems yielded products that were used to kill people sometimes kept him up at night. He had told her about nightmares he had centered on schools and children's hospitals hit by laser-guided missiles and bombs. Bleeding, screaming boys and girls being carried out, some missing limbs.

Thinking that maybe his sudden disappearance was somehow related to his job, Nan waited until after seven, again called James's best friend, Kevin, and invited him over for breakfast. A very eccentric and brilliant man, Kevin lived alone in a big house crammed with junk since his wife had left him five years ago. He and James shared the same adolescent sense of humor and obsession with mathematics and science.

To Nan's mind, Kevin was even more emotionally shut off and socially awkward than her husband. It's not that she didn't like him; he just didn't know how to behave like a normal human being. He seemed happy but dressed oddly, often ignored his personal hygiene, drove a disgusting '88 Mercedes, and almost always carried around a video camera, which he used to record people and conversations with no regard to how intrusive it was. Despite these things, Nan had learned to appreciate Kevin's sensitivity and intelligence, and his devotion to her husband.

So she showered, dressed, woke up Karen, took her to a neighbor's house, and returned home before nine, when Kevin arrived with a Sony MC Series Camcorder on his shoulder.

"Put it away, Kevin," she said at the door as she shielded her face with her hand. "I don't want to be filmed."

"Come on, Nan. You've got such a pretty smile."

"If you don't put the camera down and turn it off, I'm going to ask you to leave."

"Gee, Nan. Where's Jimmy?"

Kevin was the only one who called her husband that. Now he set the camcorder on the table with the red light still on and a mischievous look on his face.

"Turn it off!"

"Gosh, Nan," Ryan said with a grin, "you know all my tricks. Where's Jimmy? Where's that rascal?"

She placed a mug of steaming coffee in front of him. Milk and sugar were already on the table. Turning back to the stove to pour the batter, she said over her shoulder, "James still hasn't returned from Switzerland. You know that already."

"Yeah, but I thought..." His voice trailed off as pancakes sizzled.

"He's still not back. Nobody's seen him since the presentation

Thursday night. This morning I received this e-mail." She handed him a printout.

Kevin groaned and shook his head as he read. "Oh, no. No, that's not Jimmy. No..."

"I don't think so, either."

When she slipped a plate of hot pancakes in front of him, Kevin stared at them without moving. He said, "I don't know what you want from me, Nan. Maybe I shouldn't be here if Jimmy isn't here," and started to get to his feet.

"Don't be ridiculous! You're his best friend. I need your help. Sit down!"

Kevin sank back into his seat, deep in thought. "Yes, Nan, you're right."

"Is there something going on at work that I should know about?" she asked.

"What do you mean?"

"I mean, is that the real reason he went to Geneva? Work."

"What are you talking about?"

"I know you people work on things you're not supposed to tell me about. I'm asking if maybe James is related to that."

"No, Nan, I don't think so. Why do you ask?"

"Because two officers from Homeland Security came here last night and asked me some questions."

"They did? Oh, no..." Looking agitated, Kevin stood and started to pace beside the table. "I'm starting to feel uncomfortable, Nan," he said. "Very strange. Do they think Jimmy stole sensitive information?"

She stepped in front of him and blocked his path. "Stole what for whom, Kevin? What are you talking about?"

"I don't know. For, like, another country?"

She followed him and his camcorder to the front door. "Kevin, you know my husband as well as anyone. Would James ever do anything like that?"

"No, I don't think so. But you never know."

In the dark Crocker sprinted down the steps to the promenade with Cyndi's smiling face in his head. Hundreds of curious people crowded the walkway to stare at the darkened strip. Tall, unlit casino hotels loomed like ghosts. Police sirens wailed in the distance.

The crowds hindered his progress, so he hopped the waist-high barrier and ran alongside the stalled oncoming traffic. Las Vegas Boulevard had become a parking lot and provided the only light. He juked around stalled taxis, limos, and tourist minivans and through the snarl in the Flamingo Road intersection, oblivious to the gently falling rain and exhaust fumes. A car horn blared to his left and a gray-haired man leaned out. "You trying to get killed, dumbass?"

He wanted to respond but didn't have time. Bigger fish to fry. Cyndi provided plenty of distraction already. He wanted to get this over soon and get back to her.

On reaching the corner, he texted, "Sorry. I have to take care of something. Will meet u later."

He wanted to open up to her further. Maybe tell her about his family. Up the steps and past Serendipity 3 café a minute later his cell pinged. Holding it up to the reflected light, he read, "Wondered what happened. Be safe. Hope to see u soon."

"Yes" he texted as he ran across the looping driveway blocked by fire trucks, their lights washing red and white across the façade. Stepping over the yellow police tape, he entered the lobby, now harshly lit with bright emergency lights. A fireman with a megaphone was telling restless, uneasy patrons to stand back and clear the rotunda.

"What the hell's going on?" someone asked.

A woman to his right commented, "Who ever heard of a power outage in Las Vegas?"

Entering the check-in area, he saw a way around the huge crowd clogging the central atrium with its marble fountain and statues of half-naked nymphs. For once, the casino was quiet. No jangling slots, no clinking of chips. Soon, he figured, an emergency generator would be started up somewhere and the machines would be active again.

He found Walker's office, which was lit by a battery-powered torch. Jeri stood in its penumbra, the harsh light transforming her face into a Halloween mask, speaking quickly into a cell phone. "I don't care how the fuck they get here. I want all agents in the area contacted and told to report. Now!"

She sighed, took a sip of something out of a paper cup, and announced to the half-dozen people standing in the room, "NPC says the transponders at Henry Allen station overloaded. They're trying to patch in other sources now."

"Jeri—" Crocker started.

"Walker? Where's Walker?"

"Jer—"

He was cut off by a man standing in front of him. "What kind of time frame are they talking about?"

"I don't know. Has anyone seen Walker? Why are all you people standing around?"

Jeri spotted Crocker, crossed over to him, and grabbed his shoulder. "Crocker, oh god…"

"I got here as soon as I could."

"Good. Good." He could feel the anxiety coming off her body as she leaned into him and whispered, "Those slick fucks set their suite on fire and escaped."

"The guys from before? The diplomats?"

"Yeah." Remembering something, she called out, "Where the fuck is Walker? Somebody find him, now!"

Jeri took Crocker by the elbow, led him toward the door, and whispered, "Your colleague's on his way to Parking C," she said urgently. "He's trying to stop those two assholes before they got away."

"Mancini, good. I'll find him."

He turned toward the door and simultaneously reached for his cell.

Jeri shouted at his back, "Nelson here will show you the way."

She pushed a heavyset, balding man through the door toward him.

"Nelson, Crocker."

"Follow me."

Jeri shouted, "Wait!" She ran to him, pushed a walkie-talkie into his hand, and said, "Talk to me, Crocker. Channel C."

"Lead the way."

They pushed past crowds of gawkers clogging passageways to the back of the casino. Nelson knew a shortcut down a hallway, out an emergency exit, down a long concrete corridor, and up a flight of stairs.

"This way."

He held a flashlight to illuminate the floor in front of them as they ran. Crocker found his cell phone and hit Manny's number on speed dial.

"Boss, where are you?" Mancini answered.

"Headed for the garage. You?"

"Reserved parking, level two."

"Jeri told us C."

"There is no C. It's level two."

"Two. Copy."

"How far away are you?"

"I think we're close. Hang on."

He stopped and turned back. Nelson, who had been lagging with the flashlight, stood ten feet behind him clutching the back of his leg.

"What's the matter?" Crocker asked.

"I think I pulled a hamstring. You better continue without me. There's an elevator at the end to the right. The security code is 9114."

Crocker nodded. "I'll radio Jeri and tell her to send someone."

"Don't bother. I'll be okay."

"I'm calling her now."

He held down the button as he ran. "Jeri? It's Crocker."

"This is a fucking disaster. What the hell is happening?"

"I'm about to find out. Nelson pulled a muscle. I left him in the security hallway to the right of the casino. He's near the ground-floor elevator."

"I'll tell Walker to send someone if I can fucking find him."

Emerging from the elevator Crocker realized he was unarmed and wearing his best shirt, pants, and new John Varvatos shoes. Not that it mattered. He heard the echoes of men shouting, the squeal of rubber against concrete, a car horn blaring.

"Manny, position?"

"Cars are exiting onto Frank Sinatra Drive, black Escalades, Arizona plates."

"How many?"

"Two."

"What's your position?"

At the emergency stairway, he turned left toward the sound of shrieking tires. Saw a black Cadillac Escalade forty feet away whip around the corner and down the exit ramp. Mancini ran out from behind a pickup to its right and lunged toward the partially opened rear window of the SUV. Seeing him, the driver turned sharply right, smacking him with the right rear bumper and tossing him against the grille of a parked Mercedes. He bounced off and hit the pavement.

Crocker found him bleeding from the nose and disoriented. "Don't move," he instructed.

"Fuck that." Mancini pushed himself up onto all fours, rolled to his right, and stood in a crouch. "Which way did they go?"

"I only saw one."

"One individual?"

"No, one Escalade."

Crocker punched in the side window of a Ford pickup with his elbow, got in, and loosened the ring around the ignition switch with his pocketknife. Once he got the ring off, he pulled the switch out of the dash and unplugged it as Mancini slid into the passenger's seat.

"You okay?" Crocker asked.

"A little woozy. Don't worry about me."

"Anyone following them?"

"Don't think so. CP security is totally overwhelmed."

"What about the Treasury guys?"

Mancini shrugged and rubbed his ribs.

"Take the push-pull. Tell Jeri what's happening. Tell her to send a team with wheels."

He found the red wire with the green stripe around it and the black one, and stuck them both in the hole at the back of the plug, touching the red one to the one that started to crank the motor. Then he held the black one to the other wire until the engine started. He pressed down on the gas and unplugged the red one.

Mancini, who had been talking on the radio, lowered it into his lap. "Ixnay on the follow team, says Jeri."

"Why?"

"All focused on hotel security."

"You armed?" Crocker asked as he backed the truck out of the spot and Mancini wiped a stream of blood from his nose with the back of his sleeve.

"No. You?"

"Negative. Which way we going?"

"Turn right toward the back exit. There!" Mancini grimaced and pointed.

As Crocker turned onto Frank Sinatra Drive, he swerved to avoid some guy with a camera, who shot him the bird.

"Fuck you, too. You see 'em?"

"Right. Bear right," Mancini said. "Stay on this road and give me your iPhone."

"Why? You calling takeout?"

"So I can find the fuckers."

"How the hell you gonna do that?" Crocker asked.

"When the second SUV sped past, I tossed my Android in the open rear window. Made sure the volume was muted and the GPS engaged."

"What's your Android gonna do?"

"Watch."

"How many targets you see total?"

"Three subjects in the first vehicle. Two in the second. All male."

As Crocker cranked the pickup up to eighty, he saw Mancini to his right punching something into his iPhone. "What the fuck you doing now?"

"Accessing my InstaMapper account. You got a text from Cyndi. She wants to know where you want her to wait, at the Bellagio or Caesars Palace."

"Leave my shit alone!"

"Relax. She's waiting for you, buddy."

"Focus."

Mancini held the little screen to the right of Crocker's face. It showed a map with a red dot moving down a highway. "See that?"

"That them?"

"Brilliant, right? They're headed north on 15 toward Salt Lake City. You enter up ahead."

Crocker swerved left up the ramp and merged into traffic at ninety miles an hour. Multiple car horns screamed behind him.

His mind was spinning, trying to figure where the diplomats/counterfeiters were headed and how they might stop them. All they had were the phone, a pocketknife, a walkie-talkie, and the truck, which had a quarter of a tank of gas.

"Check the glove compartment," Crocker barked.

"Turning off on state route 95, toward Indian Springs."

"I see 'em."

He spotted the black Escalade two hundred feet ahead, burning down the left lane. The other Escalade was another two hundred feet ahead of it.

"Got 'em both."

"Cool. Nothing here but registration cards and a bottle of perfume," Mancini reported.

"Perfume? Radio Jeri. Tell her to contact the Las Vegas police and tell them we need help."

Mancini tried the walkie-talkie. "We're already out of range."

"Call her on my cell. Her number's on my contact list."

"You're real fucking demanding."

Manny didn't sound good. Crocker glanced right and saw blood trickling out of his ear.

"You get rung up pretty good?"

"Don't worry about me. Jeri isn't answering. You want to leave a message?"

"Hang up and try again."

Mancini glanced at InstaMapper on the phone and exclaimed, "Yo, yo, yo, cowboy! They're exiting ahead onto 95 north toward Reno."

"No problem. Keep trying Jeri."

CHAPTER SEVEN

A problem is a chance for you to do your best.
—Duke Ellington

THEY WERE twenty miles past the city limits, and the landscape had become shades of black. No moon to help out. Just the occasional pair of headlights on the highway and a canopy of stars. Polaris ahead at ten o'clock. The escaping SUVs had extinguished their lights. So had they, for that matter. The cab illuminated by the blue glow from his iPhone, Crocker leaned forward to check the gas. It was an eighth of an inch away from empty. Probably another gallon or gallon and a half, which would get them twenty more miles, max.

Manny's breathing was labored. In the glow from the little screen, Crocker saw that the left side of his face had swollen up. His eyes didn't look right, either.

They'd never gotten hold of Jeri, nor had they gotten through to an operator when they dialed 911. The city behind them was still dark.

"Dude, you remember your name?" Crocker asked. "You okay?"

"Still smarter than you, asshole, with half my brain working."

"More like a tenth, seems to me."

"Pay attention," Mancini growled as he looked at the screen. "They're turning off."

"Where? You see a road?"

"Up ahead to the right. Slow down!"

Crocker let up on the gas, applied the brake, and peered right into the darkness. All he saw was furry black and the sharper outline of a ridge in the distance.

"Turn here!" Manny shouted.

"Am I looking for a road?"

"No road. Just turn."

"Here?"

"Yes!"

The truck bounced so hard across the shoulder that they had to hold on to prevent banging their heads on the ceiling.

"Motherfucker!"

Crocker applied the brake and eased the pickup down an embankment. They found themselves on relatively flat desert terrain interrupted by the occasional boulder or shrub.

"You trying to flip this thing over?" Mancini asked.

Crocker picked up speed. It was hard to see through the dust and darkness ahead.

"Any idea where the fuck these guys are going?"

Soon as he posed the question, automatic fire rang out to their right and bullets shattered the side window and windshield. Crocker ducked behind the dash and turned left as more rounds ripped into the pickup's door and bed.

The vehicle hit a rock, dipped precipitously, and went downward fast.

"Fuck!" Mancini shouted.

"Hold on!"

They were airborne, but Crocker remained calm enough to check that both their seat belts were buckled. Twisted his torso hard right so it almost faced the seat and covered his head. Watched as Mancini did the same.

"Clench your teeth!"

The grille hit the ground hard, then the vehicle flipped over, spinning slightly right, and landed with a bang on the right side of the bed. Then it rolled onto the roof and was stopped by something hard that blew out the passenger-side window. *Bam!*

Crocker unclenched his teeth, exhaled, and shook the glass off.

"Manny?"

All he heard was a groan. Then he smelled gas.

"Manny, you all right? You hear me?"

The pickup had come to a rest on its side at a forty-degree angle, with the driver's side up. He pushed open the door with his left foot, unbuckled his seat belt, then turned to attend to Mancini. He seemed to be slipping in and out of consciousness, but was breathing freely and his pulse was only slightly slower than normal. Crocker unbuckled his seat belt, then felt carefully along his neck and back to check if anything was broken. His spine was intact.

"You hear me, buddy?"

No response, so he wrapped his arms around him and slowly lifted out the bear of a man—230 pounds of bone and muscle. Crocker managed to lug him a safe distance away from the vehicle and set him on the ground.

"Manny, can you hear me?" he whispered.

After a ten-second pause, Mancini groaned and responded, "Yeah." Then, "Fuck. My head hurts. What happened?"

"We crashed. I'm going to look for the phone and call for help."

He inspected Mancini more closely and found multiple cuts to his right arm and side, and a large contusion near his right eye. He didn't have the iPhone in his pocket or clutched in either hand.

"Wait here," Crocker whispered. "I'll be right back."

Turning and looking over his shoulder, he saw that they had fallen into a twenty-foot-deep gulch. As he took a step toward the pickup, he heard helicopter rotors echo off the incline ahead.

He scurried upward across the dirt and rocks on his hands and knees, looked up and followed the sound. The helo was drawing closer. He made out its dark form in the night sky. It hovered with lights out. Then suddenly the bright landing lights came on, illuminating a wide circle five hundred feet ahead and to the right, temporarily blinding him.

"Fuckers!"

It was descending, looking for a place to land. To the right of the circle he made out the two black SUVs. Men with automatic weapons stood around them.

"Now what?"

Without thinking he broke into a sprint, keeping his eyes on the ground ahead of him, juking to avoid boulders, holes, shrubs. Focused on his target and calculating that he should swing right of the SUVs and approach from behind. His legs and lungs burning, he pushed with everything he had left, making sure to land on the balls of his feet to minimize the sound.

The helo engines were idling now. He heard voices ahead, echoing off the mountain. They seemed to be speaking a foreign language. Sounded like barked instructions, said with urgency.

He felt urgency himself, pushing harder and closing within two hundred feet. Men were carrying suitcases from the Escalades and loading them into the helicopter. He ran as fast as his legs could take him, fighting through stiffness and pain, remembering Mancini and the pickup past his left shoulder, ignoring all the warnings that flashed in his head.

He looked up again. Saw the sides of the SUVs from a hundred feet, then the bottom of his right loafer slid across something and he lost his balance and fell forward. He tried to break the impact with his hands, but still hit his chest and chin hard enough that his teeth smacked together and he lost his breath. Ten seconds later he had recovered. He tasted blood in his mouth and felt it dripping down his chin. More alarming was the sound of the helo engine revving up as if it were about to take off. Again he ran, hobbling this time, ignoring the pain from his knee, mouth, and lungs.

Out of breath, he ducked behind the first SUV. The whine of the helo engine was deafening, the light it emitted blinding. The rotors kicked up a violent swirl of dust that stung his skin. They seemed to be waiting. Crocker saw someone emerge from the back of the other SUV carrying a suitcase and hurrying—a short man with a wrestler's body wearing a black tracksuit.

Crocker got up and sprinted toward him. Halfway there, someone screamed from the helo. Shots rang out. He fixed his eyes on the man's legs and launched himself. Hit the back of the man's knees hard and saw stars.

They were grappling in the dirt, dust in his eyes and mouth, more swirling around him, the man screaming and swearing in a language that sounded like Chinese.

Crocker located the man's head with his hands, delivered some quick, short blows to the front and right. Then the man twisted violently and kicked him in the groin. All the air went out of Crocker, and the pain was so intense he couldn't help but loosen his grip just enough for the man to squirm away.

He reached for him blindly, ignoring the pangs that shot up his back and down his legs. The helo started lifting off. Shots rained down on Crocker, tearing up the ground around him. He rolled under the helo and looked for the man but couldn't find him.

As the helicopter rose, he rolled left, then got to his feet and zigzagged sharply left and right. The helo stopped at thirty feet and hovered. Automatic-weapon fire poured from the doors and windows on both sides—like a wave of deadly bees.

Seeing a boulder ahead, he dove behind it and hugged its base, heart pounding, dirt in his mouth. The firing paused momentarily. He thought of Cyndi waiting. Jenny, Holly. Maybe the guys in the helicopter had lost sight of him. Maybe they were going to wait for him to give up, which would never fucking happen.

While the helo continued to hover as though the men inside couldn't decide whether to land and eliminate him or fly away, he quickly considered his options. There weren't any.

Past the bottom of the boulder he saw a glint from the chrome hardware on the black Pelican case the man had been carrying. Either Crocker had managed to wrestle it away or the man had left it. Didn't really matter.

Maybe the guys can't see it 'cause it's black and covered with dirt?

He hoped so as he looked for a route of escape. Any movement of his part would involve tremendous risk, so he waited, hoping that the next moment would reveal a solution, the tension stretching tauter by the second.

Looking at his dirt-covered hands, he realized he wasn't wearing his wedding ring. He felt for it in his pocket.

Yeah, it's still there.

Moments like this distilled existence to its essence—life and death, good and evil, love and hate. He loved Holly and always would.

Imagine thinking of her with my last breath.

The sound of the helo engine deepened. He saw the landing lights wash over the landscape.

Taking what he knew was a foolish risk, Crocker snuck a look. The helicopter was landing, which meant he was fucked. They would see the boulders. They would figure it was the only place in the vicinity where he could be hiding.

Just as he expected, shots rang out and pinged off the rock. He glanced behind him, looking for the route of escape. Facing forward again, he saw the flicker of flames in his periphery near the SUVs. Seconds later the sky lit up with a massive explosion that shook the ground and pushed the helo up and to the left like a toy. A large piece of metal from one of the Escalades clanged off the rocks. The closer SUV was engulfed in flames.

Manny? WTH!

He held his breath as the helo spun left. He was praying for it to crash, but the pilot managed to level it. The engine whined higher and the helo ascended and banked left. He followed its dark shape along the ridge of the mountain as the Escalade continued to burn.

He waited a minute until the sound of the rotors chopping the air receded and was replaced by the hiss and crackle of flames.

"Manny?" he called.

"Boss." His small, pained voice tripped across the landscape to his right.

He found Manny lying on his side, his face glowing orange in the reflected light.

"You saved my ass, buddy. You torch that vehicle? How?"

"Matches and my shirt."

"You better?" he asked, his chest heaving and sweat beading on his forehead.

"My whole right side is fucked, but I can move."

"Stay here. I'll be right back."

He ran and recovered the Pelican, then crossed to the intact Escalade. The handle was hot but the door wasn't locked. He took a quick look at the other Escalade burning twenty feet away and quickly catalogued the things he needed to do: hot-wire the SUV, rush his colleague to a hospital, find his phone, and call Jeri.

As he pried off the housing around the ignition box, he remembered two more things: He'd left Cyndi waiting, and he wanted to call Jenny, too. She always seemed nearby, even when she wasn't. He'd felt the same about Holly, and thought for a second that maybe there was still a chance to sort things out. Then he reminded himself that their marriage was over. He had to come to terms with that. He would.

James Dawkins woke to a continuous hum in his head, as though the song he was listening to had gotten stuck. It took effort to partially open his eyes, and when he did, he saw white and mustard colors and a shape directly in front of him. He made out a broad-shouldered Asian man sitting across from him wearing an implacable expression and sunglasses.

Dawkins sat up in the cream-colored leather seat. His left arm felt numb. As he shook blood into it, the Asian man looked past his shoulder and called to someone in a language Dawkins didn't understand.

"Where are we?" he asked.

The man didn't respond. Dawkins blinked, looked left and right, and slowly realized he was in a small jet that was airborne and probably had been for a while. Before he had a chance to think another thought, an Asian woman with sharp cheekbones and wearing a black pantsuit sat beside him, bringing a scent of soap.

"Did you rest well, Mr. Dawkins?" she asked gently in accented English.

She wasn't Dr. Nikasa, and as his brain brightened into consciousness, details began to come back—the speech in Geneva, the drinks in the hotel suite, now this. "I…uh…Where am I? How did I get here? Where is Dr. Nikasa?" he asked.

The woman's mechanical smile never left her face. "Okay, Mr. Dawkins. If you wish me to explain, I will."

His blood pressure spiked. "I…I don't know why I'm here. I must have been taken against my will."

She took a long breath and spoke quickly. "Mr. Dawkins, we have hired you for a short period of time. Two months probably. Three months at the most."

His mouth turned dry and his neck grew hot. "Hired me? I don't understand."

"Once you have completed the task we ask of you, you will be returned home safely."

Did this have something to with his job a UTC Aerospace? "Who has hired me?" he asked.

"While you are with us, we will treat you with the highest respect and take care of your needs," she said, hands folded in her lap. "At the end of your stay with us, Mr. Dawkins, we will wire-transfer a million U.S. dollars into your Chase account."

The mention of the million dollars stopped him. "No, there's been a mistake. I never agreed to this. I want to go home."

She leaned closer and slightly parted her lips expectantly. For a second he wasn't sure if she was going to bite him or kiss him. Instead, she stretched her mouth into the same mechanical smile. "I am here to answer your questions."

"Okay...First...Who do you work for?"

"There is no reason to be afraid."

"Please answer my question." An acute sense of alarm buzzed at the base of his spine.

"While you are away, Mr. Dawkins, your family will be taken care of. We have already wired one hundred thousand dollars to your joint checking account for that purpose. We have people who will attend to the needs of wife and daughter."

She seemed to be reciting from a memorized script.

"What's your name?" he asked.

"Miss Alice Wa."

"Okay, Alice. It seems that you've taken me against my will. I never signed up for this. So how do I know that anything you say is true?"

She frowned and looked confused. "There is no reason to be afraid, Mr. Dawkins."

He was dressed in the same shirt and pants as before. He un-buttoned his collar to make it easier to breathe. "You said that before, but I don't believe you. Who do you work for?"

With the mechanical smile still in place, she turned and mut-tered something to the man with the sunglasses, who picked up a laptop from the seat beside him and leaned across to hand it to her. Dawkins noted that it was a white Toshiba Satellite with a fifteen-and-a-half-inch screen.

She lowered a table out of the wall, set the laptop on it, and opened it. Turning to Dawkins and smiling, she said, "Log in to your checking account and see for yourself."

It took him a few seconds to remember his Chase password, but when he did, he saw that $100,000 had been deposited in his account on March fifth. His speaking engagement at the Swissotel Metropole had taken place the evening of the third.

"Okay," he said, sitting up again. Maybe what he had seen was real, and Nan and Karen would be taken care of. But maybe it wasn't. These people had a jet and were sophisticated. They had set up the whole charade in Geneva. If they wanted to set up a web page that looked real, they probably could.

Trying to sound as calm as he could under the circumstances, he said, "Just tell me where you're taking me, and why."

Miss Wa quickly replaced her frown with a smile. The man across from them continued to stare ahead with no expression. "I cannot tell you that, Mr. Dawkins. The mission is top secret."

The jet jolted sharply right. "What mission?" he asked as he held on to the armrests.

"I cannot tell you specific details. I can tell you that it will involve the application of your scientific and engineering skills toward solving a specific problem."

"What problem?"

"That is all I can say. I can tell you that you will be treated with the highest respect. All your accommodations and meals will be first class. All your needs will be taken care of. Anything you want."

She smiled into his eyes. For a moment he had the impression that she was including herself in the offer. In another time and place the proposal would have intrigued him, though he probably wouldn't have acted on it. Now it only added to his alarm.

He was a man of science who tried to see things as they were, without illusions. These were people with resources. He was a means to an end, not unlike what he had been at UTC. But he had chosen the UTC job and believed he was doing important work for his country.

Who were the people who had taken him? Enemies of some sort, who couldn't be trusted? What did they need from him?

"Maybe you would like food or wine now?" Miss Wa asked.

He had to think clearly. "A glass of water would be nice."

"Red, white, or rosé?"

"No wine. Just water."

"Yes. And maybe a massage afterward?"

He wouldn't allow himself to be distracted. "What about my job back home?"

She nodded as though she was trying to remember something in the script. "Yes. Your job will be waiting. This has been arranged."

"How?"

She stood and bowed. "It's an honor, Mr. Dawkins, to serve you and welcome you as our guest. I'll get your drinks now and will return to show you the movies we have downloaded for your viewing pleasure."

CHAPTER EIGHT

No one is so brave that he is not disturbed by something unexpected.

Julius Caesar

"CROCKER?"

"Yeah?"

"Crocker, you awake?"

He blinked into the stark fluorescent light. A man wearing a white polo shirt with CAESARS PALACE stitched across the pocket leaned over him. He had short sandy hair and a scar across one eyebrow.

"Sorry to wake you, sir. Ms. Blackwell sent me to see how you're doing and to take you to her if you feel well enough." He spoke in a flat midwestern accent.

"Jeri?" Crocker sat up in the bed and tried to get his bearings. "Who are you?"

"Special Agent Mike Edberg. I work with Ms. Blackwell."

He was in a light-blue hospital room with off-white curtains pulled closed. Besides a sore back, tightness in his legs, and a small bandage on his left arm, he felt okay and rested.

"She says it's important that she see you right away."

"Where am I, Mike?"

"Centennial Hills Hospital, Las Vegas."

He remembered the helicopter, the shootout, Mancini's injuries. Having seen the inside of way too many hospitals recently, he wanted to leave as soon as possible.

"The nurse I spoke to said you aren't a patient," Agent Edberg added.

"Good news. Thanks."

"You were exhausted and a little banged-up, so they gave you an empty bed to sleep in."

He checked under the blanket and saw that his shoes, pants, and shirt had been removed, but he still had on the undershirt he'd worn to dinner with Cyndi. He'd left her waiting. Not a great way to start a relationship.

The clock by the bed read 8:42.

"I need to wash up, then check on my colleague," Crocker said. "You know where I can find him?"

"Asleep in the room across the hall."

"Thanks. Give me ten minutes."

"I'll wait for you in the lobby."

Showered and dressed in the same clothes he had worn the previous night, he found the doctor who'd been treating Mancini. According to Dr. Gupta, his teammate had suffered a concussion, cuts to his arms and face, and a contusion near his right eye. "His condition is stable," Dr. Gupta said, "but we plan to keep him here another twenty-four hours for observation."

"Good luck with that."

Crocker entered Mancini's room, if only to prove to himself

that his teammate was still alive and the episode last night hadn't been a dream. He found him sitting up in bed eating breakfast and watching a documentary about General George Patton on the History Channel.

"Enjoying yourself?" Crocker asked.

"Always. You have fun last night?"

"You bet," Crocker answered, remembering the Pelican case and wondering what had happened to it. He'd never had a chance to open it and see what was inside.

"Excellent show, boss. Pull up a chair. General Patton was outstanding. You know what he said when he was asked what he loved most in life?" Mancini asked, shoveling a spoonful of cereal into his mouth.

"What?"

"Fucking and fighting."

"Really?"

"Yeah, in that order. And I agree, but would have to include learning as a close second."

"Of course you would. I've got to check on something," Crocker said as he headed for the door. "I'll call Carmen and tell her you're still as insane as ever."

Mancini grinned. "And as horny. Hospitals have that effect."

When he asked Dr. Gupta about the Pelican case, the doctor referred him to the admitting nurse—a big guy with a shaved head, glowing pink skin, and a gold hoop in one ear who looked like Mr. Clean.

"No, sir, no one reported seeing a black Pelican case."

"You sure about that?"

"I'll double-check."

Crocker reached into his pocket and found his cell phone. The front screen was cracked, but the device still worked. Checking his texts, several of which were from Cyndi, he saw he had a recent message from his daughter, Jenny.

He pressed the number next to her name.

"Hi, sweetheart, you okay?"

Her voice burst through the line like a bubble. "Yeah, Dad. Fine. What about you? Enjoying Las Vegas?"

"Oh, yeah. Fun town. What's going on?"

"Not much. Kenna's boyfriend stayed over last night, so I crashed at your apartment."

"Anytime, sweetheart. No problem. What's Kenna's boyfriend like?"

"Nice. Kind of a hipster."

He smiled at himself for asking. Knew it was a waste of time, since Jenny and her friends were grown up now and weren't going to tell him much. Still, he couldn't help trying.

"Dad, Cox cut off your cable TV service," Jenny continued in a serious tone. "I called them and they said you haven't paid your bill in months."

"Cox?" Crocker asked. "Who's that?"

"Your cable TV provider."

In the past Holly had handled all the household bills. Since she'd moved out, he'd missed several deadlines, not because he was short on funds, but with the travel and everything else that was going on, he forgot.

"Give me their number," Crocker said. "I'll call them now and pay it over the phone."

"Thanks, Dad. Hold on."

The admitting nurse returned to tell him that no one had seen a black Pelican case, nor was it noted on any admittance form.

"What about the vehicle I arrived in?" Crocker asked. "That seems to be missing, too."

"We don't keep track of patients' cars. But if you drove it here, it's probably still parked in the garage."

That sounded logical. "Thanks."

He was trying to remember the make, model, or color of the vehicle he'd arrived in when Jenny came back on the line with the Cox Communications number. She asked if he'd be home for the holiday.

"Which holiday is that?"

"Easter, Dad. It's in three weeks."

He checked his mental calendar, which was foggy at best. "Yeah, I think so. I was thinking of taking you to the Coastal Grill."

It was a fib.

"Oh, cool. But…Kenna's parents invited me. They asked if you wanted to come, too."

"Sure, if you think that's okay."

He was trying to remember whether he'd met them.

"They're excited to meet you. I'll tell 'em. Love you, Dad. I've got to go."

Apparently he hadn't. "Love you, too."

It seemed like just a few months ago that Jenny was adjusting to living with him and Holly after she'd moved east because she and her mother (Crocker's first wife) weren't getting along. Now she was a semi-independent young woman with her own car and apartment and a host of friends he'd never met. He prayed to God she wasn't as wild as he'd been at that age. Didn't think so, but it was hard to know.

He walked up the parking garage ramp remembering the

members of his family and the passage of time. His dad lived by himself in Fairfax, Virginia. His sister, her husband, and their two children lived outside of Raleigh. His brother and his family resided in a suburb of Boston.

Even though he was limping slightly from the bursitis in his left knee and tightness in his lower back, he still felt the urge to take a long run through the desert. It would clear his head, loosen his muscles, and reenergize him. But there were duties to take care of first.

He spotted the black Escalade covered in dirt and parked near the second-tier elevator. The Pelican case was resting in back.

As he exited the lot with the case, names and faces passed through his mind's eye like signs in a freeway tunnel. As soon as he had the time, he'd call the various members of his family and catch up. He owed them that. His father had just turned seventy-five. His younger brother was forty-one now. Nieces and nephews were graduating from high school and going to college. He loved them all, wished them well, and hoped they still remembered him.

The Caesars Palace casino lights shone bright again, and the cacophony of slot machines and games sounded more annoying than ever. Quite a contrast to the quiet hush of the desert. He preferred its cleansing heat to this sweet, refrigerated air. Jeri stood behind the desk in Walker's office drinking coffee and eating a doughnut, looking like she hadn't slept.

"Crocker! Ain't you a sight for sore eyes."

He shut the door behind him, rested the Pelican case on the floor, and sat. "Morning, Jeri."

It's not that she didn't work hard. It's just that she never seemed to let problems interfere with her enjoyment of life. Except now. This morning she looked worried and distracted.

"You functional? You rested?" she asked, biting into her doughnut. "I hear those dudes in the penthouse got away."

"Affirmative to all three." He knew she was married with grown kids, and wondered how she balanced work with personal life.

"Good. Good. And that's too bad. Have a doughnut. Pour yourself some java." She nodded to a Mr. Coffee on a table in the corner. Under normal circumstances he would have declined, but he hadn't eaten since the meal with Cyndi.

Jeri coughed into her hand and said, "You know I wanted to assist you guys but was working with limited resources."

"No problem. We handled it the best we could." He sipped the bitter coffee and took a bite of the doughnut, which tasted stale. He set it aside.

"Your teammate okay? Manny?"

"A little banged-up. He'll be fine."

"I appreciate everything you guys have done. We're comping your room and expenses, so there's no need to check out."

"Thanks."

She threw the empty box in the trash, stood, and wiped sugar off the front of her blue blouse. "Stay for dinner if you want. Stay over another night. This whole mission has been a disaster— no leads, just a trashed hotel suite and a shitload of unanswered questions—so who the hell cares. Follow me."

He walked beside her, carrying the Pelican case across the casino floor to a black SUV waiting out front.

"Where are we going?"

"Followup. Probably nothing." They sat beside each other in

the back. "Why does stuff like this always happen on my watch?" Jeri asked as the vehicle jolted to life.

He figured she was referring to an incident that had happened in '06 while she was on President George W. Bush's security detail during a visit to the country of Georgia when some lunatic had tossed a grenade wrapped in plaid cloth onto the podium a few feet away from the president. Jeri and the other Secret Service officers had failed to notice. Fortunately for them and the president, the grenade failed to detonate.

"We got to move on, Jeri. You know that."

"When did you start sounding like Dr. Phil?"

She looked out the window at a passing bail bond office and a massage parlor, apparently lost in thought.

"I forgot," Crocker said, slapping the top of the Pelican case that rested near his feet. "We recovered this last night." He popped it opened and Jeri's eyes widened at the sight of the shrink-wrapped hundred-dollar bills packed inside.

"Shit, Crocker! Why didn't you say something before?"

They left the case with the driver, who stayed with the vehicle as they walked into a brown brick building with the sign on the glass door that read NEVADA POWER COMPANY. Inside, a patently nervous official with a shaved head and strange-looking rectangular glasses invited them into his office.

In a pinched voice, he said, "We've completed a preliminary crisis report and concluded that whoever killed the lights last night did so by hacking into our supervisory control and data acquisition system."

Crocker didn't know what that entailed. Nor did he understand the two-page report the official handed them, which consisted mainly of computer code and terminology.

"Any idea who was behind the attack?" he asked.

The official squinted through his glasses. "In my line of work, we don't use the word 'attack.' We call them incursions. Incursions are generally difficult to trace. Sometimes the people behind them are kids showing off and gaming the system. In other instances, they're individuals or organization with more sinister motives."

"Which category do you think this incursion falls into?" asked Crocker.

The official twitched and shrugged. "I'm a power official, not a criminal investigator. I assume you would know that answer better than me."

Jeri yawned and covered her mouth. "Based on what we know now, none of the casinos were hit and nothing was stolen."

"Then it's possible the blackout was a prank," the official said.

"Makes you wonder about the guys who ran," Crocker commented. "Wong and Petroc."

Jeri stopped reading the report and looked at him over the top of her glasses. "What do you mean?"

"Makes me wonder if the whole thing was planned—the blackout to cover their escape, the helicopter to meet them in the desert." Turning to the NPC official he asked, "How often do blackouts like this happen?"

"In my eighteen years at the NPC, we've had a handful of minor incursions, but never one that shut down the entire system," the official answered.

Outside, as they prepared to climb into the SUV, Jeri turned to Crocker and said, "We knew we were looking at a counterfeiting operation that included Wong and Petroc. You think the blackout was part of it, too?"

"That's what my gut tells me."

"You're smarter than you look, honey," she said, scrunching up her face in thought. "I'll check with DC."

Dawkins had consumed half a bottle of silky, dry Clos Fourtet 2012 and enjoyed a dinner of hanger steak with Bordelaise sauce. He even had ice cream and espresso for dessert. But the hospitality ended as the jet started its descent. That's when the sunglassed guard roughly tied a blindfold over his eyes and handcuffed his wrists in front of him. There were no further explanations from Miss Wa. No announcements from the pilot. No further warnings or instructions.

The plane banked sharply and bounced, then touched down gently, braked, and taxied to a stop.

His stomach was in his throat now, and he felt more anxious and alone than at any time in his life. Worse than when he'd gotten lost in the foothills of the Adirondacks while camping with his father. At least then, he knew he was in the United States. Now he was almost certain he wasn't.

"This way, Mr. Dawkins," Miss Wa instructed.

The guard pulled him upright and wrapped some kind of parka around his shoulders. The air outside was cold and smelled of jet fuel and agriculture. People around him murmured in an Asian language: Chinese? Mongolian? Korean? He couldn't tell.

The warm room he entered smelled of rubbing alcohol. Someone checked his blood pressure. Then he felt a cold stethoscope on his chest and back.

"Is this necessary?" he asked.

No one answered.

Fear tingled upward from the base of his spine. Now he was on a bus, thinking about the trip Nan and he had made to Beijing eight and half years ago to meet their adopted daughter. At two months of age she had been placed on the steps of a bank in southern China, clad in a pink dress and wrapped in a blanket. On what the adoption agency called Gotcha Day, he was the first to hold her. The connection he made with Chun, who they renamed Karen, was powerful and immediate. He couldn't remember feeling happier. Now he missed her. He also remembered his older sister, who he hadn't spoken to in months. As kids they'd played doctor, until their mother caught them partially naked one day in the bathroom of their house in Colorado.

After a four-hour bus ride he boarded a boat. The farther he traveled, the more helpless he felt. He and Nan had been married for fifteen years now. She was his rock. All he wanted was to return home and be with his family. He told himself that he would do whatever he had to in order to make that possible. He had never thought of himself as brave, but so far he had surprised himself. Despite the fear and uncertainty, he was holding it together.

The boat docked, and he was helped off and led down a path to a concrete entrance of some kind and then an elevator. The elevator descended slowly.

He heard the shuffle of shoes against a concrete floor. He smelled mildew. A door creaked open and he was led into a room and pushed into a chair. Someone removed the handcuffs and blindfold.

He blinked into the harsh fluorescent light. The walls were painted a dull shade of green. Across from him was a metal bed covered with an olive-green blanket. A young Asian woman moved in front him wearing a white shirt and baggy black pants worn high. She bent at the waist and peered at him through wire-rimmed glasses like she was studying a strange creature in a zoo.

"Welcome, Mr. Dawkin," she said in heavily accented English. "My name is Sung. I am your assistant. I happy to meet you. It is my pleasure. Would you desire tea?"

He tried to conceal the feeling of hopelessness that was descending over him. "No, not now," he said with a tight smile. "But thank you for the offer." It felt like three times gravity was pushing down on every part of his body.

He could barely keep his eyes open and focused. A guard stood at the door like a statue, dressed in a baggy camouflage uniform and cap. Everything felt cold and strange.

"Would you like soda and crackers?"

He struggled to get the words out. "No thanks."

"You looked tired, Mr. Dawkin, so I let you rest. If you need anything, push white button on wall. I…come." She pulled the blanket back and beckoned him to the bed as if dealing with a child. He sensed humanity in her gesture. Shivering, he crossed the cold concrete floor.

He lay down with his clothes on, heard the door lock behind her, and fell asleep.

CHAPTER NINE

Character is destiny.

—Heraclitus

THE PILOT of the Blackhawk had a Steelers logo tattooed on the back of his neck. Crocker was tempted to tell him about the time two well-known Steelers defensive players showed up at his house in Virginia to work out with him. Within an hour he was just getting warmed up and both of them were puking on his front lawn. But what would be the point? He didn't want to appear to be a braggart, and it wouldn't be smart to distract the pilot, especially when they were closing in on their target, a North Korean container ship named the *Cong Son Gang*. So he dry-checked the HK416 in his lap and kept his mouth shut.

Back in DC, Jeri had started to assemble the pieces of an international conspiracy that involved counterfeit money, illegal arms shipments, and narcotics, possibly originating in China, North Korea, or Iran. Now he was chasing a North Korean ship suspected of playing a role in it. The evidence was sketchy—captured text messages about "valued goods" to an Iranian official in Singapore from a phone linked to Wong and Petroc.

Nevertheless, Crocker was back in the fray and grateful that the hearing in Fairfax County had been pushed back. Two days ago he learned that Captain Sutter had written a letter to the judge explaining the important role Crocker played in protecting the country's national security and asking that the charges against him be dropped. Hopefully, he wouldn't have to worry about it again.

Everything on the HK416 seemed secure—the AAC (Advanced Armaments Corp.) suppressor, AG416 40mm grenade launcher and AN/PVS-17 scope.

His Black Cell teammate Akil, on the bench beside him listening to "One" by Metallica through his headphones, turned to him and mouthed "Awesome."

"One" happened to be one of Crocker's favorite workout songs. Out of the side of his mouth, he said, "Won't be so awesome when you shred your eardrums."

"What?"

"Your mama's so fat the back of her neck looks like a package of hot dogs."

Akil nodded to the beat of the music and flashed a thumbs-up. A couple of SEALs on the opposite bench laughed. Akil was a knucklehead, but Crocker loved him. Appreciated his family, too, a tight-knit group of Egyptian Americans employed in Akil's father's jewelry shops in and around Detroit.

Crocker tucked the gold ankh good luck symbol Akil's father had given him under his combat vest. Last time he was in Michigan, Akil's old man had told him about the incidences of anti-Muslim prejudice directed against them—slurs painted on their car, rocks thrown through windows, garbage dumped on their front stoop. It pissed Crocker off.

He tried to be objective. With ISIS radicals routinely hacking off people's heads and raping women, he understood why many Americans felt outraged and angry. But the guys in ISIS and al-Qaeda occupied the lunatic fringe. Most Muslims were decent people who wanted a better life for their families. Some were freedom-loving Americans, and a few, like Akil, played an important and heroic role in the war on terrorism.

The copilot barked through Crocker's headset, "Zero Alpha, Tango Two. Eyes on target, one o'clock."

He jolted to attention. "Copy, Tango. Over."

Crocker slapped Akil on the shoulder, then pumped his fist up and down and pointed at the forward windshield to tell the members of Team Alpha to get ready. Filling out Alpha were four other SEALs from DEVGRU (Team Six)—Jenks, Tré, Pauly, and Sam. Most of them were guys Crocker had never worked with before. His Black Cell teammates Mancini, Suarez, Davis, and Cal were either on medical or personal leave and therefore unavailable.

A light southeast wind rocked the Blackhawk. They were currently fifteen miles off the coast of Singapore in the Strait of Malacca—a busy shipping lane that had been the scene of hundreds of pirate attacks from 2001 to 2004. Now it was regularly patrolled by the Indonesian, Indian, Malaysian, and Singaporean navies.

Because their target was still in Singaporean waters, the Singapore Maritime Police cutter *White Shark,* commanded by Captain Kin Han, would do the initial intercept. Earlier this morning Captain Han and Crocker had traded sets of 350-pound bench presses at the SMP gym. It wasn't something Crocker did often. Instead of adding bulk, he preferred to remain lean so he could shoot and scoot.

The SEALs were in the air to provide backup should the crew of the *Cong Son Gang* try to evade the Marine Police or things get noisy. Given that this was a North Korean freighter headed for Iran and that the North Koreans had a reputation for being crazy, they had to be prepared for anything.

Crocker slammed a twenty-round 5.56mmx45mm mag in his weapon, checked that everything in his assault vest was secure, then turned left and tried to locate the vessel through the forward windows. The early morning yellow-orange haze obscured the water, making it hard to spot anything, even something the size of a 295-meter-long container ship.

His last week and a half had involved a whirlwind of travel— Vegas to Virginia Beach; Virginia Beach to DC; DC to Coronado, CA; Coronado to Honolulu; Honolulu to Okinawa; Okinawa to the USS *Ronald Reagan,* stationed in the Indian Ocean off the island of Sumatra.

"Zero Alpha, this is White Shark One, do you read me? Over."

"Send, White Shark One. Over."

"Moving into position. Ready to initiate radio contact."

"Copy. Over."

The Blackhawk hovering at three hundred meters flattened the chop in a circular pattern. Even with the engines roaring, Crocker could hear EDM blasting through Akil's headphones. He shoved his shoulder.

Akil turned to him and lifted his grizzled square chin. "What?"

"You're not gonna be able to hear anything," he said, pointing at Akil's headphones.

Akil pulled them down. "This? It's Swedish House Mafia." He sang off-key, "'We're gonna save the world tonight...'"

"Not like that, you won't."

"Whadda you know about music?"

Crocker preferred classic rock like the Stones and sixties-era jazz. Brubeck, Getz, Monk, and Davis were his current faves. He regretted leaving his iPod in the locker back at SMP headquarters.

The haze was starting to burn off, so he lifted the binos and could now make out the long container ship with the rusted white hull and yellow-blue-and-red stack. Looked like it was badly in need of some TLC. Pulling up to one side was a much smaller and sharper-looking white-red-and-blue Singapore Maritime Police cutter.

Five minutes passed without the *Cong Son Gang* appearing to reduce speed and Crocker growing antsy.

"Zero Alpha, this is White Shark One. The target is not responding to our radio signals, so we're going to initiate blocking maneuvers."

"Copy, White Shark One," Crocker responded. "We're standing by. Over."

He wasn't surprised. North Korean vessels were notorious for not responding to internationally accepted maritime signals and conduct.

"What the fuck we waiting for?" Akil asked as he removed his shiny new Beats headphones.

"For you to get your shit together. Ready?"

"Always, boss."

"Put your toys away and inspect the rope," Crocker said, nodding toward the back of the helo.

"Copy that."

Through his Steiner binos, Crocker watched as the Marine Police cutter positioned itself in the path of the container ship and the ship changed course to steer around it. He glanced down at his Suunto watch to start to measure how long this would last when he heard a rip from the *White Shark*'s 25mm Bushmaster chain gun and looked up.

Captain Han wasn't playing. Either that, or the *Cong Son Gang* was nearing the limit of Singaporean territorial waters and Han was taking this bit of United States–Singapore cooperation seriously. Maybe he had a personal motive. At the gym that morning, he'd talked about wanting to get his daughter admitted to MIT.

Crocker removed the Hellstorm SOLAG gloves from the carabiner on his web belt and pulled them on. The four SEALs on the opposite bench followed suit. On hearing the gunfire, the pilot of the U.S. Navy Blackhawk moved in closer so they were only a hundred meters behind the North Korean freighter and two hundred meters overhead.

Crocker felt the adrenaline building in his system. Below he saw the *Cong Son Gang* tack left past the *White Shark* and closer to the eastern edge of Sumatra, which glistened in the distance. *Interesting corner of the world,* Crocker thought. And one he wanted to explore further. He'd read a lot about Borneo and its rain forests and diverse species, which included orangutans, barking deer, pig-tailed macaques, and huge flying fox bats. It lay about six hundred nautical miles to the southeast.

Below, the *White Shark*'s Bushmaster and twin 12.7mm machine guns echoed in unison. When the smoke cleared, the *Cong Son Gang* showed no signs of slowing down.

Stubborn fucks.

Through his headset he heard, "Zero Alpha, this is White Shark One. The target is not responding. Engage! Engage!"

The Blackhawk pilot swooped down and hovered over the forward deck of the *Gang* at forty meters. A patchwork of orange, rusty-white, and dark-blue shipping containers bobbed and swayed below.

"Ready!" Akil shouted.

"Ready!"

On a hand signal from Akil the copilot disengaged the hatch, whereupon Akil threw the braided-nylon 1.7-inch-diameter fast rope out, located a container to land on, and went down first, expertly and fast. Crocker felt a burst of pride. The other SEALs followed in designated order, ten feet apart. Crocker went last, using his hands and feet to hold the rope and slide down smoothly. Once on deck, he scanned 360 degrees through the AN/PVS-17 scope.

No greeting party or targets in sight. The ship itself looked old and tired. The foremast was literally coming apart and listed to one side. Some of the shoe-fit latches on the hatch covers didn't close properly, and the bridge tower front was pitted with rust.

Move and cover.

He signaled Akil and Jenks to wait while he, Tré, Pauly, and Sam took the bridge. They slipped past a dozen forty-foot containers, the rubber composition soles of their Merrell boots muffling the sound. Entering the tower, they climbed five levels of metal steps to the bridge. Crocker tried the metal door, but it was locked.

He banged on it and called out, "We're U.S. Navy working with the Singapore Maritime Police. We're here to inspect your ship."

"Door no work!" came the answer.

"Either you open this door or we blow it in."

"Door no work!"

He signaled to the breacher, Sam, to apply the charges—strips of C-4—then shouted through the door, "Tell all your crew members to stand back!"

As Sam readied the strips and detonators someone unlatched the door from within and let it slowly creak open. Confronting them was a skinny Asian man in black pajama pants and an old white T-shirt with a defiant look on his face. He was holding a .38 revolver in his right hand, currently aimed at the floor but alarming nonetheless.

"Drop the weapon!" Crocker ordered, his HK aimed dead center on the man's chest, his left hand gesturing down to the metal floor.

The man, who appeared to be in his late forties, grunted disgustedly and lowered the pistol to his side. Crocker noticed he was wearing flip-flops.

"Are you the captain of this vessel?" he asked, stepping forward with his weapon still pointing at the man's chest.

The Asian man shrugged.

"Sir, are you the captain?"

This time the man stuck out his chin and growled, "Cap-tain."

"You speak English? What's your name?"

The man sneered something in a foreign language. Beyond him, Crocker saw Tré, Pauly, and Sam checking a group of crew members huddled near the ship's command console. Sam shook his head, indicating that they weren't armed.

Simultaneously, he heard Han over the radio: "Zero Alpha, White Shark One here. What's the situation onboard?"

"Stand by, White Shark. Situation developing. Over."

Crocker never took his eyes off the captain. He said, "I'm going to ask you one more time to drop the pistol. Then my men and I are going to inspect the ship."

The captain didn't respond. Crocker was trying to decide whether he should shoot him in the leg, smack him with the butt of his HK, or forcibly remove the pistol from his hand. In the last-minute lead-up to the op, this contingency hadn't been discussed.

He stepped forward until they were within three feet of each other. Suddenly the captain lifted the pistol to his head and pulled the trigger. *Blam!* Blood and brain matter splattered across the bridge wall and floor as the captain's knees gave way and his body folded.

The gunshot reverberating in Crocker's ears, cordite cleaving to the inside of his nostrils, he stepped over the body and stood next to Tré, who was facing five frightened-looking crew members. Pauly and Sam peeled away to inspect the rest of the tower.

"Who's the next in command?" Crocker asked.

The tallest of the men, with a wisp of dark beard on his chin, held up his index finger and said, "My name…Lu. First officer."

"You speak English," Crocker responded. "Good." He pointed to the body bleeding out behind him. "First, I want him covered. Then I want to see your cargo manifest."

According to the manifest, the *Cong Son Gang* was transporting rice from Hamhung, North Korea, to Bandar Abbas on the Persian Gulf. The only other cargo was two small containers of "bicycle parts." Remembering that Bandar Abbas was a port city in Iran and that Iran was one of North Korea's few trading partners, Crocker radioed Captain Han of the SMP to board the ship and lead the inspection.

That's when Pauly and Sam returned, holding a dark-haired man by the collar of his dirty white shirt.

"Who's he?" Crocker asked.

"Banasheh Nasari, according to his ID," Pauly said. "We found him hiding in the mess."

It was a Persian name, which made sense, since the ship was headed to Iran and Jeri had said the Iranians might be behind the larger conspiracy. Nasari was a man of about fifty with a high forehead, black-framed glasses, and a sly, somewhat intellectual appearance.

"Do you speak English?"

He looked back at Crocker with dead eyes.

"Who are you working for? Why are you on this ship?"

No answer again.

Akil tried addressing him in Persian and then Arabic. Nasari didn't respond to either. Not that it really mattered to Crocker, who had decided that even if Nasari offered information, he couldn't be trusted.

Once Captain Han boarded, the SEALs descended to the cargo deck and stood guard as Lu and other crew members opened the large deck containers one by one. Han's men slit open some of the 22.6-kilo (50-pound) bags of rice and crawled through the containers. Satisfied that they were filled only with rice, the group climbed down the metal galley ladder to the hold.

The smaller twenty-foot containers in holds 1, 2, and 3 did in fact hold rubber bicycle seats and pedals. According to First Mate Lu, so did the containers in forward holds 4, 5, and 6. But the door to the forward hold area was double-padlocked shut, and he claimed not to have a key.

"I bet this asshole has it," Akil said, nodding toward Nasari.

"Do you?" Crocker asked.

Again no answer, just a blank stare.

Instead of searching the ship for the keys, one of the policemen on Captain Han's team produced a Rotorazer saw with a carbonized blade that cut through the locks like they were butter. Then he swung open the first container and sliced through a thick black plastic lining. Stacked inside were metal barrels packed with a white crystalline substance.

Han put some on the tip of his tongue, tasted it, and spit it out. "Crystal meth," he announced.

Behind the barrels they found a wooden crate. Stacked inside it were rows of shrink-wrapped hundred-dollar bills.

Lu claimed he hadn't known they were there, and Nasari didn't change his expression even when Crocker got in his face and asked, "You knew nothing about this either, did you?"

The SEALs escorted the bills back to Singapore harbor, where they guarded them until U.S. Treasury officials arrived and took possession. Crocker later learned that they were counterfeit, amounted to nearly $1 million, and fit the same 2HK1 profile as the bills seized in Vegas.

Even though Nasari claimed diplomatic immunity and had to be released, it wasn't a bad day's work.

CHAPTER TEN

The mind is a universe and can make a heaven of hell,
a hell of heaven.

—John Milton

JAMES DAWKINS sat in the chilly underground workroom in the company of three male assistants and confronted the task in front of him. Basically he was being asked to miniaturize and calibrate the inertial guidance system that would fit directly under the warhead of a newly developed Unha-3 rocket. According to the mockups and schematics he'd seen, the Unha-3 was a three-stage 110-foot rocket that weighed about eighty-five metric tons.

Dawkins shivered and sneezed into the sleeve of his dirty gray lab tunic. His nose started running.

The first stage of the Unha-3 used a Nodong engine similar to those deployed on the Pakistani Ghauri-I and Iranian Shahab-3 missiles. It borrowed from the design of the Scud missile engine, but was at least 140 percent larger and featured more finely calibrated nozzles and combustors. Dawkins knew that the Nodong had originally been designed by the Soviets. He was also aware that a man who looked Russian, and who Dawkins suspected was a rocket engineer, appeared to be working in another part of this same underground complex.

He had seen the man once, by mistake apparently, when he emerged from the bathroom with his watchers and assistants while Dawkins was being escorted to his room. They had exchanged quick looks.

The second stage of the Unha-3 was almost identical in design to the old Soviet R-27 ballistic missile deployed in Soviet nuclear subs during the Cold War.

Without even considering the third stage, which was the part Dawkins was charged with working on, he realized three things: One, he was almost certainly in North Korea. Two, he probably knew more about the progress of the North Korean missile program than anyone in Western intelligence. And, three, the North Koreans were close to developing an intercontinental ballistic missile that was capable of hitting the continental United States.

His job was to provide the gyro-stabilized platform (GSP), missile guidance set control (MGSC), and amplifier assembly that would direct the warhead to within feet of its target. The GSP, which was the platform that needed the most work, acted to measure acceleration and velocity and maintain proper flight control. It was stabilized by dual-axis, free-rotor gyros whose rotors were supported on self-generated gas bearings. One gyro helped to stabilize pitch and roll, and the second provided azimuth stabilization.

Dawkins knew all the details of this particular GSP system based on his work on a host of U.S. military rocket systems for UTC Aerospace. He was therefore able to identify the challenges immediately. In this case, this meant generating and regulating the proper gas cushions so the gyros would operate properly during startup.

If he accomplished this, he knew he would be giving the North Koreans the ability to hit targets more than five thousand miles away with pinpoint accuracy. It's something he absolutely didn't want to do. But he also desperately wanted to get out of North Korea alive. This was the conundrum that confronted him now as he stood in the cold lab looking at the GSP on the table in front of him. It resembled a large stainless-steel ball with two bands encircling it at perpendicular angles. Each band housed a torque motor and a digital resolver.

Somehow the supposedly backward North Koreans had chosen the perfect engineer for the task. How they had managed to identify Dawkins and snatch him so easily gave him pause. Clearly, these weren't the bumbling fools spoofed in Western movies and comic books. They were dangerous, ingenious men who also ran very active uranium and plutonium enrichment programs, and therefore in Dawkins's mind probably had sufficient amounts of weaponized uranium and plutonium to create numerous nuclear weapons.

Dawkins had read published reports about the North Korean nuclear program. He also understood that one of the most difficult challenges in building an ICBM capable of delivering a nuclear weapon was reducing the size of the warhead so it could fit over the guidance system and atop the Unha-3 rocket. He wondered if they had other engineers, like the one he had seen in the hallway, engaged in that task as well.

Of course, there was the Russian. One of Dawkins's assistants, Pak Ju, referred to him as Dr. Soderov, formerly employed by the Makeev Design Bureau in Moscow, and boasted that Soderov had volunteered to help the Democratic People's Republic of Korea without remuneration. Whether this was the scientist's real name, and whether he had worked at the Makeev Design Bureau or not, was impossible for Dawkins to tell.

Clearly there had been a large amount of outside input. In Dawkins's opinion, the North Korean engineers and technicians he had met weren't capable of bringing the program to the advanced state it was in now. He concluded this based on the knowledge and capabilities of the North Koreans he'd met, particularly his two assistants—Pak Ju and Yi-Thaek, both of whom spoke some English and were veterans of the program.

Pak Ju was the older and more experienced of the two—a guarded, slow-moving, heavyset man in his late fifties with tiny slits for eyes that he hid behind yellow-tinted, black-rimmed glasses. Yi, Pak Ju's subordinate in age and rank, had trained as a mathematician. He had a more agreeable manner, stuttered when he spoke, and was thinner, slightly taller, and balding. Dawkins's third assistant was a guard or minder named Kwon, who stood about five eight, was thickly muscled, and rarely spoke. At least two of these three men accompanied Dawkins everywhere, including to the bathroom.

At the end of each workday Kwon would lock the lab and the three of them would walk him down the hallway, down a flight of stairs and along another dank hall to his quarters, where Sung would be waiting. She prepared his meals, washed his clothes, and attended to his other needs. At night after he fell asleep, she'd leave quietly and lock the door behind her. She returned promptly every morning at seven to help him dress and serve him breakfast.

It was a strange, simple routine, but one that he adjusted to relatively easily. At the end of the first week, Sung dressed in him in a suit—black and badly made—shirt, and hooded parka.

"Think about you family," Sung whispered before she turned off the electric space heater and pointed outside.

"My family? What do you mean by that?"

Kwon stood waiting in the hallway. The two North Koreans led him to a large freight elevator that lifted them to ground level. It was the first time Dawkins had seen the entrance to the underground complex, which looked unimpressive—a twenty-foot-high concrete structure with large metal doors hidden in a grove of tall pine trees. The air outside was thin and freezing cold. The sun shone weakly through a thick layer of gray clouds.

He sneezed again, and his legs and head felt heavy as he walked beside Sung along a dirt path that ended at what appeared to be a very large body of water with islands in the distance shrouded in mist. Ice covered the rocks along the shore.

As he shivered, he remembered that today was Karen's ninth birthday. After muttering a prayer to her under his breath, he sighed. He wanted her to be proud of him, and sensed that whatever he did or didn't do here would greatly affect her future.

"Very peaceful, Mr. Dawkin," Sung said, lingering at his side. He had asked her to call him James.

"In the spring and fall the cranes come. They are sacred."

"Sacred? Are you sure you're using the correct word?"

"A thousand of cranes appeared when our Supreme Leader's father died four years ago. They tried to carry him to heaven, but the people cried and despaired so much that the Supreme Leader's father returned."

Dawkins assumed she was talking about Kim Jong-il, who had

died of a heart attack in December 2011. "Where is he now?" he asked.

"Living in special palace in Pyongyang."

"Do people see him?"

She didn't answer. He wanted to believe that Sung was a sensible woman, but this kind of talk troubled him. Changing the subject, he said, "I assume we're on an island. Is that correct?"

Sung turned slightly to glance back at Kwon. When she saw that Kwon wasn't looking, she nodded. It was a very slight gesture of independence, he thought.

He heard dry leaves crunch behind him and smelled cigarette smoke.

Sung said loud enough for Kwon to hear, "Today is important day for you, Mr. Dawkin. Some very important man want to meet you." It was the first indication Dawkins had that Kwon understood English.

"Oh, really? Who?"

"This is the great man who direct our program and is trusted by the Supreme Leader. This will be very great honor for you. We call him *Jang-gun-nim.*"

"Am I correct to assume that's his name?"

"There is no word in English for this. Maybe…marshal, or honored general."

Presented with a choice, Dawkins would have preferred to remain outside, but he wasn't. So he followed Kwon and Sung as they walked back to the complex, descended one level instead of two, and turned right. The hallways here were narrower, and they soon came to a door with two soldiers outside. Kwon saluted and they entered a waiting room with a large framed photo of Kim Jong-un on the wall, smiling and wearing sunglasses. In another image he wore a white tracksuit and held a basketball under his arm. Dawkins thought he looked like a puffed-up infant in adult clothes.

A military orderly wearing white gloves showed him into an office.`A square-shouldered, square-jawed man in a stiff green military uniform with red piping around the lapels and collar rose to greet him. His hand felt soft and lifeless. Behind him stood a wizened older man in a black suit and white shirt smoking a cigarette and sizing him up through thick glasses.

Dawkins bent at the waist to show respect and was led to a sofa behind a round glass table in the corner. The honored general sat in an overstuffed chair opposite him, with the older man in another upholstered chair to his left and the jittery young aide/interpreter perched on a metal chair to his right.

The aide picked up a piece of white paper and started to read in a high, strained voice: "The most honored general welcomes you, Mr. James Dawkins. He is joined today by Minister Kim Gun-san. The most honored general brings greeting from the Supreme Leader, who is brilliant and benevolent in all things. He wants to tell you that the project that you are privileged to work on is of utmost importance to our people and those who oppose imperialism throughout the world."

The word "privileged" grated on Dawkins's nerves. The aide paused and seemed to be waiting for his response.

After an awkward silence Dawkins muttered, "Thank you."

The young man leaned across the glass table and handed him a document. "The most honored general has prepared this schedule. When the tasks are completed, you will be paid one million dollars into your bank account and will be allowed to fly home in first-class accommodations. If you finish the task on time, you will get an extra bonus of one million dollars. Two million dollars in total, plus whatever gifts the Supreme Leader decides to give you. Does that please you, Mr. Dawkins?"

The general smiled at him like a kindly grandfather and waited for his response. Dawkins noticed that he was wearing a gold Breitling Chronomat watch, which seemed at odds with the spare, functional surroundings. A large gold, jade, and diamond ring adorned the index finger of his right hand.

"Mr. Dawkins?" the aide asked.

Dawkins scanned the typed schedule, which had him completing all work on the gyro-stabilized platform, missile guidance set control, and amplifier assembly by September 15—approximately six months away. It was doable if everything went well.

Dawkins cleared his throat and said, "I will do the best I can, honored general, but I hope you understand that some things are out of my control. Specifically, the delivery of parts. I've given my assistants a list of components with precise measurements and instructions in terms of composition and materials."

"Very good," the aide gushed. He turned to the general and translated.

As the general listened, he nodded and smiled so that his eyes became hidden. Despite his gentle manner, he exuded menace.

A military aide arrived and served jasmine tea and almond cookies. As Dawkins drank, his entire body started to tremble. He didn't know whether he had been drugged with something, was simply unnerved by the situation, or was coming down with a cold.

Crocker was sitting on the edge on his bed in his apartment in Virginia Beach watching a *Frontline* documentary entitled "The Secret State of North Korea" when he heard a knock.

"Dad?" his daughter asked through the door.

He pulled a black *World's Fastest Indian* T-shirt over his head and used the remote to lower the sound. "Yeah? What is it?"

"Grandpa's on the phone. He wants to know time of the hearing tomorrow."

"Ten." He paused the TV, opened the door, and faced Jenny, who had recently added pink streaks to her long fawn-colored hair. He thought it cheapened her but refrained from commenting. At least it wasn't a tattoo, though she already had at least two of them—a butterfly on her right ankle and what his buddies referred to as a "tramp stamp" on her lower back.

"Grandpa's coming?" he asked. "Is he sure he wants to do that? Does he need a ride?"

"No, he said he'll see you at the courthouse."

Jenny went off to answer her grandfather's question, and Crocker stood thinking that the trial would be uncomfortable enough without his father's presence. He'd probably be so focused on the proceedings he wouldn't notice.

When he looked up, Jenny was standing in the doorway again. "Dad, you gonna be okay tomorrow?" she asked.

"Yeah, yeah. You working tonight?" He wanted to change the subject.

"I've got to close up, which means I won't get out until eleven. After that, Kenna and I are going to stop by a friend's birthday party. So I'll be crashing at my place."

"Okay..." He reminded himself once again that she was eighteen now and semi-independent. "I'll be in the DC area tomorrow. When will I see you again?"

"Wednesday night, I'm off. It's two-for-one night at Outback. You wanna go?"

"Sure, honey." It was her favorite restaurant.

"Cool, Dad." She kissed him quickly on the cheek and left.

"Be good."

Sweet kid, he thought. *Despite her uninterested manner she knows I'm lonely and is making an effort to spend more time with me, even though she'd rather be with her friends.*

Next morning he sat at the defendant's table in Courtroom C of the Fairfax County Court sweating through his suit as the assistant district attorney read the charges. "Your honor, under the authority entrusted us by the State of Virginia, we believe we have sufficient evidence to prove that the defendant Thomas Michael Crocker is guilty of breaking and entering, and aggravated assault."

Judge Doris Whitney looked like she was in her late forties, with a helmet of short brown hair and a pretty face. She asked her clerk to read through the police report on the incident. "On the night in question, the defendant, Thomas Michael Crocker, forcefully gained entry to the apartment of Carla Ruiz on 267 Mulberry Drive. Entering the bedroom, the defendant confronted Ms. Ruiz and Bill Atherton, who is a deputy sergeant with the Fairfax County Police Department. Deputy Sergeant Atherton identified himself and asked the defendant to leave the apartment, whereupon the defendant assaulted the police officer with a lamp and proceeded to knock him unconscious. He subsequently assaulted Ms. Ruiz and threatened to kill her."

"Jesus, Tom," Crocker's father whispered behind him. "You lost control."

Crocker half turned and whispered back, "Quiet, Dad."

He was confused and annoyed that Captain Sutter's letter

seemed to have had no effect on the judge. His attorney, John Nestor, offered no explanation for the judge's indifference except to say, "Each judge is different. Some consider mitigating factors like that; some don't."

What annoyed Crocker even further was the sight of Carla in a white dress sitting beside his father.

What the fuck is she doing there?

He was trying to remain calm and resist the powerful impulse to throttle Deputy Sergeant Atherton, who sat behind the prosecutor's table in a freshly pressed uniform, looking like an altar boy.

Judge Whitney turned a stern face to Crocker and asked, "Does the defendant have anything to say before he enters a plea?"

Crocker's attorney stood. "No, your honor."

Crocker rose right behind him. "Yes, I do."

"Proceed, Mr. Crocker."

Nestor shot him a confused look that didn't stop him. Crocker's charcoal-gray suit felt like a straitjacket. "Your honor," he said, "my father, Mr. William Crocker, seated behind me, is a military veteran and holds the position of commander at his local VFW. Several months before the incident, I had become aware that he was helping out a young Gulf War vet named Carla and her son. Your honor, he was helping them out financially to the tune of over twenty thousand dollars. I became concerned because my father is a man of modest means who basically lives off his military pension. He's also a very empathetic man, and I suspected that Ms. Ruiz was taking advantage of him."

The female assistant district attorney stood and asked, "Your honor, can I approach the bench?"

"Let the defendant finish his statement."

"A day or so before the incident, I learned from my father that he had given Ms. Ruiz an additional ten thousand dollars to attend a private drug rehab facility to kick her dependence to Vicodin and other drugs. My father told me that she was attending the facility at the time. That night I drove by Ms. Ruiz's apartment and noticed that the lights were on. When I rang the bell, she didn't answer, despite the fact that I could see her in the apartment through the kitchen window. I saw her in the company of another man. When they left the kitchen, I entered through the open window."

"You entered her apartment illegally?" the judge asked.

"I did, your honor."

"You admit that?"

"I do. When I entered Ms. Ruiz's bedroom, I found her and Officer Atherton sitting on her bed smoking crystal meth."

"Objection!"

The judge pounded her gavel, then, turning to Crocker, asked, "How did you know it was crystal meth?"

"They were smoking it through a glass meth pipe, and it had that unmistakable smell like oven cleaner or burning plastic."

"What happened next?"

"Officer Atherton identified himself as a cop and told me to leave immediately. When I didn't, he assaulted me with his fists. I stepped out of his way, causing him to lose his balance and crash into a wall. While that was happening, Ms. Ruiz reached into a drawer by her bed and produced a pistol. She threatened me with it, and I disarmed her."

"Did you threaten to kill her, Mr. Crocker?"

"I told her that if she took another penny from my dad under false pretenses, I'd break every bone in her body."

"So you did."

Both Crocker's attorney and the assistant district attorney jumped to their feet and called for the judge's attention. Just then a man in a shabby gray suit entered from behind them, spoke to one of the court officers, approached the judge, and handed her a document. As the people in the courtroom waited, she unfolded it and read it, then called both attorneys and Crocker into her chambers.

Crocker emerged thirty minutes later. Finding his father sitting on a bench in the hallway looking worried, he said, "Let's get out of here and get lunch."

He escorted his father out of the building and down the steps, and his father stopped and asked, "Tom, what happened with the judge?"

"It was pretty straightforward. She handed me a warning and dismissed the charges."

"Gee, Tom, that's terrific news."

A very relieved Crocker opened the passenger door to his pickup and watched his dad climb in. Soon as he settled on the backseat, his father asked, "She dismissed the charges, just like that? No explanation?"

"Apparently Deputy Sergeant Atherton was caught on video this weekend selling meth to an undercover DC police officer," Crocker answered. "I dodged a bullet."

"Thank God."

"From now on you're not giving any more money to that Carla Ruiz piece of shit, are you?"

"Don't you dare talk to me like that. I'm still your father."

"Sorry, Dad. But what were you thinking, sitting with her in court?"

"Carla wants to talk to you. She feels badly."

"I bet she does."

As soon as Crocker started the engine, his cell phone rang. It was Jim Anders, deputy director of CIA operations. He put him on speaker.

"Crocker, you still in the DC area?"

"Yes I am."

"Good. There's someone I want you to meet, this afternoon at four. A safe house in Arlington. I'll text you the address."

"I'll be there."

Crocker hung up, shifted into first, and pulled out into traffic.

"What's going on?" his father asked.

"You didn't hear that, okay?"

"You need to lighten up."

CHAPTER ELEVEN

*When men speak ill of you, live so nobody may believe
them.*

—Plato

IT WAS a ranch house off Wilson Boulevard with a white gravel
driveway and a FOR SALE sign on the front lawn. Looked like it
had been built in the late sixties. Two big Scorpion CIA private
security guards checked Crocker's ID through the half-open
screen door.

"Come in," one of them said gruffly.

He peeled off the suit jacket and set it on the back of one of
the living room chairs. The air was stale and reeked of cigarettes.

"You think one of you guys could crack a window?" Crocker
asked.

"You're a guest here. Take a seat."

Choosing the path of least resistance, he sat and checked his
texts. One of them had come from Cyndi, wishing him luck in
court.

He used his thumbs to text back "All good. Charges dismissed!
Tnx."

They talked on the phone practically every night. He was hoping to get an opportunity in the next week or so to travel back to Vegas and meet her daughter. She also had a nephew who was interested in going to BUD/S and wanted to meet him.

If all went well, he was thinking of flying himself, Jenny, Cyndi, and her daughter to Hawaii for Christmas. They'd stay on Maui, his favorite island. If he could afford it, he'd rent a house away from the hotels on the south shore for a week—windsurfing, exploring, eating fresh fruit and fish.

He was trying to imagine how Jenny would respond to the idea when Anders entered in a burst of energy. Broad-shouldered and clean-cut, he walked with a slight limp—the result of a bullet wound at the hands of Syrian agents in a Paris hotel elevator—and spoke into a cell phone. Behind him followed a short, thin Asian man wearing a porkpie hat, sunglasses, and Bermuda shorts even though it had barely cracked fifty outside, and two more large security men.

Anders was arguing on the phone with someone. "I know. I've heard that, but I don't agree. Look, I've got to go now. Print it out and leave it on my desk."

They clasped hands and bumped chests, military style. The two had gone through a lot together over the past three years. Adversity had drawn them closer.

"Crocker. Real good to see you. What's with the suit?"

"It's a long story. How's the knee?"

Anders rolled up the leg of his khaki pants to show the fresh scar. "Bullet entered here and shattered the patella. Took four hours of surgery and pins, screw, and wire to put it back together. Rehab's been a bitch. But the knee's working again, so I can't complain."

"Glad to hear it."

One of the Scorpions entered with bottles of water, which he placed on the table. He pulled the shades closed and left as Anders introduced the Asian dude who was scrolling through something on his iPhone.

"Crocker, I want you to meet Terry."

"Konnichiwa," Terry said in Japanese, bowing from the waist.

"Nice to meet you, too."

He still wore the plaid hat, which clashed with his shorts.

"Terry is Japanese," Anders explained, "but he's spent a lot of time in Pyongyang and developed a close relationship with Kim Jong-il and his son Kim Jung-un."

"Eighteen years altogether," Terry said, nodding and removing his hat. His head was as smooth as a cue ball.

"Terry here served as the Supreme Leader's fitness and karate instructor. He taught his son as well."

"I first meet Jong-un...twelve years old. No shit."

"You must have stories," said Crocker.

"Oh yes. Many stories. Stories to curl the hair on your head."

Without prompting, he described his first trip to Pyongyang for a karate competition back in the '90s, how he had been approached by an aide to Kim Jong-il, and how the Supreme Leader himself enticed him with money and gifts to become his personal fitness instructor. He spent six years in North Korea, returned to the town he grew up in Japan, and was later lured back. He eventually became part of the Supreme Leader's inner circle and participated in wild karaoke parties, orgies with teenage sex slaves, and feasts with delicacies flown in from all over the world.

"Off-the-hook shit," he commented. "You can't make this stuff up."

Terry explained that while the majority of the twenty million residents of North Korea lived in abject poverty and others starved to death, the Supreme Leader surrounded himself with a carefully selected coterie of military and party officials who lived in extreme luxury. He basically bought their loyalty with apartments, houses, cars, special privileges, and gifts. Terry himself had been given hundreds of thousands of dollars, gold watches, fine clothes and shoes, jewelry, any pretty girl he wanted, and the wife of his choice.

In return, those allowed close to power first had to pledge absolute loyalty to the Supreme Leader. He was deified by state media and treated like a god. The slightest hint of disloyalty would result in one being tossed into a reeducation camp or one of the country's 180 political prisons, or having to face some form of execution.

In December 2013 Kim Jong-hu's uncle and top economic advisor Jang Song-thaek was abruptly removed from all official posts and dubbed "despicable human scum" by state media. A week later he and his top aides were stripped naked and fed to over a hundred dogs that had been starved for three days. Hundreds of top Kim Jong-un aides were forced to watch as the men's bodies were ripped apart and eaten in a process that is reported to have taken over an hour.

North Korean citizens were routinely executed for routine offenses, including the possession of a Bible or watching South Korean–produced videos.

Crocker shook his head in disgust, despite that fact that he had heard much of this before.

Turning to Terry, Anders asked, "Tell us where Kim Jong-un gets the money to support his nuclear program, his million-soldier-strong military, and also to support his inner circle in luxury when the economy is dismal, most people are starving, and the country lives under a strict UN economic embargo that blocks practically all international currency from flowing into the country."

"Illegal activities."

"What does that mean, exactly?"

"The government has a branch that is a criminal enterprise to make money and accrue power to the regime by any means possible."

"For example?" Anders asked.

"Killing people, torture, kidnapping for ransom, selling drugs, hacking into bank accounts, spying. All the things criminal organizations do."

"How do you know about this?"

"I became friendly with the general who runs it. We call him the Dragon."

As he lay on the bed Dawkins's mind roiled with ghastly scenes of postnuclear Nagasaki and Hiroshima—buildings vaporized, people reduced to dust, mothers and children covered with oozing radiation sores and burns, wandering through rubble like zombies. Dawkins hovered over them like a giant bird. Hot, ionized air burned his feathers and skin. Ashes clogged his throat, causing him to choke.

The coughing pulled him into a level of semiconsciousness. He opened his eyes into darkness—just a glowing ribbon from under the door to his right and the hum of a ventilation system.

Something rustled nearby.

"Sung?"

He had trouble breathing and grabbed at his throat. Then felt warm hands on his chest.

"Sung, is that you?"

"Breathe, Mr. Dawkin. You have bad dream. Relax."

He turned and saw her sitting beside him, her shiny black hair falling over her eyes, her neck long and arched like a swan's.

It all came back to him—his kidnapping, his family, the missile program he was being forced to work on, and his terrible moral conundrum. For the second time in his life, he thought of killing himself. Junior year in high school he had swallowed a bottle of aspirin after his girlfriend dumped him for his best friend.

He told himself that this time he would do it right, and considered the means at his disposal, the cord of the space heater in the corner, the sharp edge of the metal bathroom sink.

But even as he did, Sung's hands and words soothed him. "You need…relax, Mr. Dawkin. Go to sleep. Clear you head. You work in the morning."

"Sung, I can't sleep."

"You miss family. Family okay?"

"I don't know."

She leaned in until their faces almost touched. "I stay with you, Mr. Dawkin. You want pill for sleep? I give you pill."

"No pill, please."

"You good man, Mr. Dawkin. You love family."

He pictured Nan and Karen in his head and sighed. "Yes, I do."

"You sick in you heart."

"I am."

"I know, Mr. Dawkin. I know."

It was reassuring to hear her say so. His week of captivity had caused him to partially shed his sense of self because his very existence had become a problem. Dangerous men wanted his mind and the knowledge it contained. He had gone to Geneva with a plan to help save the planet and had been lured away by an offer to put the plan into operation. Now he was being asked to help destroy it.

The irony crushed him.

He blamed himself and the choices he had made. And then he argued that this current situation wasn't his fault. He was a scientist and an engineer with no desire to hurt others. Could he help it if his expertise was used for sinister purposes? Yes, he had trained to become an expert in missile guidance systems. Yes, he had benefited from the money he earned from working for the U.S. government. It's true that he could have gone into another field of endeavor.

"Sung, is there light at the end of the tunnel?" he asked out loud.

"I no understand," she whispered back.

"Will I ever see my family again? Will I be able to face them when I do?"

He felt lost in a gray, formless muddle with nothing to hold on to. Death waited and watched. In many ways it seemed preferable to the dying ghostlike creatures that stumbled through the shadows of his consciousness at night.

"Mr. Dawkin...You family need you."

This woman he knew almost nothing about had become his only real human contact. His nurse and angel of sorts. She sang him songs and told him stories, and massaged his legs, back, and shoulders to try to get him to relax.

In the far, far distance, over continents and oceans and beyond the moral quagmire he currently faced, waited his wife and daughter. He had no way of reaching them, or explaining why it might be better if he never came home.

His North Korean captors had cut him off completely from the outside world. No Internet, no phones, no newspapers, magazines, books, gossip. Nothing. Only Sung and the VCR, the TV monitor and a box of porno videos sitting in the corner.

She knelt beside him on the bed kneading his neck and shoulders, and singing what sounded like a lullaby. Her voice reminded him of a bird climbing and swooping through the branches of trees.

"What's the song about?" he asked when she finished.

"It's about a mother who goes to the shore to look for food for her baby and has to leave the baby alone in the house."

"The melody reminds me of something…"

"She need the food for her baby. She has to have faith her baby will be safe. And her baby has to trust that the mother will be back. The same as us, Mr. Dawkin. We have our work."

He noted that she had included herself.

"Sung, is that why you're doing this, so you can return to *your* family?"

"This is my duty," she answered sadly. "I return to family if Supreme Leader give permission."

He had never really considered her situation. As sweet and attentive as she was, and as much as her words touched him, he wasn't sure he could trust her.

"We need faith, Mr. Dawkin," she said.

"In what?"

She didn't answer. Did she secretly believe in God? Or did she believe the bullshit about the benevolence of the Supreme Leader?

He decided not to ask. In the darkness he heard her stand and the rustle of fabric. Then she pulled the blanket aside and slipped onto the bed beside him.

He felt her cool skin against his and her ribs against his chest. She held on to him and whispered, "Close you eyes and sleep, Mr. Dawkin. Tomorrow maybe bring you something good."

"Freedom, I hope."

"Sleep, Mr. Dawkin. Tomorrow maybe you have better news."

Crocker passed through the lobby of CIA headquarters, stopped at the Memorial Wall, and looked at the 111 stars carved into the white Alabama marble, placed there in honor of CIA employees who had died in the line of duty. He knew that one of the stars was there to commemorate Mike Spann, who he had known when Mike was a young marine and he was a young navy recruit stationed in Okinawa. Mike had died tragically, killed by rioting Taliban and al-Qaeda prisoners at the Qala-i-Jangi fortress in Afghanistan in November 2001. Stars also paid tribute to Glen Doherty and Tyrone Woods, who had died in Benghazi, and Elizabeth Hanson, Darren Labonte, and Jennifer Matthews, who had been killed during a suicide bombing in Camp Chapman in Afghanistan.

Crocker had worked with all of them at one point, and now said a silent prayer and moved on. There would be more stars on the wall as the war on terror spread from Afghanistan and Iraq to Syria, Kurdistan, Libya, Somalia, Nigeria, and Yemen. And that didn't include state-supported terrorists and insurgents from countries like Russia, Iran, and North Korea.

Upstairs a security agent scanned his badge and ID, then led him into a conference room. Twenty or so people sat two deep around a long oval table. He looked for Jeri's face. Instead, he saw Jim Anders waving from the end of the table and pointing to a free chair beside him.

He didn't recognize the other attendees. They seemed to be government analysts and operations officers from various branches, ranging in ages from late twenties to midsixties, and all wearing suits.

The meeting started with a detailed presentation on the counterfeit U.S. currency seized from the *Cong Son Gang*. According to the Secret Service's director of Investigations, the counterfeit hundreds matched the same 2HK1 profile as counterfeits that had surfaced over the past several months in places like Hawaii, Macau, and Las Vegas. The counterfeit bills were of very high quality and had passed inspection at some of the world's high-end casinos, including the Park Hyatt in Mendoza, Argentina, the Ibiza Gran Hotel in Spain, the Marina Bay Sands in Singapore, the Hôtel de Paris in Monte Carlo, the Ritz Carlton in San Juan, Puerto Rico, and the Casino El Jadida in Morocco.

Millions of dollars of the bogus currency had passed through the Banco Delta Asia in Macau. Treasury estimated that there was currently as much as $1.5 billion in fake 2HK1 bills now in circulation. If they continued to enter the global economy at the current rate, they would act to devalue the dollar and cause inflation to rise. The long-term effects, according to the Secret Service's director of investigations, could be catastrophic.

She explained that the seized bills had been examined under a microscope, scrutinized in ultraviolet light, and otherwise inspected to reveal flaws, composition, and printing techniques. The paper they were printed on matched the three-quarters cotton / one-quarter linen mix used for real U.S. currency. The bills had been manufactured using an intaglio press, which was the most advanced form of currency-printing technology available and far more expensive than offset, typographic, or lithographic presses.

While counterfeits manufactured by intaglio press had been seen before, they were very rare. Only a handful of companies made intaglio presses. Not only were they extremely expensive, they were also seldom sold to any entities except governments.

"Any idea which government we're talking about here?" Anders asked.

"I can't answer that specifically," the female director answered. "But we do have several clues. Because of the number of high-quality imitations that were starting to appear in worldwide circulation at the end of the past century, we did a complete redesign of our currency starting in 1996. The new designs included a security thread embedded in the paper, a watermark featuring a shadow portrait of the figure on the bill, and microprinting. All these features were put in place to frustrate potential counterfeiters. The most significant and sophisticated change was a shift to optically variable inks known as OVIs. If you hold up one of today's twenty-dollar bills and hold it one way, it appears bronze-green. If you turn it another, it looks black. That's because of the OVIs."

"Why is that important?"

"Because only one Swiss company, named SICPA, manufactures the types of OVIs used in printing currency, and the U.S. purchased the exclusive rights to green-to-black OVIs in ninety-six. That same year, North Korea purchased the exclusive rights to green-to-magenta ink, which can be easily manipulated to imitate green-to-black. It doesn't prove anything, but we think it is significant."

The next official who spoke was the head of the CIA's Iranian desk. He speculated that the sudden spread of 2HK1 bills was an unintended consequence of international economic sanctions against Iran. They had been imposed starting in 2006 as a result of Iran's efforts to develop nuclear weapons and had been expanded over the years. Not only had the international sanctions acted to strangle the Iranian economy; they also had the intended effect of shutting off sources of international currency, which the Iranian government could then use to buy foreign goods and services, including parts and matériel for their nuclear weapons program.

As the CIA officer spoke, Crocker considered the Persian man they had found on the *Cong Son Gang*.

"So the sanctions are working," Anders remarked.

"Yes, most are still in place and have been quite effective," said the officer from the Iranian desk. "And even if the Senate votes to roll them back in accordance with the new U.S.-Iran agreement, the fact remains that the Iranians have been cut off from the regular sources of international currency for years. Even if the sanctions were to end today, it would take the Iranians at least a year to earn enough international currency to make a difference in their economy. So they've resorted to illegal and extraordinary measures. Specifically, they made a devil's bargain with the leadership of the Democratic People's Republic of Korea."

"Kim Jong-un."

"Yes."

"Iran needs international currency, and the North Koreans want advanced rocket technology. Following a visit by North

Korean ceremonial head of state Kim Yong-nam to Tehran and a meeting with Iranian president Mahmoud Ahmadinejad, the two countries signed a trade agreement. The Iranians would start sending military parts and technology to North Korea, and the North Koreans would revive their production of counterfeit U.S. currency in order to supply the Iranians with much-needed dollars. Iran also dispatched a group of construction engineers to help build and expand their underground military and research facilities."

"Those two countries have had a history of military and economic cooperation," an official from the State Department remarked.

"It dates back to the 1980s, when the North Koreans supplied weapons to Iran during the Iran-Iraq War. They included artillery, antitank weapons, naval mines, antiaircraft machine guns, mortars, tanks, and surface-to-air missiles. As late as 2010, a Russian-built cargo jet filled with North Korean weapons bound for Tehran was seized at the Suvarnabhumi Airport in Bangkok."

During a break, Crocker found Anders talking to an aide in the hallway. When the aide left, Crocker asked, "What am I doing here?"

"Background," Anders replied. "I'll explain later. In the meantime, select a teammate to go with you and prepare to deploy to China."

"China? We spent the last hour talking about Iran and North Korea."

"You're going to China. I'll brief you as soon as this meeting is over. You're leaving tonight."

CHAPTER TWELVE

Truth exists; only lies are invented.

—Georges Braque

ALMOST FOUR weeks had gone by since her husband's disappearance, and Nan Dawkins was starting to wonder if he'd ever return. What surprised her was that her daughter, who was extremely close to her father, seemed to be taking his disappearance in stride. Maybe she appeared more withdrawn than usual, but otherwise she seemed fine.

James almost never left Nan's mind. She had pored through his personal e-mails, notes, and journals for an answer to the mystery but hadn't discovered a single clue. She had queried colleagues at work, trainers at the local gym where he occasionally worked out, and neighbors. They all said pretty much same thing: James was a friendly, modest guy who seemed content with his life.

FBI agents had traveled to Geneva and retraced all of his movements. They had coordinated with the local Geneva police and the Swiss Federal Intelligence Service, which had done their own investigations. They had found no evidence of wrongdoing, foul play, or accidental death. James was last seen talking to people from the audience after his speech at the Swissotel Metropole. He hadn't spoken to anyone after 7 p.m. the night of the third, or used his credit cards. No one at the hotel had seen him leave that night, nor did he return to his room.

So what had happened? The mystery deepened, and it perplexed her.

Priding herself in being a very rational, practical woman, Nan knew there had to be an answer. She tried to lose herself in work and looking after Karen.

But nothing seemed to pull her mind away from James and the mystery. At night, unable to sleep, she'd troll the Internet for possible answers. She learned that an astounding 900,000 people disappeared in the United States every year—approximately 2,300 a day. The majority of them were children and teens. Many of them surfaced later in hospitals, shelters, and morgues. Some were sold into sexual slavery. A portion were men and women running away from their families or escaping severe financial problems.

A number of them, like James, disappeared without explanation and were never found. She read stories of farmers working in fields, or housewives doing the laundry, who seemed to vanish in broad daylight and never return. People speculated that they had accidentally slipped into an alternate universe or some kind of time warp. Nan, though, highly skeptical of things like that, wanted an explanation.

A colleague at work suggested that she consult a psychic friend of hers who sometimes worked as a consultant to the DC police in helping to locate missing people. The psychic worked out of a building on Wisconsin Avenue that also housed a commercial real estate firm. Her office was furnished simply—no crystals hanging from the ceiling or strange pictures on the walls. In fact, she looked like many of the housewives Nan knew in her neighborhood—pretty, midforties, and fit, carefully dressed, with shoulder-length brown hair.

The psychic explained that five years ago she had been working as a sales director at a printing company, and was happily married with two young children, when a neighbor died and she started to sense that he was trying to communicate with her. That's when she got in touch with and started to develop her psychic abilities. Since then, she'd been helping people contact loved ones on "the other side" and consult with spirit guides.

Nan remained skeptical. The psychic moved from behind her desk, sat across from her, and asked her to concentrate on her missing husband while she consulted people and spirits on the other side.

She closed her eyes, then said out loud, "Have you seen him? Is he there?"

She seemed to be waiting for an answer, and nodded as though she was receiving information. "You're sure of that?" she asked.

This communication with unseen people or spirits went on for about ten minutes. Then the psychic opened her eyes, looked at Nan, and smiled. "Okay," she started. "I'm almost certain your husband's not dead, so that's a relief. No one on the other side has seen him."

She said it matter-of-factly, as though she were reporting the weather.

"If he's not dead, where is he?" Nan asked.

"I'm not sure. He feels far away. I know this sounds strange, but I get the sense that he's in a cave."

"A cave?"

"He doesn't want to be there, but he's healthy. He's okay."

"Do you think this cave is in Switzerland, or somewhere in Europe?"

"I don't know for sure, but I don't think so."

"Is there any way I can reach him?" Nan asked.

"All you can really do is send him your love and support, psychically," the psychic instructed. "It will reach him. By the way, he's doing the same for you."

Surprisingly, Nan left her session with the psychic feeling relieved. Even though she wasn't sure what had just happened, she was more convinced than ever that James was still alive.

Sara, the young brunette CIA operative at the wheel of the silver Chinese BYD F3 sedan, turned off the two-lane asphalt road and entered a small dirt parking lot adjacent to the Tumen River. Sitting next to her was Crocker's blond teammate Davis. Crocker, in the backseat, looked through the rear window and saw the black Chery QQ minicar that had been following them stop ten feet short of the turnoff and cut its lights.

"What happens now?" Crocker asked as he checked his watch.

"We wait for Choi," she answered. "He'll signal from the other side of the river before he crosses to let us know all's clear. That should happen at ten o'clock."

It was now 1946 hours local time. They were in Liaoning province (the southernmost part of Manchuria) in northeastern China, about sixty miles east of the Chinese city of Dandong. North Korea sat on the other side of the Tumen River, which gurgled to their right.

Crocker and Davis had traveled here under aliases as Canadian trade officials interested in the local mining industry. According to Sara, Chinese Ministry of State Security (MSS) knew the real purpose of their visit to Liaoning province. Although the Chinese officially supported the Kim regime in North Korea, they would not be unhappy to see it replaced with a less belligerent government.

"When Choi arrives, one of you will get out, go to the trunk, and hand him the bags filled with shrink-wrapped thumb drives," Sara explained. "He'll hand you back the information we requested."

The thumb drives were loaded with U.S. and South Korean movies and TV shows, including *22 Jump Street, Cinderella, The Matrix, Friends,* and the North Korean favorite, *Desperate Housewives.* They were part of a CIA program to expose North Koreans to Western culture and break through almost sixty years of draconian restrictions on any information about the world beyond its borders.

"When North Koreans watch *Desperate Housewives,*" Sara said, "they realize Americans aren't all war-loving imperialists. They're just people having affairs and enjoying their freedom. When they see that reality, they want it for themselves."

"What about the guys in the vehicle behind us?" Crocker asked.

"They're with MSS. They're here to observe and file a report on what we do but won't interfere. Their bosses and local police officials have already been paid off."

She sounded like she knew what she was talking about. Crocker hoped so as he looked at his watch again: 1952. "We're getting close," he said. "Are the MSS guys gonna follow us?"

"They might."

"What do we do if they stop us?"

"They won't."

"You sure of that?"

"Yep. It's time."

Crocker and Davis met at the trunk, where Davis removed the two bags loaded with thumb drives and Crocker grabbed a laser marker. It felt strange being in this remote area of China and operating in such an exposed manner at a time when China and the United States were accusing each other of cyberattacks. Crocker would have preferred a deeper cover and to be carrying a sidearm. The two men entered a stand of twenty-foot-high Japanese celtis trees and reached the two-hundred-foot-wide, rushing Tumen River.

Davis zipped up his thin nylon jacket and shivered.

"You okay?" Crocker asked, the chicken with spicy garlic, green chili, and ginger sauce turning in his stomach.

"That deep-fried carp didn't agree with me."

"You probably didn't like the fact that its mouth and gills were still moving."

"Not really. No. The waiter recommended it."

"Could be he's working for the MSS."

Neither stars nor moon were visible through the low clouds. The temperature hovered in the middle fifties. No wind. Only the deep gurgle of the river.

"How many guys we expecting?" Davis asked, pulling the collar of his jacket up around his neck.

"One, I believe."

Two hundred feet away, on the opposite side of the river, Crocker watched as someone drew a large *O* in the air with a red laser marker.

He drew one too, about shoulder width.

"You playing tic-tac-toe?" Davis asked.

"No, dude. That's the signal. Here he comes."

"Where?"

Crocker peered through the compact night binoculars he carried and made out two individuals dressed in hoodies and shorts. They entered the water, stopped to look behind, and started to cross.

Crocker pointed. "There, and I stand corrected. It's two pax, not one."

"Whatever."

They watched them pick their way through the river that at the deepest part came up to their waists.

"Fucking cold, I bet."

"One of them is named Choi. He's our man," Crocker reminded him.

The two men, both about five foot five, emerged from the river, shook the water off their legs, then stopped in front of them and bowed. Crocker bowed back and said, *"An-nyung-ha-se-yo."*

"An-nyung-ha-se-yo," the young men responded. They seemed delighted and surprised to be seeing two large Western men. The stouter of the two said something in Korean that Crocker didn't understand.

He grinned and shook his head. "I don't speak Korean."

The same man reached into the backpack he carried over his shoulder and handed Crocker a large envelope wrapped in plastic.

Davis offered them the two large bundles of thumb drives. They slipped them in their backpacks and bowed again.

"Choi?" Crocker asked.

The slightly stouter of the two nodded.

"Here." Crocker reached into his pocket and handed him 6,000 Chinese yuan, which came to about $1,000 U.S.

Choi stuffed the money into the backpack and without saying another word turned and waded back into the river with his partner. Soon they became dark shadows.

"That was easy," Davis said.

"Sure was."

Seconds after Crocker took a step back toward the car, he heard something above the rush of the river that sounded like a helicopter. He stopped and listened.

"You hear that?"

"Yeah, boss," Davis answered. "We'd better split."

Then he caught it out of the corner of his left eye, coming in fast and low over the river. It was small and snub-nosed, with twin turbine engines mounted overhead.

"Looks like a Polish-made Mi-2," Davis said.

Crocker was hoping it was only an observation craft when he heard the 23mm rip through the air.

"Stand back!"

Through the night-vision binos Crocker made out one of the dark figures veering right and scrambling to shore, while the other seemed to turn back as the helo passed. He ran about fifty feet until he was near the middle of the river, then stumbled and fell.

"Fuck."

"What?" Davis asked.

"I think one of them got hit."

The young man was up again and struggling forward. When he stopped and went down again, Crocker handed the binos to Davis.

"Hold these."

"Boss...What are you doing?"

He was already running into the river, trying to keep his balance on slippery rocks and locate the downed kid in the water. He thought he saw him ahead when he neared the center, but it turned out to be a pile of rocks. Then, thirty degrees to his left, he saw a splash and an arm sticking up, fingers spread. Crocker pushed toward it, found the kid, and pulled him up like rag doll. Saw a large splotch of blood starting on his chest, about four inches from his armpit. Quickly checked his pulse—he was alive.

Tucking him under his arm, he turned and pushed through the water, barely aware of the roar of the helo returning for another pass. It was coming in even lower this time. He felt the downdraft from the rotors slapping the top of his head and went under with the kid. Counted to sixty and came up.

The kid was coughing up water. The red light on the helo tail blinked and disappeared around a bend. He hurried forward to the Chinese side, where Davis had waded out to help.

"Where's he hit?"

"Left shoulder and chest. Passed right through. We've got to get him to a hospital."

When they reached the shore and carried him up, Crocker saw two men in black watching from under a celtis tree, probably MSS officials. They didn't move or lend a hand. In their heads, Crocker imagined, they were already writing their report.

Sara looked alarmed when she saw the young man and the blood. "What's he doing here? What happened?"

"The kid got shot."

"Choi?"

"No, I think it's the other one."

"Holy fuck!"

She turned and gunned the BYD down the road while Crocker checked the kid's vitals on the backseat and held his balled-up shirt over the wound. It appeared that the two bullets that entered his back had missed the arteries around the heart. "Lucky guy."

He wrapped his belt under the kid's arm and over the T-shirt and tightened it.

"Where's the closest hospital? He's lost a lot of blood."

When they reached the outskirts of Dandong, Sara stopped in front of the first taxi stand she could find. "Have the driver take you straight to the airport. I'll take care of him."

"You better move fast!"

"Okay. Call me from Beijing, Shanghai, or wherever you land!"

CHAPTER THIRTEEN

*Sometimes the questions are complicated and the
answers are simple.*

—Dr. Seuss

IT WAS a beautiful late-March night fragrant with the first
scents of spring, so Nan Dawkins decided to fire up the barbecue
and dine outside—chicken, strips of red pepper and zucchini,
and new potatoes. It reminded her of James, who often sat outside alone in the summer looking at the stars. Astronomy was one
of his passions. The Celestron CPC 1100 XLT computerized
telescope that he had bought recently sat under a plastic cover in
his home office.

After dinner she sat sipping chardonnay and half listening to
Karen talk about the poems they had read that day in school.
One of them was Edgar Allan Poe's "Annabel Lee." Normally,
anything having to do with literature was a favorite topic of dis-
cussion, but tonight Nan seemed drawn to the stars trying to
break through the city haze. She wondered if James was looking
at them, too, wherever he was.

Her current theory was that he was working somewhere on a top-secret government program and would return soon. Maybe he had wanted to tell her but couldn't. Maybe he'd forgotten, which was characteristic of James. He kept different aspects of his life in separate compartments.

"Mom?" her daughter called.

She drifted to their wedding day and his shy, handsome face, and returned.

"Yes, 'Annabel Lee' is a beautiful poem..." Nan started, and then stopped. When she looked for Karen's oval face across the table, she found an empty chair. Turning, she saw her back passing through the gap in the sliding glass doors. She was carrying dirty plates.

"That's very kind of you, darling," Nan said. "Thank you."

"You're welcome, Mom."

Wonderful girl, she thought. *Cleaning up...because she sees I'm preoccupied. Where would I be without her?*

Karen's emotional steadiness through the ordeal continued to amaze her. Nan refilled her glass with wine and looked up at the stars. James, she knew, would be able to name them and recount the legends behind them. She located the Big Dipper and remembered that James had showed her how to connect the outer stars in the bowl and use them to locate Polaris, which marked the end of the Little Dipper's handle.

During a summer vacation in the Adirondacks ten years ago, he had explained that the Big Dipper was actually an abbreviated version of the constellation Ursa Major—the Great Bear. The three stars that made up the bowl were thought to be hunters chasing the bear. The constellation served as both a calendar and storybook. In the fall the hunter would catch up with the bear.

According to the Iroquois, it was blood from the dead bear that colored the autumn landscape.

As Nan lowered her gaze, she noticed something gold flickering. At first she thought it was a reflection off the sliding glass door, but when she looked closer she saw that it originated inside the house. Then she noticed smoke wafting out of the crack between the sliding glass doors.

Alarmed, she called, "Karen?"

Hearing a cry from inside that sounded more like a wounded cat than a child, she let go of the wineglass and sprang. As she squeezed through the doors, smoke and the smell of burning plastic stung her eyes. To her right, red and orange flames rose from the living room rug and sofa.

"Karen, oh my God! Where are you?"

A strangled sound resounded from the front hall.

Turning, she spotted a can of lighter fluid on the wooden end table and a box of matches. A picture of what had transpired flashed in her head as flames danced three feet away.

"Karen!"

She grabbed hold of the can, screamed as the heat seared her hand, and running back three steps, tossed it out the door onto the patio.

"Karen, sweetheart! Where are you? Say something!"

The smoke made it very difficult to see. When Karen shouted "Mommy, help!" Nan turned right and saw her daughter rolling on the wooden hallway floor, trying to extinguish flames at the bottom of her pants.

She threw herself on her daughter like a wild animal, then attacked the fire furiously with her hands. The flames were stubborn, but Nan smothered them out. Ignoring the burns on her hands and the seething, tightening sensation in her throat and lungs, she scooped up her daughter and ran out the front door, collapsing on the lawn.

She was still lying there in the same position when the paramedics revived her minutes later. She saw flashes of firemen passing, lights, smoke, and hoses. Rough hands lifted her onto a stretcher. She looked up at someone but had trouble getting the words out.

"My dau…"

A male voice said, "Relax, ma'am. You'll be fine."

"My daughter. Where's Karen?" She felt panic.

"She's okay, ma'am," the man said in a reassuring voice. "We've got her. We're taking you both to the hospital now."

"I want to see her. I've got to see her!"

"Hold on, ma'am. You will."

Her panic grew with every face they passed and jostle of the stretcher. Blue, red, and white flashed across the front lawn and driveway. Neighbors stood in silence and watched.

In the back of a red ambulance, she blinked into the bright light. To her left she saw Karen seated on a gurney. An EMT was using scissors to cut away the right leg of her pants.

"Karen, is that really you?" Nan shouted.

As soon as Karen saw her mother, she started to cry.

Restraints prevented Nan from sitting up, so she reached out and touched her daughter with the back of her injured hand. "It's okay, darling. The doctors will take care of us now."

"I'm sorry, Mommy," Karen cried. "I'm so sorry. I started the fire, Mommy. I'm sorry."

"It's okay, darling. I don't care about that. But…why?"

Karen's chest heaved and tears poured down her soot-covered

cheeks. "I thought that maybe if Daddy heard about the fire on the news...he'd come home."

Dawkins shuffled down the drab, cold hallway with Kwon behind him, trying to convince himself that he had accomplished something, which brought him a step closer to freedom. The new platform shroud that had been machined in a nearby shop under his supervision fit perfectly around the gyro compass and torque motors. Another couple of months and the GSP system would be fully functional and ready to insert into the Unha-3 missile. Allowing for several more months for testing and adjustments, he figured the process would be complete by September, at which time his service wouldn't be needed anymore.

The seventeenth of September was Nan's birthday. Maybe, just maybe, Dawkins thought, he'd make it home by then. As soon as he did, he'd contact the FBI and CIA, and brief them about the underground facility and the progress the North Koreans had made in their nuclear missile program. He'd spill all the information and impressions he'd stored in his brain.

He told himself that under the circumstances, informing U.S. authorities was the best he could do. He wanted to believe that the North Koreans were still a year or more away from building a nuclear missile that could hit the mainland United States. He based his estimate on the numerous other engineering problems they still had to solve, including miniaturizing the warhead, finding the right mix of fuel, and engineering the warhead housing so it wouldn't burn up on reentry into the atmosphere.

Back in his room, he sat at the square wooden table as Sung prepared his dinner in the kitchen down the hall. He opened the journal he kept on the shelf that he assumed was read daily by NK officials, and wrote. "Day 25. Milestone day. The shroud fits...Goal accomplished! Tomorrow we begin testing. No. Tomorrow is my day off. Looking forward to another walk with Sung. Hope to see more red-crowned cranes. The fresh air gives me energy."

Sung entered quietly in a dark blue tunic and matching pants, and slid the plastic plate in front of him. It was *ton-yuk-kui*, rice with pork strips, and *banchan*, spicy cabbage and cucumber. As she had explained, a good meal was one that harmonized warm and cold, spicy and mild, rough and soft, solid and liquid. This seemed to accomplish that.

"You like, Mr. Dawkin?" Sung asked. She had her hair pulled back and held with a rubber band. The skin over her high cheekbones was pulled tight. No makeup to conceal the brown circles under her eyes.

"Yes. Very good."

"You watch movie after?" She pointed to the new videos the honored general had given him, stacked on top of the box of pornos from Japan, Thailand, South Korea, and the Philippines.

The North Korean films he'd watched so far were stagey, propagandistic tropes with names Sung had translated as *Order No. 27, The Kites Flying in the Sky,* and *The Respected Supreme Commander Is Our Destiny.*

"No thank you," he responded.

When he finished, she took the plate and chopsticks away and waited for Kwon outside to inspect them. Nothing that could possibly be used as a weapon was allowed to remain in the room. Every morning he had to request a razor. Kwon would carry it in and watch Dawkins while he shaved, and then take it away.

"I think I'll meditate a little, then get ready for bed," Dawkins said.

Sung had taught him how to sit quietly on the chair with the lights out and monitor the thoughts and images that floated into his head. Pushing away the negative ones, she said, would give him a healthier mind and body.

Dawkins sat quietly. He found the time between dinner and bedtime to be the most difficult, because he had nothing to engage his mind. He wasn't allowed music to listen to, or books to read, and the videos were awful. The first thoughts that drifted into his minds were concerns about Nan and Karen. It felt wrong to try to will them away.

Three mornings after the op in China, Crocker hopped a cab from Honolulu International Airport to Pearl Harbor. During the drive he listened to the balding driver talk excitedly about how he had driven a famous pop star named Iggy Azalea back to her hotel last night and how she had tipped him twenty dollars. Crocker pretended to care, even though he didn't know who she was. He was thinking about how he had missed Easter dinner and had to call Jenny.

Even at 0740 the sun was blinding. He got out at the entrance to the base, stretched, and looked out over the harbor, which still seemed filled with ghosts. His grandfather had passed through here on his way to Guam back in '43. His dad had billeted here often while serving on various destroyers and aircraft carriers in the Pacific fleet.

Inside, he found a mess where he fortified himself with a cup of coffee and scrambled eggs, then hustled over to the CINCPAC building, where he checked through security again and was escorted to a third-floor conference room.

Anders looked up from some papers, saw Crocker in his customary black jeans and T-shirt, and said, "You're on time. Good. How was China?"

"Strange."

"How come you can't execute a mission without causing complications?"

"Shit happens. How's the kid?"

"Alive. Still in Dandong. Interesting that you inquire about some North Korean boy you barely know before you ask about the intel."

"People come first. You got a problem with that?"

"No. But the Chinese aren't happy."

"They'll get over it. Choi get you the intel you wanted?"

"He did. Thanks. Our guests should be here any minute. Get yourself some coffee and a muffin and relax."

He didn't want coffee or a muffin. He'd rather be running along Waikiki Beach, which he spied out the window on the left. Staring at the breaking surf, he remembered his honeymoon with Holly and happier times—the two of them splashing one another, the time he broke a surfboard in two on a monster wave while he was showing off.

The door opened and three serious-looking Asian gentlemen and a guy wearing a white hockey mask marched in. Two of the Asians were wearing uniforms, one had on a suit. The dude with the mask sported a white polo shirt and pants.

Any doubts Crocker might have had that the subject was North Korea were dispelled the moment Anders introduced one of the men in uniform as Park Yong-koo of South Korea's National Intelligence Service—NIS, their equivalent to our CIA. They took their places in upholstered chairs around the oval table and without ceremony or small talk got down to business. They were here to pick the brain of the man wearing the hockey mask—Min Sang Fu—a recent defector from North Korea and colonel in the North Korean Special Operation Force (NKSOF), an elite military unit trained to perform military, political, and psychological operations. He had served as personal liaison to Supreme Leader Kim Jong-un since 2013 and had defected during a recent visit to Beijing to consult with his Chinese counterparts.

Min was compact, with a square head and close-cropped black hair. Through an interpreter, he said he was currently a target of the North Korean secret police. He had decided to cooperate with U.S. officials, he explained, after hearing about the brave action Crocker had taken on the Tumen River.

"The kid was going to drown. I had to do something," Crocker said, and turned to glance at Anders as if to remind him that in the end everything was personal, even covert ops.

Min proceeded to warn them about the dirty tricks of Office 39, which he described as a criminal enterprise run like the Mafia, designed to raise revenue for all of the Supreme Leader's special programs and activities, including a very large gift and privilege system designed to buy the loyalty of his top lieutenants and military leaders and keep the regime in place. Office 39 also funded the regime's aggressive nuclear missile program, which the North Koreans viewed as the key to their survival. The enterprise was run by one of Kim's right-hand men, a former criminal and businessman named Chou Jang Hee. Chou, according to Min, was the most feared man in North Korea and had been given the title Honored General. His elite staff at Office 39 headquarters in Pyongyang consisted of about 150 operatives, planners, managers, and accountants.

Office 39 also employed another fifty to a hundred men and

women who worked overseas—some in front companies in Switzerland, Thailand, and Dubai, which were used to buy and sell military equipment and procure parts and technology for the nuclear weapons program. Others ran operations including selling cigarettes and counterfeit currency, and drug trafficking. In recent years, according to Min, Office 39 had made billions of dollars manufacturing crystal meth and selling it in places like the Czech Republic, Sweden, Latvia, Slovakia, Finland, Thailand (where it is known as *yaba*), and the Philippines (where it is called *shabu*).

Office 39 also kidnapped young women from places like Thailand, Vietnam, and the Ukraine to serve as sex slaves to top regime officials, managed a large Internet hacking operation, and stole industrial secrets. Illegal activities in foreign countries, Min explained, were often farmed out to local criminals and gangs. Chou's code name was the Dragon, and he called all the shots.

He also had a hand in managing Office 99, which raised funds by selling missiles and military equipment to countries like Syria and Iran, and Office 35, whose focus was to undermine the government of South Korea. Many of the billions of dollars in assets Chou accrued annually were stored in bank accounts in Switzerland, Dubai, and Macau.

Anders opened a folder and spread across the table the documents that had been smuggled over the border. They appeared to be hand-drawn plans of the various Office 39 facilities. As Min started to explain what they were and how Office 39 worked with other branches of the North Korean government and military, the air conditioning died and the lights went out.

The South Korean officials fidgeted and chattered nervously, but Min kept his eyes focused on Crocker across the table. A few minutes later a navy orderly knocked on the door and reported that the city of Honolulu had suffered a large-scale power outage. If the electricity wasn't restored shortly, he said, the base would begin firing up its emergency generators.

"How long do you expect that to take?" Anders asked.

"Five minutes tops, sir."

His mind quieted, Dawkins turned off the light and slipped under the coarse sheets. Usually when he got in bed, Sung left quietly, except on those rare occasions when he asked her to stay. He hadn't done so tonight, which was why he watched with curiosity as she entered the bathroom through the door beyond the foot of his bed.

He knew almost nothing about her life. Judging from her appearance, he assumed she was in her late twenties. In conversation she sometimes referred to her family, but she never talked about how big it was, or whether she had a husband or children. Dawkins had always been introspective and self-involved, but during his captivity he spent even more time thinking about his own family.

Now he lay on his back with his eyes closed, remembering a picnic with Nan and Karen on the shore of the Potomac. Karen, who was five at the time, had been given a pink Barbie kite for her birthday. He watched her run with it attached to a string, trying to get it to take flight as the sun glistened off the river and her dark hair flew behind her. He heard her squeal with excitement, "Daddy! Mommy! Look at me!"

Sensing something moving above him, he half opened his eyes and saw a shadow. Sung leaned over him and whispered, "Mr. Dawkin, I show you something."

"In the morning, Sung."

"Important. I show now."

The breeze along the Potomac carried the faint scent of cherry blossoms. Sung shook him. "Come to bathroom. Bring you glasses. I show you, Mr. Dawkin."

Her aggressive behavior surprised him. He sat up and watched her beckon him with her hand.

"Okay, Sung. You sure this can't wait?"

He put on his glasses and shuffled across the cold tile floor. Sung had entered the small five-by-five-foot space ahead of him. He saw the planes of her face shift under the bare light.

"What?"

She held a thin finger up to her lips, reached behind the rust-stained shower curtain, and turned on the water. He had always assumed his quarters were bugged and had been careful never to talk about anything that could get him in trouble. Now he watched her unscrew a five-inch-long plastic cylinder, reach inside it, and remove a piece of paper. He assumed the cylinder had been hidden somewhere on her body.

She carefully unfolded a small sheet of paper with blue handwriting on both sides.

"Where did you get this?" he asked.

Sung pushed the paper under his nose. "For you, Mr. Dawkin…for you."

He squinted through his glasses and started to read:

"Sir, my name is Dr. R. S. Shivan. I was a professor of nuclear engineering at the Tata Institute of Fundamental Research in Mumbai before I was kidnapped and forced to come here. TIFR is the Indian version of MIT. Part of my university training was at the University of Rochester. I have a PhD in nuclear engineering from the University of Michigan. I was brought to NK against my will over a year ago. Since then and after some delays due to illness, I have been working to solve the challenge of miniaturizing a nuclear weapon to fit in the warhead of an Unha-3 intercontinental missile. I don't know if you know this, but that is an important component of what the NKs are trying to achieve. As of this week, that critical engineering problem has been solved, which is both good and bad. The good part is that soon, God willing, I will be allowed to return to my home in India. It is my understanding from being privy to many details of the Unha-3 program that there are very few engineering and rocketry issues left to solve before NK is able to launch a nuclear strike at targets in China and the US. It is my fear that this is what the NKs are planning to do. Based on numerous things I have seen and experienced during my year in captivity I believe that they are going to foment a war between China and the US and use this as a cover to invade and take over SK. This isn't a theory. I have spoken to people here who have told me this. It's a very alarming situation. I have several questions for you:

1. How long have you been in NK?
2. What are you working on?
3. What is the status of your project?
4. Do you know anything else about NK plans?

"As I mentioned above, my project has been completed. I am hoping to be allowed to return to India soon. Once I am home I will talk to officials of my government and tell them to alert the US. I have heard you are American. I don't know if that is true or not. If you tell me your name and where you live, I will communicate with your government and your family. I am a faithful servant of God and your colleague in captivity, Dr. R. S. Shivan."

As Dawkins finished reading, his entire body started to tremble. With the shower hissing to his right he stared at Sung, who seemed more psychologically complex than she had moments before. Maybe daring, maybe cunning or deceitful. Perhaps some of all three.

He tried to grasp the choices he faced and their implications. "Have you read this?" he whispered so close that their noses almost touched.

"No, Mr. Dawkin."

"Do you know what it says?"

"No."

"Where did you get it from?"

"Woman like me. Work here for different man."

"Do you know this man?"

"No."

"Have you seen him?"

"Yes."

"What does he look like?"

"Black hair. Brown skin. Same height as you."

"And this woman, does she have a name?"

Sung nodded. "Chiang-su."

Dawkins had never heard of her. "Does she perform the same functions for that engineer as you do for me?"

She looked confused.

"Do you trust her?"

Sung nodded.

CHAPTER FOURTEEN

To get the full value of joy you must have someone to
divide it with.

—Mark Twain

FIVE MINUTES had passed, and Crocker was starting to sweat through his shirt. He kept thinking about the blackout in Las Vegas, and couldn't help wondering whether that event and this power outage were connected. Across the table, Min was describing the elaborate underground facility on the island of Ung-do, off the east coast of North Korea, that housed Office 39's new high-tech money counterfeiting facility, complete with intaglio press.

Crocker started to see where this was headed, which excited him. He'd been to North Korea once before, in '03, on a mission to knock out a radar and listening station in the north. He and his ST-6 teammates parachuted at night into freezing water, climbed into a Zodiac, and motored to shore. By the time they reached land the six men were suffering from hypothermia, their feet and hands were numb, and their clothes and gear had frozen. They spent the next three days climbing icy mountain trails. At night they slept huddled together on a bed of sticks to stay off the frozen ground. One night, one of Crocker's feet slipped off the bed and was frostbitten.

He still felt it more than a decade later. That mission to North Korea, three hundred miles north of Ung-do near the city of Kimchaek, had ended in success. Ung-do, according to the map Anders brought up on his computer, was approximately 102 miles east of the capital of Pyongyang and roughly on the same 39th parallel of north latitude. The island was covered with a forest of pine trees, which provided perfect cover for the large excavation project started in 2007. With the help of Iranian and Russian construction engineers, the North Koreans had expanded a series of natural caves. It was here, according to Min, that 2HK1 counterfeit hundred-dollar bills were being printed.

Interestingly, it was off Ung-do where the spy ship USS *Pueblo* had been seized by the North Koreans in 1968, sparking a very tense international standoff. One American sailor was killed when the ship was fired upon by a North Korean submarine chaser. The remaining eighty-two crew members and officers were captured and held in North Korean prisons, where they were starved and tortured. Almost a year later, the officers and crew were released. The vessel itself was never returned and was publicly displayed in North Korea as a monument to resisting the American imperialists.

All this had happened a year before Crocker was born. The United States had issued an apology and a promise never to spy on North Korea again. Thinking about it now pissed him off. Why do we back away when rogue countries like North Korea act aggressively? He didn't pretend to understand international politics, but he knew that you couldn't allow a criminal regime like the one that ruled North Korea to get away with anything without risking a much bigger challenge later. It was one of the laws of the streets he'd learned as a teenager. You couldn't let a punk insult you in public and walk away. You had to punch him in the mouth.

"What are we going to do about the presses?" Crocker asked when the emergency power finally came on.

Anders blinked and frowned. "We'll get to that now. Be patient."

Dawkins sat at the wooden table raking his hand through his thinning hair. He'd been staring at the blank page in his notebook for almost an hour and hadn't written a single word. If he responded to Dr. Shivan in any way, he'd be revealing himself. There was no question about it. What if Dr. Shivan didn't exist? What if the note was a ruse by the North Koreans to test him?

Any reply—even "I wish you well but have nothing to say"—could be construed as an act of complicity. And he didn't want that.

On the other hand, judging from the tone and content of the letter, which he had reread a dozen times, Dawkins believed there was an eighty percent chance that Dr. Shivan was who he said he was. Assuming that was true, the temptation to tell him details about himself so that he could communicate them to U.S. authorities upon his release was very strong. He desperately wanted his government to know where he was, and he wanted his captivity to end. But if the letter was fake, any response would serve to diminish his chances of ever reuniting with his family.

Dawkins wasn't adept at rational thinking in difficult emotional circumstances. He usually did everything he could to avoid situations like this, and if he failed, he relied on Nan. Now, no matter how he examined the dilemma, the biggest, loudest part of him told him to think about his survival. The safest course was best. His release and return home had to be the paramount goal. The voice in his head argued that he wasn't only thinking of himself. His return to the States would be good for everyone—him, Nan, Karen, and even his countrymen. If Sung and Chiang-su were doing this of their own volition, they were taking an enormous risk for reasons that weren't apparent to him. If, on the other hand, they were doing this on the regime's orders, they were being cruel.

But what did he know about their lives and the political and personal pressures they were under? He hadn't been aware of Chiang-su's existence before tonight. And if he had to character-ize Sung's behavior over the many hours they'd spent together, he would have to say gentle and sympathetic. Nothing she had said or done had given him any indication that she harbored any hostility toward him or the United States.

Nor was she naive. Sung had to know that the note put her in danger. He wanted to convince himself that by not responding to Dr. Shivan, he would be doing the best thing for her, too.

But he couldn't. A quieter, more contemplative part of his psyche wanted to learn more from Dr. Shivan about the under-ground facility and the state of the North Korean nuclear missile program. It urged him to somehow take advantage of the oppor-tunity offered by Sung and Chiang-su. He spent the rest of the night trying to come up with a plan that would afford him maxi-mum deniability and the greatest chance of success.

In the morning when Sung arrived with his breakfast, he sum-moned her to the bathroom and turned on the shower. With the water hissing, he said, "Tell Dr. Shivan to call this number…seven, zero, three, seven, one, five, eight, two, eight, seven. Ask to speak to Bird, and tell her where I am."

Late the following night in a secure room at Naval Amphibious Base in Coronado, CA, Crocker met with James Anders, his assistant Dina Brooke, an analyst from the CIA North Korean desk, and another analyst from FBI Cyber Division.

Anders said, "Everything we discuss here will be preliminary and subject to executive approval, because of the mounting atmosphere of hostility between us and China. I want to talk about that, and I also want us to start looking at possibly launching an op against the printing presses on Ung-do."

"It's about time we did something," remarked Crocker.

Dina Brooke, a very serious young woman with long dark hair and glasses, reviewed the causes of the recent tensions between the two superpowers. Over the past month a dozen cities in the United States had experienced power outages similar to the ones he had witnessed in Las Vegas and Honolulu. All of them had occurred when an unauthorized person or entity hacked into the local power utility's supervisory control and data acquisition system.

They had done this, the FBI Cyber Division expert explained, by bypassing the local power utilities' security measures and compromising the Domain Name System (DNS). By changing the mapping between the utilities and the IP addresses of their physical servers, the intruders were able to direct traffic heading for the utilities' domains to the wrong IP addresses—addresses of servers under their control.

The hackers then fired massive amounts of network traffic at the host, which caused it to become overwhelmed and drop legitimate traffic. Using these protocols and others, they essentially took over the local utilities' computer systems and directed them to power down the outflow of electricity.

Why the hackers had done this was unclear. Analysts at the FBI and CIA theorized that the people behind the cyberattacks were either operatives of an enemy state or a terrorist organization trying to spread fear throughout the United States.

After hundreds of man-hours of tracking and investigation, the FBI Cyber Division had identified People's Liberation Army (PLA) Unit 61398 near Shanghai as the likely source of the attacks. Unit 61398 was a viable candidate, the FBI expert explained, because it had been the source of previous hacking attacks on U.S. government agencies and businesses. Since 2000, ninety percent of cyberespionage on the U.S. originated in China.

Public utilities were particularly vulnerable, according to the FBI expert. "All it takes is the right Google search terms to find a way into the systems of U.S. water and power utilities. And this isn't unusual. Many industrial control systems are hooked up to the Internet. If they don't change their default passwords and you know the right keywords, you can find their control panels easily."

When White House officials lodged a formal complaint with the Chinese government, the Chinese responded angrily, in part because they had been experiencing cyberattacks of their own, targeting banks, businesses, and government agencies, including PLA offices and installations. They pointed a finger at the United States and the same top-secret U.S. cyberwar units that had created the computer worm Stuxnet, which had infected the software of at least fourteen industrial sites in Iran, including a uranium-enrichment plant.

This worm, first discovered in June 2010, was an unprecedentedly masterful and malicious piece of code that attacked in three phases. First, it targeted Microsoft Windows machines and networks, repeatedly replicating itself. Then it sought out Siemens Step 7 software, used to program industrial control systems that operate equipment such as centrifuges. Finally, it compromised the programmable logic controllers. The worm's authors could thus spy on the industrial systems unbeknown to the human op erators at the plant and even cause the fast-spinning centrifuges to tear themselves apart.

Two years later the International Telecommunication Union, the UN agency that manages information and communication technologies, discovered another very sophisticated piece of malware forty times larger than Stuxnet, which they called Flame. On investigation it turned out to be a precursor to Stuxnet that had somehow gone undetected.

While Stuxnet's purpose was to destroy things, Flame's was to spy on people. It spread through USB sticks and infected printers shared by the same network. It could also exchange data with any Bluetooth device, and through directional tunnels linked to Bluetooth enabled computers to steal information from other devices and embed itself from two kilometers away.

The scariest and most revealing aspect of Flame was how it got into computers in the first place—through an update in the Windows 7 operating system.

Because of the enormous amount of time, money, and resources needed to develop malware like Stuxnet and Flame, cyber experts around the world suspected that a large government was behind their development. And because Stuxnet had been targeted to disrupt Iran's nuclear enrichment program and Flame had infected millions of computers throughout the Middle East, international experts suspected the United States and Israel, either working separately or together.

The Chinese had reason to be suspicious of the United States. But this time, according to Dina Brooke and the FBI expert, the United States was innocent. "The charges directed at us have been thoroughly investigated," Brooke said, "and are absolutely untrue. It's possible that the hackers involved are acting for some third party and are using the U.S. and Chinese servers as proxies."

Crocker, who understood very little about computer systems, found all this fascinating. Before the cyber experts were dismissed, he asked one question.

"If it's possible, as you say, to hide behind or piggyback off someone else's server, could some other country, like Iran or North Korea, be behind these attacks?"

"The short answer is yes," Brooke said. "With all the available stolen credit cards and Internet proxies, it's really quite easy for attackers to become invisible."

Crocker smelled a rat. He thought the North Koreans were up to something, maybe with the help of the Iranians, maybe on their own. He didn't want to hear more hedging from Anders, who was now saying that given the recent tensions with China, the White House would be averse to any contingency in terms of North Korea that could directly or indirectly serve to further offend the Chinese.

Fuck Chinese sensibilities, he said to himself. *If the North Koreans are counterfeiting our currency and hacking into our power grid, let's kick their butts.*

*   *   *

During a coffee break, Crocker stood on the steps of National Amphibious Base headquarters looking out on San Diego harbor. Seventeen years ago he had suffered through BUD/S training a few hundred yards from where he stood now—eight months of ass-kicking that involved endless runs on the beach, calisthenics, obstacle courses, swimming, boat drills, fast roping, land navigation, and dive training. Out of a hundred guys in his class, twenty-three had graduated.

Seventeen years ago he had driven cross-country in a beat-up TR6 with no brakes. Since then he had suffered all kinds of scars and bruises in places all over the world. As he watched Anders talking into a cell phone on the lawn, he marveled at how much the world had changed in seventeen years. When he received his SEAL Trident there was no war on terrorism, no ISIS, no Homeland Security, no FBI Cyber Division, and no cyberespionage.

Who knows what the next seventeen years will bring?

Whatever the new threats were or where they came from, he knew it was imperative that the United States respond with intelligent, decisive action. Dithering over a reply to al-Qaeda after the bombing of the U.S. embassies in Dar-es-Salaam and Nairobi and the attack on the USS *Cole* had led to tragedy. An ill-advised invasion of Iraq and the failure to act in Syria had encouraged the rise of ISIS.

If you saw warnings and didn't heed them, you could expect bad things to follow. That was the hard, hard truth of life. Blaming people was a waste of time. You had to learn from your mistakes, take responsibility, and get better and smarter. The cold reality was that the world was becoming increasingly complex, dangerous, and interdependent. When rogue actors behaved badly, they had to be put in their place.

He watched Anders put the phone away and climb the steps. Crocker stepped into his path.

"If we're not going to do something, you don't need me here," he said, scowling into the setting sun.

"Come on, Crocker," Anders responded. "You've been around long enough to know how this works. We collect intel, analyze it, make plans, and recommend that the White House takes action. All we can do is hope they make the right decision this time."

Day by day, Dawkins was growing increasingly anxious. He'd made it through nearly a week of ignoring the pleading look in Sung's eyes when she brought him breakfast in the morning, and had gone about his business without mentioning the note from Dr. Shivan or the phone number he'd given her.

But today was different. For one thing, Sung hadn't arrived at his room at 7 a.m. An older woman with gray streaks in her hair showed up instead. She spoke less English than Sung and offered no explanation for Sung's absence. Instead, she served him a rolled egg omelet with kelp and carrots, and rice cakes, set out his clothes, and escorted him out to the waiting Kwon as though she had been doing this all along.

The second odd thing was that when Dawkins arrived in his workshop, his assistants weren't there. So while he spun the gyro compass to test that it met no resistance from the digital resolver and platform shrouds, he wondered what was going on.

Maybe today was a holiday or some special government function was being held. Or perhaps Chiang-su and Sung had been caught passing another note. Or Dr. Shivan had spilled the beans during interrogation.

Normally, at lunchtime his junior assistant, Yi-Thaek, would roll in a small metal cart bearing hot soup, noodles, and some kind of salad. But today no food arrived. So he sat at the bench sipping rusty-tasting water from a plastic bottle while Kwon waited by the door reading a book in a weathered leather sleeve.

"Food?" he asked as he mimed putting something in his mouth and chewing. "Lunch?"

Kwon looked up at him sullenly, then removed a cell phone from the pouch on his belt and punched in a number.

Dawkins was adjusting the platform shroud when someone rapped on the door and handed Kwon two bowls of soup. The hot broth tasted greasy, and the slices of meat in it were as tough as shoe leather, but at least the soup spread warmth throughout his body, and with warmth came confidence and hope.

He'd almost convinced himself that there was a logical and nonalarming explanation for Sung's absence when a crackly announcement came over the PA system.

He looked at Kwon to try to gauge his reaction. Kwon worked a piece of food out of his teeth, stood, and waved to Dawkins to follow him.

"Where are we going?"

Kwon didn't answer. Dawkins hoped they were on their way back to his room, where he would be given time to fetch his parka and then be escorted outside. But when they reached the end of the hallway, Kwon turned right instead of left, grabbed Dawkins by the elbow, and led him down a short flight of steps and into a darkened room.

When the light came on, he saw that it was an oval amphitheater with about a dozen rows of chairs. The floor was concrete, and thick metal fencing separated the stage area from the seats. Two men entered and set a ten-foot-tall metal pole into a hole in the floor and secured it with bolts. As they worked, people started to file in silently and sit.

He noticed Sung across from him with her eyes cast down. She looked up, met his gaze, and quickly lowered her head. He thought he saw fear in her eyes.

When the space was half full, the same man's voice came over the PA system. This time it took on a scolding tone. Dawkins noticed the eyes of the spectators shifting to him—the lone Westerner. Panic started to worm into his stomach. When he found the courage to glance up, he couldn't see anyone familiar besides Sung across the way and Kwon, who sat next to him, upright and rigid, with his hands folded in his lap.

Martial music played, then a metal door slammed and he heard a man barking orders. Four soldiers in olive uniforms marched in from his left. They stopped at the metal pole, turned with precision, and two men split off to each side and stood at attention with their automatic weapons held in front of them.

Then eight more soldiers marched in. The last two held metal chains that were attached to the wrists of a woman. Her long hair obscured her face, and she wore a plain gray sack-type dress. The soldiers chained the woman's ankles and wrists to the metal pole. Then two of them used scissors to cut apart her dress until it fell off and she was naked. Dawkins still couldn't see her face.

The soldiers left, leaving the chained, exposed woman alone in the pit. Then the man's voice came over the loudspeaker again and began a long, loud harangue that seemed to go on for an hour.

Dawkins noticed that some spectators were visibly shaking and others started to weep. None of them dared make a sound. He started to feel sick. When he tried get up to find a bathroom, Kwon pushed him roughly back into the seat.

The harangue stopped and there was a long silence. He heard a low groan from the crowd and saw that the woman had peed down her trembling legs.

The metal door slid open again and a man wearing a black mask and carrying some kind of backpack emerged. At his side he held what looked like a hose with a nozzle. He stopped ten feet away from the woman, pointed the nozzle at her, and pulled a lever.

With a loud whoosh a bolt of fire shot out of the nozzle, hit the woman, and then subsided. The spectators groaned in unison. The flame had lasted only seconds, but it was enough to singe off all the woman's hair and melt her ears and lips. She screamed in agony as her skin continued to burn. When the smell hit Dawkins's nostrils, he lurched forward from the waist and threw up onto his pants and shoes.

He tried again to stand up, but Kwon slapped him violently on the side of his head. The voice came over the speaker again and harangued the crowd. They responded with groans of agony as the man with the hose released another bolt of fire.

This one hit one of the woman's arms, which burned and snapped off at the shoulder. Dawkins covered his eyes. He couldn't look anymore. The woman wailed like a castrated animal. Was she Chiang-su? Waves of shame and fear passed through his body as he felt a sharp slap across his ear and face, then another.

When he tried to cover his head, Kwon pulled his arms away

and punched him in the mouth. One of Dawkins's front teeth gave way. He tasted blood.

The crowd groaned louder this time. He heard another whoosh of flame and passed out.

Nan sat outside the burn unit of the Reston Hospital Center, waiting for Karen and feeling increasingly anxious. She wasn't sure why, because this was a routine checkup, and so far Karen's recovery had gone well. But she sensed that something was wrong. When she saw one of the burn unit nurses leave a room farther down the hallway, she hurried to catch up with her.

"Is Karen responding to treatment?" she asked. "Are there complications?"

"No, Mrs. Dawkins. She's fine. An excellent patient. The doctor is changing the dressing on her ankle. She'll be out in a minute or two."

"Will there be much scarring?"

"Maybe a little on the outside of her ankle. It can be addressed with plastic surgery, if it's a concern."

"Thank you."

The conversation with the nurse hadn't lessened her anxiety. Maybe all the worrying about James and the incident with the fire had frayed her nerves. Thinking that she was about to have a panic attack, she crossed to the water cooler in the waiting area, filled a paper cup, and downed it.

She was about to refill the cup when her cell phone rang. She expected it to be a call from work, but the screen read "Unknown."

The voice on the other end asked, "Bird?"

"Yes. Who is this?" No one called her Bird except for James and her stepsister, who she hadn't spoken to in months.

"I'm calling in regard to Mr. James Dawkins." It was a man's voice with an Asian accent.

"Oh, oh…Yes! He's my husband."

"Mrs. Dawkins, I work for an antigovernment organization called the North Korean Strategy Center based in Seoul, South Korea."

"Are you with my husband? Is that where he is now?" Nan asked.

"I am not with Mr. Dawkins. I'm sorry. He's at a location called Ung-do. He's been held prisoner there by the North Korean government."

A dozen questions crowded her brain. "North Korea? Do you know why? Is he being treated well and in good health?"

"He is alive. Unfortunately, I have very few details. He's living in an underground complex and is being forced to work on North Korea's nuclear weapons program."

"Oh…What is the name of his location again?"

"Ung-do. It's an island."

CHAPTER FIFTEEN

A great river does not refuse any small streams.
—Korean proverb

AFTER DAYS of hanging around San Diego and growing increasingly frustrated, Crocker was summoned to NAB headquarters again. As he sat texting Cyndi, Captain Sutter arrived, all spit and polish, with every Kentucky-bred hair in place. The same group of analysts that had been meeting all week took their places—minus the FBI cyber expert and the analyst from the NK desk. Dina Brooke had a lizard tattooed on the back of her wrist and something that looked like computer code on her upper arm.

What it meant, he had no clue. Seeing the document stamped TOP SECRET that she set in front of him and the burn bag by the door, his mood brightened. Looked like they were finally getting down to business.

Sutter dove in, explaining that SOCOM—Special Operations Command—had been considering three military options for dealing with North Korean aggression:

1. A cruise missile attack launched from U.S. warships stationed in the South China Sea.
2. A laser-guided high-altitude aerial bombing with special bunker-busting bombs.
3. A small amphibious landing by a SEAL demolition team.

"But given recent developments, options one and two have been shelved," Sutter explained.

"What recent developments?" asked Crocker.

"We learned last night that a missing U.S. advanced missile guidance engineer was kidnapped by the DPRK and is being forced to work on their nuclear missile program."

"How long has he been held?" Crocker asked.

"About a month," Anders answered. "The DPRK kidnapped at least one other missile engineer, an Indian gentleman, who we believe was killed recently. There might be others."

"The blackouts, the counterfeit currency, now the kidnapped engineers...I knew they were up to something."

"Analysts at CIA believe that these acts are all part of a campaign initiated by Kim Jong-un," Anders explained. "His endgame isn't clear. Maybe some form of nuclear blackmail, or an attempt to lure the United States and China into military conflict that he can take advantage of."

Crocker's blood pressure had started to spike. He said, "We've got to respond decisively. I hope that's why we're here."

"DPRK's missile tech operation is run out of the Ung-do complex," Anders continued. "We believe it's the same place where our guidance engineer is being held."

He didn't explain who that important piece of information had come from—specifically, an FBI agent who had received a call from the engineer's wife, who had been contacted by a DPRK dissident, who got the information from a woman working in the Ung-do complex.

"We're prioritizing option three," Sutter announced. "It's yours, Crocker. We need you to lead the planning and assemble a team."

"What size team are we talking about?" he asked, getting fired up.

"Small," Sutter answered. "Probably no more than four men, but totally contingent on how you infil."

He left the infil part dangling for the time being. "Why only four?"

"Because we want to keep the footprint as small as possible," replied Anders. "Optimally, we'd like the mission to have no U.S. footprint at all. But that's probably outside the realm of possibility, because the South Koreans want no part of this."

Crocker deduced from his answer that they'd already been asked and had declined.

"Why's that?" he asked.

"One, they say they're committed to a political program of normalizing relations with North Korea. And, two, they're obviously worried about military repercussions, though they won't admit that. Suffice it to say, the DPRK has an army of over a million, a lot of them are deployed within a hundred miles of Seoul, and they're fucking crazy."

"Got it."

Anders rubbed his square chin. "There's several other aspects of this to consider," he stated. "One is that Min has offered to be part of the mission."

"Min, the defector?" Sutter asked. "Are we sure that's wise? Can we trust him?"

Anders turned to Brooke, who answered, "Based on everything we know, yes. The South Koreans are extremely thorough in the way they vet DPRK defectors."

"But loyalties in that part of the world are tricky, so there's always a chance, correct?" Sutter asked.

"I would characterize it as slight probability," hedged Anders.

Crocker spoke up. "Whatever the odds, it means we could be screwed the moment we launch."

"That's one way to put it," Anders replied. "Nevertheless, Min has given us a detailed picture of the layout, entrance and egress points, and resources on the island. All of which has been matched against drawings that Choi smuggled out."

"Sat and electronic surveillance?" Crocker asked.

"The full three-sixty package of surveillance assets have been deployed, as well as a complete target profile amalgamated from other DPRK defectors."

"When was the last time Min was physically on the island?" Crocker asked.

"Roughly a year ago," Anders answered.

"How sure are we that the presses, missile research program, and U.S. engineer are still there?"

"In terms of the first two, ninety-nine percent. Obviously, we can't see them from the air, but the heat signatures around the entrance continue to be strong. Obviously, the engineer is easier to move, so his location is very difficult to confirm."

"He have a name?" asked Crocker.

"James Dawkins," Dina Brooke answered, reaching into a folder and producing a photo of the engineer, which she handed to Crocker.

Crocker had been in this business long enough to know he had to discount all CIA odds by at least twenty percent. Which meant that there was a better than even chance that the presses and missile program were still on Ung-do and operational. In terms of the engineer, it was anybody's guess.

"How well fortified is the facility and how far underground?" Crocker asked.

"You'll find all that detail in the document in front of you. Page three."

"Thanks." He jotted down some facts in his notebook: reinforced concrete walls, bomb-resistant roof, target approximately thirty meters underground.

"What are we looking at in terms of possible exposure to radiation?"

Brooke jumped in. "It's a missile research facility that according to what we know is devoted to two important tasks, reducing the size of the warheads and increasing the accuracy of their missile guidance systems. We can't confirm the presence of active nuclear material."

"Nothing has been picked up by airborne monitoring," added Anders.

"But we don't know for sure?"

"No."

"I'm assuming that we'll be taking out the complex with explosives," Crocker said.

"Correct. And you'll probably have to carry the material in yourself. Because of the high level of local security, we don't think it's possible to drop anything on the island or immediate vicinity."

Sutter spoke up. "DARPA has developed something that you'll want to get your hands on. It's currently the most powerful nonnuclear explosive in existence. Insensitive to shock like TNT, and has twenty-five percent more explosive power than HMX."

"What's it called?"

"CL-20. Like HMX, it has an extremely fast explosive velocity."

"Suarez know about it?" Crocker asked, referring to Black Cell's explosives expert.

"I believe so. Yes."

"Then I want him included," Crocker concluded. "We have anyone on the teams who speaks Korean?"

"There's a sniper on Team Three named Sam Lee," Sutter reported. "Strong, smart kid. Good reputation. He's a native speaker."

"I want to meet him this afternoon."

"Done."

Dawkins awoke seated in a chair in his room. He couldn't tell if he was dreaming or what he saw was real. Kwon was holding his mouth open with one hand and a flashlight in the other, as a man with a very thin face and bad breath used a dental instrument to examine his teeth.

The man muttered something and nodded, and Dawkins drifted off.

Next thing he remembered was Kwon helping him into bed. The box of videos, VCR, and TV were gone. So were his pens and notebooks. With his tongue he felt the empty space where his tooth had been.

Sung emerged from the bathroom carrying a wet washcloth. When he sat up and blinked, the older woman was in her place instead.

"Where's Sung?" he asked in a weak voice.

Kwon barked something in Korean and left.

Dawkins's body felt like it was burning. Someone placed a cool washcloth on his forehead. He looked up and thought he saw Sung.

"Sung, I'm so sorry."

He heard someone humming the lullaby she had sung to him about the mother going out to look for food for her infant son. But when he focused on the woman's face, it didn't belong to Sung, and her lips weren't moving.

Crocker was sitting in his rental car in the Doheny State Beach parking lot, just south of Dana Point, reviewing the mental checklist in his head, when a guy who met Sam's description pulled up in a late-model pickup and got out. He strode like an athlete and stood about six two, with a sidewall haircut and a SEAL Trident tattooed on his shoulder. His size and large nose were the only clues that he wasn't a hundred percent Korean.

"Sam?"

He smiled. "Warrant Officer Crocker."

"Thanks for coming. You ready to run?"

Crocker led the way across the sand, down past San Clemente to San Onofre, sweet ocean air in his face, the sun shining over his shoulder, enjoying the pulse of movement, freedom, and space. Surfers to their right, sunbathers on their left. Nature at full astonishment. He didn't even think of stopping to buy a bottle of water until they reached Camp Pendleton South, by which time they had covered more than twenty miles.

Sam had kept stride the whole way. When he finally stopped, Crocker slapped him on the back.

"You okay?"

"Yes, sir. I was warned about you. We running back?"

"Let's talk first."

They stretched their legs on a dune looking out over the ocean and Sam started telling him about his family. Both mother and stepfather were immigrants from poor farming communities in South Korea. At nineteen his stepdad got a job as a cook and mechanic with the U.S. Navy. A friendly commander sponsored his immigration to the States. He arrived in North Carolina and worked in the retired commander's nursery business. Just when he started to think of moving on, he met his former wife, Sam's mother, rifling through a trash bin outside a Winston-Salem supermarket. He was twenty-six and gainfully employed. She had just turned twenty-eight, was a single mother, homeless, and completely broke.

"He took us in that day and we've been together since," Sam said. "My parents just celebrated their twentieth anniversary. They also gave me a younger brother and sister."

Crocker tried to focus, but he kept returning to the long checklist in his head—comms, weapons, medical kits, et cetera. "Tell me about your father," he said, reminding himself that his men would be arriving in an hour and his first task would be to talk to Suarez about the CL-20.

"Supersolid; never complains. My mother is my inspiration. She started working in rice paddies at the age of five, where she had to slice leeches off her leg with a machete. At sixteen she was discovered one night making out in the backseat of a rich boy's car, which caused her to be shunned by her family and kicked out of school."

Crocker flashed back to his own high school in Massachusetts and one of several times he'd been expelled—for punching the captain of the football team and breaking his nose.

"The only way she could support herself was by working as a prostitute at a nearby U.S. Navy base. At eighteen she met a young American ensign who fell in love with her and took her back home with him to Pensacola. That's where they married and where I was born. But my dad's parents shunned their Korean daughter-in-law, and my mother had big dreams. She wanted to go to college, so she started her own business, which was selling cosmetics door-to-door.

"My father imagined a more traditional role for her. They fought and separated. She met another man, who moved us up to Winston-Salem and then abandoned us. Today she's a successful businesswoman with a college degree and a dozen stores throughout Southern California. Next year she's planning on running for mayor of Newport Beach."

"Sounds like an amazing lady," Crocker said.

"Thanks."

"I'd like to meet them when we get back."

"Absolutely, chief. Where are we going?"

"The mission is top secret. I'll tell you later. After we run back to our vehicles, grab your gear and meet me at NAB Coronado. Be there at 2100."

"Yes, sir."

Nan sat in the bedroom of her temporary apartment Google-mapping the island of Ung-do, North Korea. A rough gray oval surrounded by light blue appeared on the screen of her laptop. Shifting to "Earth" mode, she saw the shape turn green and the water surrounding it dark blue. When she zoomed in closer, a few concrete structures became visible in the middle of the island.

She wondered if James was living in one of them and what he was doing. For a few seconds she felt close to him, as though they were communicating telepathically and focusing on him had caused him to think of her.

The FBI agents she'd met that afternoon had told her that the United States was taking steps to get her husband back. But they wouldn't specify what that meant, nor would they give her a timetable. She'd heard about American prisoners held in captivity in the jungles of South America for a dozen or more years before a rescue or exchange, or until the guerrillas holding them got tired of doing so and let them go.

How long would it be before she saw James again?

Knowing he was alive made waiting more difficult. Part of her had been preparing for a life without him. Now she understood that the story of their lives together, as intricately woven as it was already, would continue and grow more complex.

It was natural to idealize those who had died. The living were far more challenging. In the past she'd respected James more than she had loved him. But the grim reality of what they were both going through had changed her. She sensed that it wouldn't be enough for either of them to comfortably coexist the way they had before. They had to either love each other honestly and completely, or move on. It scared her, but it excited her, too.

CHAPTER SIXTEEN

Always bear in mind that your own resolution to
succeed is more important than any other one thing.
—Abraham Lincoln

CROCKER'S HEAD hurt as he sat in the operations room of the USS *Carl Vinson* 340 miles west of the Japanese island of Sado in the Sea of Japan. He wasn't sure if the source of his discomfort was lack of sleep, dehydration, or the massive amount of information he'd been trying to cram into his brain.

The logistics of an op this complex and difficult were daunting to say the least, and because the new moon was three nights away and the threat was that some sort of nuclear test or strike might be imminent, they wanted to launch soon. Five men—Davis, Suarez, Sam, Akil, and himself—would be entering enemy territory to perform a sabotage mission. Everything they carried had to be impossible to trace. Since they would be infiltrating in a very tight SEAL Delivery Vehicle (SDV), the amount of gear they could carry was severely restricted. Additionally, they would be traveling in what was essentially an open-water underwater vehicle, so all comms, weapons, ammo, medical equipment, electronic devices, and explosives had to be sealed in waterproof bags.

Crocker hated the very cramped SDVs. He would have much preferred to parachute in or swim. But given the parameters of the mission, the fact that they expected a high level of security on and around Ung-do, any other type of boat, scuba, or air insertion seemed out of the question.

For what seemed like the hundredth time in the past several hours, Crocker pored over the hand-drawn layouts of the complex and satellite photos of the island that Akil and the ship's operations officers had blown up and marked with colored stickers and pins. The real issue was whether they should drive the SDV to the more desolate and less fortified Ryo-do, about three-quarters of a mile south, and swim from there, or infil directly to the southeastern shore of Ung-do itself.

Ung-do, sometimes referred to as Ungdo-ri, was one of the smaller islands in the Pansong Archipelago, located off the coast of Cholsan county. It had an average elevation of fifty-six feet and stood at 36°16'77" north latitude and 127°37'23" east longitude. Given the probability that they would be dealing with cold water and strong currents between the two islands, Crocker chose a direct landing as the preferred option.

How they would proceed once they got on the island was more problematic. Based on the intel he had at his disposal, it was impossible to tell how well fortified the underground facility was and what kind of resistance they would meet when they got there. Heat signature profiles indicated that there were armed guards stationed at the main entrance and around all four corners of the complex 24/7. Also, the road that ran up the middle of the island and along the western shore was patrolled by armed vehicles at least every half hour.

Crocker marked a small cove and beach on the eastern side, almost due east of the facility. "I propose that we land here."

Min, who sat to Crocker's right, unwrapped a piece of chewing gum and popped it through the hole in his white hockey mask. He seemed distracted by the framed photos of F-15s on the walls.

"Min?"

He slowly turned to Crocker like a character in a horror movie.

"Sam, ask him how far this is from the complex," Crocker said, pointing at the proposed landing site. Min leaned forward and frowned as though he were seeing the map for the first time. He said something in Korean and groaned.

Crocker was starting to worry about Min's state of mind. He'd already decided not to take the North Korean defector on the mission, but he still had to rely on him for critical information. The U.S. intelligence community hadn't been able to locate a single other individual who had visited Ung-do.

"About a quarter mile," Sam translated. "Getting from there to the complex means we have to cross the road."

"Got it."

"Only trees and a little stream here," Sam added. "The island is relatively flat."

There appeared to be no other man-made structures or geographic obstacles in the way.

"What's your opinion, Min?" Crocker asked.

Sitting there in an olive-green flight suit and rubbing the stubble on his neck, he seemed a million miles away.

"Min, are you with us? Is something wrong?"

Min mumbled something to Sam, who translated. "Yes. He thinks it is a logical choice. The buildings here south of the complex…this is housing for the guards. The only way to reach the island is by boat. Boat is best for us, too. The dock is here."

Min pointed to a small man-made cove on the southwestern side, facing the mainland and the city of Munchon.

"Is the dock well guarded?" Crocker asked.

"Yes. Machine guns. DShK antiaircraft."

Crocker didn't want to have to mess with them. "So the east side is better?" he asked.

"Yes, better. Yes."

Gaining entrance to the complex itself presented another set of challenges. The layout showed two entrances, front and back, a large ventilation shaft at the north end of the complex and a long underground drain that emptied into the north end of the bay.

"I assume both entrances are heavily guarded," said Crocker, turning to Sam and Min, and trying to squeeze as much info out of Min as he could.

Sam translated again. (He was proving to be extremely useful.) "Always two soldiers in the front, two in the back. Sometimes more. Inside there is a vestibule with a stairwell and two elevators. We might find other soldiers…or patrols…inside. The printing presses are one level down…to the north. So you enter from the front…turn right. If we go in at night, the door will probably be locked."

"What about the labs?"

"Those are located on the second floor."

"Any idea where the hostage is being held?"

Min shook his head.

The *Vinson*'s operations officer appeared at the door to announce that a Blackhawk helicopter would be ready at 2130 to ferry the insertion team to the USS *Dallas,* a nuclear-powered attack submarine currently twenty-one miles off Ung-do.

Crocker looked at his watch: 2041.

"Okay, grab your gear and assemble on the flight deck at 2115. You have any messages to send home, best do it now, because comms will be restricted when we get closer to our target."

"Roger."

"Akil, make sure you collect all maps and charts."

"On it like white on rice."

"Davis, recheck the comms."

"Got it."

"Sam, double-check all first-, second-, and third-line gear. I'll eyeball the med kits and the big bag. Suarez, check the CL-20, detonators, all that stuff is critical. Make sure it's triple-sealed in case we capsize and hit the water."

"Done, boss."

"I'll see you gorillas in half an hour."

Despite the hundreds of things on his mind and the several dozen he had to get done, he shoehorned in a minute to contact Cyndi on Skype—then realized it was something like 4 a.m. in Las Vegas. So he tried Jenny back home, instead.

It was just after 7 a.m. in Virginia.

"Dad?" Jenny answered.

"Sweetheart, I hope I didn't wake you. How's everything? You okay?"

"All good. No problem. I'm up early studying for a civics exam. You talk to grandpa?"

Crocker reminded himself that he had to huddle with the SDV pilot as soon as they reached the *Dallas*. SDVs usually ran with a two-man crew and carried a maximum of four operators with gear. Since both Davis and Akil had served a tour at SDV Team One, he was hoping that under these extraordinary circumstances one of them could replace the copilot.

"No. Why?" he asked back. The team already felt thin without Mancini and Cal. Cutting another operator on an op this perilous would make them even more vulnerable.

"You didn't get my texts?" Jenny asked.

"No, sweetheart. I've been off the grid a while. What's going on?"

"Yesterday he was exercising after he woke up, and started having trouble breathing and was getting sharp pains in his chest. So he called some lady friend of his."

Crocker tensed up. "Carla?"

"Yes, Carla. She drove him to the ER. Turns out one of his arteries was like ninety percent blocked, and they caught it just in time."

He could already feel the guilt burrowing into him. "He okay?"

"Yeah, Dad, thank God. They had to insert something called a stent. He's probably sleeping now. I talked to him last night and he was really out of it."

"What did the doctor say?

"I didn't speak to the doctor, but Carla said the procedure went well. She seems like a really nice woman. Uncle Bob is driving down now. He'll be there in the morning."

A quick glance at his Suunto told Crocker he was running short on time. "Where is grandpa now?"

"Inova Fair Oaks Hospital."

Someone started rapping on the door behind him. "You have a number I can call?"

"Seven oh three, three nine one, three six oh six."

Akil, on the other side, was summoning him urgently.

"Thanks, sweetheart. Tell Grandpa I'll call him first chance I get. I've got to run now. I love you, and good luck on your test tomorrow."

"Thanks, Dad. Love you, too."

The wind hit the helo and rocked it, causing the fuselage to twist right and the tail to dip. Across from him, he watched Sam lean forward and throw up into the yellow bucket at his feet. Great kid so far, smart, focused, and thorough. Excellent command of Korean. His face had assumed a greenish tinge in the dim cabin light.

Beside him Davis listened to music through earbuds, seemingly oblivious to the noise, danger, and stench. Eyes closed, he didn't even flinch when the helo was buffeted a second time, even harder.

Crocker was thinking about his father, who had served in the navy as a pilot and was one of the kindest, gentlest men he'd ever known. Proof of that was the fact that he'd put up with Crocker's raucous rowdiness as a teenager, including various gang fights and arrests. Never stopped believing in him.

God, please look after my father, and help him heal quickly and fully.

Crocker reminded himself that he hadn't been with his mom either when she'd died in a fire. In fact, he'd left her side hours earlier.

What kind of a shitty son am I?

All the birthdays, weddings, and special events he had missed because he was busy training or deployed overseas with ST-6 unreeled in his head.

What am I supposed to do, cancel the mission and jeopardize thousands of lives because Dad is in the hospital?

Questions like this were the most agonizing part of SEAL work. The long hours, danger, and physical hardships were easy in comparison.

Over the roar of the engine, he heard the copilot establishing comms with the USS *Dallas*.

"SNN-700, Bravo Tiger Seven, do you read me? Over."

"Copy, Bravo Tiger Seven. SNN-700. Read you loud and clear. Currently waiting above at 36-16-77 lat, 127-37-23 long. Over."

Seconds later a bald man in a flight suit turned back to Crocker and held up ten fingers followed by a thumbs-up.

Crocker said into his headset, "Five minutes to ready. Ten minutes to launch."

The SEALs to his right and across from him started to get their gear ready and pull on their gloves. Davis didn't budge. Crocker reached his foot across and kicked Davis's boot. The blond SEAL opened his eyes and nodded. Cool as a fucking cucumber, like he wrestled harder shit than this in his sleep.

Out the window at his back Crocker made out the dark outline of the sub tower. It looked as though the SDV and launch pad had already been secured to the deck. Deckhands wearing helmets and earphones were using high-lumen red-lens flashlights to signal to the pilot.

The helo circled into position and hovered at twenty feet, bouncing and shifting in the heavy wind. Then the green cabin light came on, and Crocker shouted, "Go! Let's go!"

Men jumped up, grabbed bags and packs. Boots scraped against the metal floor. The hatch opened and Akil fast-roped down first, followed by Davis and Suarez.

Sam, wearing a helmet that looked too small for him, was next. Crocker shouted into his ear, "You okay? You need help?"

The draft off the rotors dented Sam's face. Instead of answering, he grabbed the rope with both hands and jumped. But he never managed to secure his legs around it, so he descended too fast. And when he tried to engage his right leg it got tangled in the rope, causing him to jerk to a stop, wrench free, and tumble the remaining ten feet.

"Watch out, below! Man falling!" Crocker shouted.

In the helo landing light, he saw Sam somersault and Akil reach out to catch him—a seemingly impossible task, given Sam's mass and the speed of his descent. There were wind conditions to deal with, too. A gust yanked Sam right, so that his shoulder glanced off Akil's chest. Akil lost his balance and the two men fell backward into the soup.

Jesus!

"Man overboard!"

"Two men in the water!"

Crocker slid down fast, dropped his gear on the deck, bent his knees, and dove in in one continuous motion. He was airborne, looking for objects, when the water hit him like a bucket of ice. He almost passed out from the impact and extreme cold. When he came up and gasped for air, his mind scrambled and blanked.

His body slammed into automatic, kicking and flailing arms to stay above water. With his right he held on to the white floatation device someone had tossed in. He saw two guys on deck pulling

Akil out with the help of a pole. Suarez knelt and shouted as he pointed to something beyond Crocker.

"What?" he shouted back.

The helo rotor tore at the surface and whipped water into his face and eyes. The salt and cold stung. He fought not to go into shock.

"Boss! Boss!"

Something heavy bumped into his left leg, and he reached down through the frigid water and felt an arm that slipped out of his grasp.

"Boss!!!!"

The light from the helo blinding him, he took a big gulp of air and dove. His hands, arms, and legs turned completely numb. In a matter of seconds he knew muscle coordination would go. Seconds after that, his brain and body would shut down. He surfaced.

Balls to that! I'm not losing Sam!

His eyes and limbs becoming rigid, Crocker reached left and right until he felt something round like a human head and dove again until his hands found a neck and shoulder. The cold salt water welled up his nostrils and hit his brain like a hammer. Trying the best he could with numb hands to grab on to fabric, he pushed up until he reached the surface and was blinded again. Sam gasped, spitting water into his eyes.

"Some fucking thanks…"

He couldn't believe he actually had him. The muscles in his legs and shoulder were so badly cramped that his tears were mixing with the water.

"Boss! Hold on!"

Sam's lips and nose had turned deep blue. Crocker's legs

were starting to spasm. He figured he had a few more seconds left, and then strong hands pulled him toward a boat. He welcomed the smell of rubber. With his last ounce of strength, he pushed Sam up.

Crocker came to minutes later, upright in a chair and wrapped in a thick wool blanket. Someone was rubbing his feet and another person massaged his hands. Their faces and his surroundings were a blur of light and color.

"You hear me, Crocker?" someone asked.

He didn't recognize the voice. Shivered and clenched his teeth. His tongue felt like a piece of leather. "Ye…ah."

"Open your mouth and sip this slowly."

It took several seconds for the signal from his brain to reach his jaw and lips. Then his mouth and throat suddenly came alive and starting burning.

He heard someone say, "Pulse rising. Body temp at eighty-nine."

"I didn't know he had a pulse." He recognized Akil's voice. "DARPA told us they assembled him out of parts."

"That's not funny. He was down to eighty-two when you brought him up. In most circumstances that means you're dead."

"He's our leader, doc," Akil said. "He ain't going nowhere."

Waves of warmth spread from Crocker's throat and stomach out to his limbs and head. His consciousness sharpened. He made out a clock on the wall and the face of a nurse—square jaw, green eyes, black hair with bangs.

"You remember your name, sir?"

"Chief Warrant Crocker. What's yours?"

"Luci."

"Hi, Luci. How's Sam?"

"He's resting. Recovered fast. Terrible fast-roper from what I hear, but the hide of a walrus."

In the morning after he'd showered and dressed, Crocker met with the commander, a rail-thin African American with short hair and a black-and-silver mustache. They sat in the sub's tiny ops room, sipped tea, and pored over nautical charts and satellite photos as the ship's doctor checked Crocker's vitals. A very serious looking lieutenant waited at a laptop ready to take notes. A photo of the commander playing golf with the president hung on the wall.

"You play?" Commander Thompson asked.

"Not my game. Don't have the patience."

"Teaches self-control and the need for precision."

"Vital signs back to normal," the doctor announced, cleaning the stethoscope with the hem of his tunic. "Can't tell how it affected his brain without a scan."

"One-two-seven-thirteen-ten," Crocker joked. "I can still count to ten. I'll be fine."

"I believe we've crossed paths before," the doctor said, peering at Crocker through round glasses. "Tikrit, '04. We were both staying in a safe house that came under attack. You and two other SEALs fought off Iraq insurgents for five hours until a QRF rescued us."

It wasn't a happy memory. One of Crocker's best buds, Sean, had taken a bullet in the stomach that night and died from complications.

The doctor seemed to be remembering that, too, as he quickly loaded his instruments into his bag. "Good to see you again."

"Thanks. You, too."

Commander Thompson cleared his throat and said, "SOCOM had the mission slated for a 2100 launch, but given events last night and the new moon, they figure you're going to want to wait twenty-four hours."

"Wait another day? For what?" It jarred Crocker back to the mission. In the recesses of his mind lurked the emergency with his father. Sensing that the mission was going to be difficult, he wanted to get it started as soon as possible so he could return home. "No. No, screw that. That won't be necessary as long as the other members of my team are accounted for and in one piece."

"What's the determination on their fitness, doc?" asked the commander in his rich baritone, freezing the doctor in the doorway.

"Uh, sir…um, yes. They're all fine, except maybe Sam, who could use another day of rest."

"No time for that," Crocker pronounced, fixing his eyes on the red phone in the middle of the metal table and wondering if he could use it to reach his father. "That connect to the States?"

"We're in a red zone, so only official calls, and they have to be encrypted," the commander answered.

"Got it."

Crocker quickly pushed his concern for his father to a corner of his mind and shifted focus. "Can we back up a minute? Am I correct to infer from what you said that SOCOM has given me the last word on when we launch?"

"That's correct."

"Then I need to talk to the SDV pilot. Where can I find him?"

"Get Warrant Naylor in here," Commander Thompson ordered, turning to the lieutenant.

"Yes, sir."

"Call the members of my team, too," Crocker added. "I need to know if we lost any gear. I'm assuming we still have time to get things flown in from the *Vinson* if we need to."

"We should be able to accommodate that. Yes."

Warrant Naylor appeared to be navy-issue all the way—medium height, thinning light brown hair, watery blue eyes, straight back. As he sat across from him sipping from a mug of coffee, Crocker laid out the reasons it made sense to swap the copilot out for Akil or Davis, both of whom had completed advanced SDV training after BUD/S.

But Naylor wasn't buying any part of it. "Chief, I appreciate where you're coming from. But this mission will be pushing the envelope as is. Taking into account ocean currents, possible live ordnance in the water around the island, and other considerations, guiding *Sleeping Beauty* to the target will be a sphincter-tightening two-person job. Any additional pressures could push the mission past the breaking point."

"*Sleeping Beauty?*" Crocker asked. "That's the name of the vessel?"

"We named it that because it resembles the coffin from the movie."

"Never saw it."

"My copilot Hutchins has got a six-year-old daughter."

"Naylor, here's the long and short. This is gonna be a tough mission, and one where we'll be facing lot of unknowns when we reach our target. That's why I need you to work with me and squeeze in five operators."

"Nope. Not happening. I hear we might be taking a hostage out. So four operators max. That's the law."

"What law?" Crocker asked, trying to remain calm.

"I'm not trying to bust your balls, chief. Even with four, you're gonna feel like you're squeezed. The fifth means you'll have to severely minimize your gear."

"How about flying in a second SDV and crew?" suggested Crocker. "What would be the timetable on that?"

Naylor thought for a minute and answered, "The closest one is in Hawaii, and its electrical system is down."

"Never mind."

"We're looking at a four-hour ride through frigid seas in wet suits breathing through tanks, and a two- or three-hour ride back. Any weather could throw us off course and kill our chances of returning."

Crocker, who had taken long rides in SDVs before, didn't need to be reminded of the conditions. Without Davis, he'd be depending on three other operators, one of whom he'd never worked with before. "What's the weather look like?" he asked.

"Clean and calm tonight," answered Commander Thompson. "Tomorrow fifty percent chance of precipitation and accompanying winds blowing in from the north."

"Then we're launching tonight. Show my teammate Akil the amount of cargo space we're dealing with, and prepare to deploy at 2100."

"Chief," Naylor started, "I just want to say that my co-pilot and I have heard a lot about you, and we're both honored to be working together."

"Thanks, Naylor. Let's get it done."

CHAPTER SEVENTEEN

Sometimes you gotta let shit go and say "to hell with it"
and move on.

—Eminem

DAWKINS HADN'T been the same since the episode in the amphitheater. Something inside him had shut down, severely reducing his energy and affecting his ability to remember simple things—like the names of his assistants or how long he had been held in captivity. He sat for hours in the workshop staring at the partially assembled missile guidance system, vaguely aware of the engineering problems involved in fitting the gyro-stabilized platform, battery, power distribution unit, and missile guidance system together. His assistants Pak Ju and Yi-Thaek stood at his side, looking concerned.

"Battery work, yes?" Pak Ju asked, pointing to the wires running from the lithium pack to the laptop-sized computer that had been specially configured to slip into the platform. Sometimes the ingenuity of the NK engineers surprised him. On other occasions they seemed useless.

"What battery?" he asked, remembering the lullaby Sung had taught him about the peasant woman leaving her baby to search for food.

He found the lithium pack on the bench, and as he picked it up he imagined her looking at the infant's face, trying to communicate without words. Then he was holding baby Karen and recalling the sense of connection between them as strong as anything he'd ever felt.

"How do you measure that?" he asked out loud.

"Measure what, Mr. Dawkins?" Pak Ju asked.

"Is there a way to correlate that to newtons?"

Pak Ju and Yi-Thaek looked confused. The baby-faced interpreter leaned over Dawkins's shoulder and said, "They don't understand."

"Newtons," Dawkins answered, rubbing his forehead. "It's how we measure gravity. The acceleration on Earth is 9.8m/s_2. On the Earth's surface 0.98 newtons equal the force of gravity of 100 grams mass, right?"

"Yes..."

What he felt for Karen and Nan was even stronger. Did it transcend time and distance, too? Didn't it compel him to behave in certain ways?

"I mean...is there any way to measure that?" he asked out loud.

As the interpreter translated, Pak Ju and Yi-Thaek shook their heads. The both seemed to be saying the same thing: the American has lost it.

"According to Einstein, the measurement of space and time are altered by the motion of the observer," he said, looking from one assistant to the other. "What about the observer's emotional state? Mustn't that alter the perception of space and time as well?"

"Excuse me, Mr. Dawkins. I don't understand."

Dawkins wasn't sure he did, either. He was reaching for something. "I mean…attraction and repulsion. They are forces. But do we measure them in a scientific way? Do we understand how they imprint the universe and affect physical time and space?"

He seemed to be getting emotional as he stood with his hands on his hips, looking down at his feet.

Pak Ju stepped closer and, squinting through his glasses, asked, "Mr. Dawkins, you feel sick?"

A tear rolled down his cheek. He turned away and brushed it off with his sleeve. "Ju, you have children, don't you?"

Ju nodded. "Yes."

"You love them?"

"I love children, correct. But job…to complete guidance system. We fall behind schedule. This bad for us."

Dawkins furrowed his forehead and nose and nodded. "Sometimes you have to leave the people you love…It's not necessarily of your own volition. There's a need you have to fill. A responsibility. Like the mother in the lullaby. I'm sure you know it. When the mother left her baby, do you think the infant understood that she would return?"

Pak Ju looked at him like he'd lost his mind. Now Dawkins placed his hand on his shoulders and leaned into him. "Of course he did," Dawkins said emphatically. "Because the baby saw something in his mother's eyes."

"Mr. Dawkins…"

"That's the force I'm talking about. That's the one that I believe is more powerful than gravity. It pulls us together. It ensures the survival of our species. Through time and distance, past this life and into the next. We have no way to measure this force, even though it's the most powerful in the universe. The best word we have to describe it is…love."

Crocker and his team faced a series of complications, mostly having to do with the volume of gear that could fit into the tight cargo space of the Mk 8 Mod 1 SDV. Now crouched in the very tight Dry Doc Shelter (DDS)—the sledlike device mounted on top of the sub that held the SDV in place—he pushed the button that illuminated the face of his Suunto dive watch and saw that it read 2142.

Through the headset connected to the Motorola radio clipped to his vest, he said, "We're already forty minutes late. What's the problem now?"

"Trying to squeeze the second med bag in," Davis reported. "Not gonna fit."

Ideally, he wanted as much redundancy as possible. According to the saying on the teams, "Two is one and one is none"—which meant two or three of everything, extra batteries, plenty of mags, flashlights, radios. But space was so limited this time, and there were some things they absolutely had to carry. A second complete medical bag, though it could prove to be critical, wasn't at the top of his list of priorities.

"All right, give me the second bag and I'll go through it."

With the *Dallas* floating on the surface, they moved back and forth in the DDS attached to the sub's forward escape hatch. The DDS allowed the operators to prepare for the op in a dry environment, but it gave them very little room to maneuver. Still, it was a hell of a lot better than trying to load the SDV in the water, with tanks on their backs.

Crocker set the second med bag on the metal floor of the DDS and started tearing through it. As he did, the pilot and the copilot ran a final check.

"O^2 tanks?"

"Check."

"Backup rebreathers?"

"Check."

"Level on the lithium ion?"

"Fully charged at nine-point-nine-nine-five."

"Backup battery?"

"Charged to the max."

"Sonar?"

"Working."

Crocker removed everything except two SAM splints to stabilize broken bones, four rolls of tape, four chest seals with one-way valves so that air could escape but not enter the pleural lining, four packs of gauze, tourniquets, pressure dressings, IVs, and fluids. He tossed the rest of the gear down the forward hatch to one of the sub's sailors. Then he repacked the med bag so it was about half its previous size.

He passed it to Davis. "Try it now."

Davis stuffed the bag and his big body into the sled-shaped SDV and came out a minute later flashing a thumbs-up.

"That should do it, then."

Davis, on his hands and knees, got into Crocker's face. He said, "Boss, I don't care what these tight assholes say. You and I can drive this crate ourselves."

Crocker couldn't help but smile. He knew what Davis was

doing—lobbying to be included on the mission even though there wasn't any room. "Sorry, Davis," he said. "Not this time."

"Fuck all, boss, I just don't feel good about you going out there without me to watch your flank and run comms."

"I appreciate that, buddy. I need you to helo back to the *Carl Vinson* and stay with Min, and monitor us from the tactical ops center."

"Aye, aye, boss. Call me if you need me. I'll parachute in. Good luck."

The man in front of Dawkins with the red mole on his chin was using a direct ophthalmoscope to examine Dawkins's eyes and test the reflexes of his pupils. He didn't tell him that he was looking for signs of a stroke.

"Doctor, can I ask you something?" Dawkins asked.

Finding no evidence of a major neurological event, the doctor picked up a small syringe from the table behind him that was filled with a yellow dye called fluorescein. He swabbed the inside of Dawkins's forearm with rubbing alcohol and inserted it.

"Why are you doing this?"

The doctor didn't answer. Nor did the young aide who stood behind him watching. Dawkins felt the liquid enter his vein and waited for its effect. He didn't know whether it was an amphetamine, a truth serum, or some medicine to get him to sleep.

He told himself to stay as still as possible. That had been his default defense since he was a kid. Like the time his father had scolded him for taking apart the living room stereo, and he stood perfectly still on the carpet, looking down at his sneakers. He understood that movement in his current circumstance wasn't good.

It would bring completion, and completion could bring horror and death.

Now the doctor rolled an elaborate device in front of him and maneuvered Dawkins's head so his chin rested on a metal bar in front of a lens.

The aide said, "Keep you head still, Mr. Dawkins."

A light flashed in front of him, blinding his right eye. For a split second he saw Nan standing in front of him in a white slip. He heard the click of a camera and willed himself to register only immediate impressions—the scrape of the chair across the floor, the diffuse quality of the light, the smoothness of the metal bar under his chin, the creases in the doctor's face.

The configuration of the SDV made it impossible for Crocker to sit up comfortably. Instead, he had to lean forward and drop his head. He sat shoulder to shoulder with Sam, his knees pressed into the space between Suarez and Akil in front.

I fucking hate these things, he said to himself, wondering how he could endure three and a half more hours of this. The twenty-one-foot-long aluminum alloy submersible looked like a flattened torpedo with an open top. Beyond a thin aluminum partition the pilot and copilot sat before a panel of glowing dials that indicated Doppler navigation sonar, speed, heading, depth, and distance traveled. The pilot used a joystick to control vertical and horizontal angles by manipulating the forward bow planes and aft elevators. All the electronic instruments were sealed within watertight compartments. But the rest of the interior, crew, and passengers were exposed to the ocean water, which hovered at around fifty-six degrees. Crocker kept a close eye on that measurement, because given the operators' inability to move their limbs, long-term exposure to temps below fifty could produce symptoms of diver degradation and hypothermia.

It helped enormously that underneath his 5mm triple-stitched wet suit, he wore a specially designed "smart" suit made of a polymer membrane that adapted to changes in the air or water temperature. It had been developed at the Natick Soldier Systems Center specifically for SEAL use in a wide variety of environments.

While he breathed through the regulator connected to the SDV's compressed air supply in tanks behind him, the vehicle's electronic engine pulled them through the ocean at 18 knots (21 miles an hour) at a depth of 10.5 feet.

Crocker glanced at his watch, which read 2156, and spoke into the mike embedded in his silicon/plastic Oceanpro dive mask: "Tiger One, this is Deadwood. What are we looking at in terms of EST?"

"Deadwood, EST to the lovely vacation destination of Keno currently stands at 0109," Naylor responded in code. "That breaks down to approximately three kilos, thirteen mikes traveling time. Sit back and enjoy the ride. The stewardess will be by soon to take your drink order. Dinner service is available at any time by simply reaching out and grabbing any of the sea life that swims past. Over."

"Roger, Tiger One. We got shit we need to get done. Can't we kick this baby up any faster? Over."

"Deadwood, that's a negative. Remember, half the fun is getting there."

"Forget the fun part. You got this crate cranked up to max?"

"Pedal to the metal, Deadwood."

He busied himself by checking to make sure his depth gauge

was attached to his belt, along with dive gloves, MK3 underwater signal flares, strobe light, dive hood, and M4 combat knife. At his feet sat ScubaPro Jet dive fins, a laser target designator, TAC-200 diver swim board, and a waterproof pack that he could strap to his shin to carry his pistol, a specially modified AK-47 with suppressor and extra mags. A Draeger LAR V rebreather unit waited in the cargo space should it be needed, along with a larger waterproof backpack with med pack, grenades, mags, chemical canisters, batteries, MREs, a water bladder, comms, and Dragon Skin tactical vest made from overlapping silicon-carbon-ceramic disks and capable of stopping 7.62.x51 full metal rounds fired at an impact velocity of 2,810 feet per second.

Everything accounted for and in place. He checked his watch and saw that a mere fifteen minutes had passed.

Screw this!

Dawkins clutched his arms across his chest and shivered. The room he was sitting in felt and looked like the inside of a refrigerator, with light blue walls and strong fluorescent light. At first he didn't recognize the face across from him, a severe one with round cheekbones and sallow gray skin that matched the color of his jumbled front teeth.

When the man stepped back, Dawkins saw that he was wearing a green uniform with gold-and-red epaulets, and realized that this was the honored general he had met weeks before. Then, he'd appeared kindly. Now he kicked the chair in front of him so that it spun across the dark blue linoleum floor and hit the wall. He leaned into Dawkins's face and shouted.

Dawkins tried to cover his ears, but the general's angry aide and translator slapped his hands away.

"Most honored general say you liar and coward. He want to know why you delay?"

"I'm not delaying. Everything is going well. I have solved most problems, and a few minor ones remain. I will solve them."

"What problem?"

"It's complicated. Optical mechanics...the challenges of dealing with very limited space and weight. Tell the honored general that for every problem there is a solution...up here." He pointed to his head.

The aide translated, and the general muttered something and threw his hands up in disgust.

"When? How many weeks? Most honored general want date."

"It's hard to say. So much depends on things outside my—"

The aide screamed, "He want specific date written down on paper!"

Dawkins didn't want to show fear, but he couldn't help himself. He started to tremble.

"When? *When?* WHEN???"

The shouting felt like lashes. Dawkins raised his head to see the general standing over him, bent at the waist, hands on his hips, handing him a pen. A jagged vein on his temple pulsed. The sparse hair on his head bristled. Everything about him spoke anger, cruelty, and pain.

"Most honored general insist you write date!"

Dawkins looked at the pen and the yellow sheet of paper in front of him.

"He want you to write the date and sign."

"I...I can't."

"You can't?" the interpreter asked. "Now the general want to know if you crazy?"

"No...no."

"If you crazy, you no good. He get rid of you."

For a second he imagined the general holding a flamethrower and flashed to the flesh burning off the woman in the amphitheater. The smell filled his nostrils, and he started to feel sick.

"You crazy. He think you either crazy or liar!"

Dawkins opened his mouth but was so upset he had trouble speaking. "No, no...not crazy. Tell him—Please tell him I'm doing my best."

CHAPTER EIGHTEEN

*Endurance is one of the most difficult disciplines, but it
is to the one who endures that the final victory comes.*
—Buddha

THE SEALS had entered Yonghung Bay in the Sea of Japan and
had drawn within two miles of Ung-do. While Crocker remained
alert to every hiss, groan, and creak of the SDV, Suarez and Akil
were amusing themselves by trading "yo mama" jokes over team
comms.

Akil: "Yo mama so fat she's got two watches, one for each time
zone she's in."

Suarez: "Yo mama so ugly they filmed *Gorillas in the Mist* in her
shower."

"Yo mama so ugly that when One Direction saw her they went
the other way."

"She's so mean her name in a text is autocorrected to 'bitch.' "

Crocker tuned them out. He was attempting to visualize
the mission in his head, but with so little information to work
with, he was having a bitch of a time filling in the details.
Obviously it was imperative that they quickly set the charges,

recover the hostage, return to the SDV, and beat a rapid path back to the sub.

What he couldn't imagine were the steps in between—the number of DPRK soldiers they'd encounter, how well they'd be armed and trained, how quickly the army and air force would respond, the complexity of the security system around the installation, how quickly and freely he and his men would be able to move from one side of the island to the other, how far into the mission they could venture before they were detected. Nor did he have any information on where the hostage was being held.

What he did know was that he and his men were going in zero footprint. That meant no dog tags or personal information that could identify them as American soldiers. It also meant that they could expect no backup, or QRF to rescue them should something go wrong. They were four operators completely on their own. Any life-threatening injury to any of the men could jeopardize the entire mission. Whatever happened, he wouldn't leave anyone behind.

Akil had regressed from trading jokes with Suarez to taking the piss out of Sam.

Akil: "What team are you on again?"

Sam: "Five."

Akil: "I hear you guys kicked ass in Iraq. Have you gotten into the shit since then?"

Sam: "All the time, dude."

Akil: "I mean outside of jerking each other off in the shower."

Crocker growled, "Akil, stop fucking around and pay attention."

"Ten-four, boss. My dick is shriveled up and my entire body is numb. What else do you want to know?"

"You and Suarez triple-check the opsec, detonators, det cord, CL-20?"

"We checked them twenty times. All's good except for my dick. If it's not working, I'll be really ticked off."

"You won't need it where we're going."

"You never know, boss. Maybe I run into some ninja North Korean fox."

"And maybe she kicks your ass."

Naylor broke in. "Deadwood, Tiger One. Currently three-twenty-two meters west northwest of Keno. We're going to start moving south and keeping an eye on sonar. Possible underwater ordnance in the area. Over."

"Underwater ordnance" meant mines. "Copy, Tiger. Over and out."

He couldn't wait to get out of the sardine can and start moving. Even though the SDV made very little noise, the bubbles produced from the tanks left a trail on the surface. Nothing they could do about that except hope no one was watching.

Dawkins had spent hours bent at the knees in a pigeonlike position with his wrists pulled above his head and tied to the wall behind him. He was alone in the cold room except for a sinister-looking guard at the door. His knees, back, and arms were in agony. Still, every time he tried to close his eyes and rest, the guard crossed over to him and punched him hard in the stomach.

Hurting, exhausted, and trying not to give in to negative thoughts, he attempted to recall every detail of his life with Nan, starting with their meeting near the front desk of the University of California at Berkeley library, where he had been studying for a physics test and she was waiting to meet a friend. She was wearing a black skirt and a yellow blouse. Minus her glasses and with her dark hair pulled back, she reminded him of the title character Rodelinda in Handel's opera.

He ignored the pain of his arms being pulled from their sockets and played the melody in his head. That weekend, Nan and her friend Deirdre had accompanied a group of his friends on a trip down Route 1 to Big Sur. They rode in a powder-blue Impala with Ohio plates and spent the afternoon at a cove and beach off an unmarked road. She wore a black-and-white polka-dot two-piece bathing suit. He wore cutoffs. Her eyes turned amber in the sunlight. They sat on a blanket on the sand talking for hours about school and life while the others climbed a path that took them to another cove.

He was a bookish, awkward, shy grad student who at night fell asleep to arias. Nan was gentle and intelligent. She seemed interested in him in ways no one else had been before. He opened up to her about his passion for music, physics, and mathematics, and how he thought they represented a key to understanding existence. Dawkins had become so completely absorbed in their conversation that he forgot to put on sunblock. That evening, running a fever and feeling uncomfortable, he sat on the sofa in the rented cabin in Pfeiffer State Park while the others went out for dinner and drinks. Nan stayed and looked after him.

She seemed to have chosen him. Why, he wasn't sure. But he accepted her kindness with gratitude, and her interest in him gave him confidence. They'd been together ever since.

Crocker held on to the back of the seat in front of him as the SDV ground to a stop. Pilot Naylor cut the engine so that all he could hear was the sound of the regulator, his own breath, and the sloshing of the water.

Anticipation grew. "Tiger One, Deadwood here. How far are we from the shoreline? Over."

"Deadwood, you're looking at a little more than eight meters, or twenty-four feet. We're resting at a depth of three-point-two meters, roughly ten feet. Over."

"Okay, guys," Crocker said. "Put on our Draegers and prepare to deploy. Akil and I will recce first."

"Roger."

"Quiet, fast, and small."

"Copy."

Akil led the way, swimming underwater with Crocker directly behind him. Nearing shore, they came up slowly, holding their heads just above the water. Through his mask Crocker saw the dark island looming before him like a sleeping elephant. A handful of stars peeked through the overcast sky. Aside from the low whistle of an occasional gust of wind, the area was completely quiet. No lights appeared in the distance, only the faint glow of the fishing port of Munchon through the mist to his left. The stories he'd heard about the millions of starving North Korean peasants and the gulags filled with political prisoners stirred in his head.

He said into his mike, "Romeo, I'll stand watch. You go and help the guys bring out the gear."

"Copy."

Akil turned and dove in one smooth motion as Crocker moved forward until he was standing in three feet of water.

North fucking Korea…

Crouching, he removed the AK from the waterproof bag slung

over his shoulder, inserted a mag, chambered a round, and scanned left and right. He was looking along the shore for signs of a guard post, an electric fence, video cameras, or patrol boats. But he saw nothing except little waves slapping the rocky shoreline and the dark silhouettes of clouds.

"Gents, you read me? All clear above. Over."

"Copy, Deadwood, over."

Sam came out first, carrying Crocker's seventy-pound pack and his combat vest and belt in a separate watertight bag. Crocker pointed to the sand beside him. Sam dropped them. His eye never left his AK's SR-25 scope. He held up his hand and waved Sam back.

The young man hardly made a sound as Crocker took cover behind a clump of shrubs, peeled off the dive suit to the smart suit underneath, and went into the pack for his NVGs. From the watertight he removed his Merrell boots and combat vest. Quickly he taped inside the various pockets extra mags, smoke and frag grenades, Israeli bandages, a backup radio, flares, flashlights, and tape. On his combat belt hung a holster containing his SIG Sauer P226, M4 knife, a coil of nylon rope, more flares, and a pair of gloves.

The temp seemed mild—low fifties. The air carried the pungent smell of sage and rotting shellfish. The wind rattled through the shrubs and kicked up wisps of sand.

The operators assembled around him and quickly readied themselves. According to his Suunto it was 0148. His goal was to return to the SDV by 0230, which he communicated now to Naylor, who had come up to guard their Draegers.

"The CO and I will take twenty-minute shifts," Naylor explained. "If we see or hear anything, we'll alert you."

"Good." Crocker put a hand on Akil's shoulder. "Okay, Romeo, show us the way." As primary navigator/point man, Akil had studied the maps, drawings, and charts provided by Choi and Min with greater urgency and focus than anyone on the team. In terms of the facility itself, the drawings that Min had said were approximately a year old were all they had to go on.

Akil looked back at Crocker and said, "Remember that in the intel briefing we were warned about the presence of poisonous snakes. So keep an eye out for snakes."

"Fuck the snakes. Look for sensors, wires, cameras, booby traps."

"Roger."

The pain was so intense that Dawkins wanted to die. He'd already been sick and soiled his pants. His body disgusted him. Now he heard the door to the refrigerator-like room open and the honored general's voice like a dog growling. It pulled Dawkins out of the movie of his wedding that had been unreeling in his head.

Someone was untying the ropes around his wrists. His head became woozy from the shooting pain up his back and the burning sensation of blood returning to his arms. He tried but couldn't straighten his legs, so the guard led him in a monkey crouch to a metal chair. There was someone sitting across from him, but he couldn't focus his eyes. Then the guard slipped his glasses onto his head and he saw the general holding an olive-green file folder.

The general slapped it on the table, pointed, and growled something.

"He wants you to look!" his aide said.

It hurt to move his fingers but he slowly opened the folder and started to shuffle through the two dozen pictures of Karen and Nan getting out of Nan's Toyota RAV4, shopping at the local supermarket, getting into the car again, and driving to an apartment near Tysons Corner, Virginia. The pictures seemed to be recent. Karen appeared taller. Nan looked thinner and older. He wondered why they were living in an apartment and not in their home.

The general pounded the metal table with his fist and spit at his head, causing Dawkins to look up. Hunger and fear gnawed at the lining of his stomach.

The general held up two fat fingers and thrust them under Dawkins's nose.

"Two days," the aide shouted. "You have two days to finish project."

Dawkins was panicking before he even knew what that meant. "Two days? I don't understand...Two days to do what?"

"Two days to complete project!" the aide growled.

It all rushed back on him—the reason he was here, the gyro compass and guidance system, the engineering tasks and adjustments that were still required.

His mouth and hands trembling, he said, "It will probably take longer than that, but I'll—"

"Two days! We know where your wife and daughter are. After two days they will both be dead!"

Snakes were the least of Crocker's worries as they humped over sandy land and skirted to the right around a clump of trees—Suarez, Akil, Sam, and Crocker in staggered formation, fingers on trigger guards, barrels pointed to the ground, scanning up, down, left, right. An owl hooted, the wind hissed. Otherwise the island remained eerily quiet.

Through the NVGs everything appeared in shades of green. Crocker didn't see any evidence of civilization until they reached a narrow bend of asphalt road, which was cool to the touch. They crossed quickly and entered a thicket of tall trees rustling and clattering in the wind. Pines and oaks. The wildness of the island heightened his sense of anticipation.

They were about a hundred meters into the grove when Akil stopped, crouched, and pointed ahead and to his right. It took Crocker several seconds to make out the ventilation stack rising about twenty feet from a short concrete structure.

"That the stack on the map?" he whispered.

Akil nodded vigorously.

"Getting close."

The stack wasn't nearly as big or elaborate as the one in the diagram provided in the packet Choi had smuggled out. It looked barely wide enough to accommodate a man Crocker's size and was topped by a little aluminum hat. Nor was the entrance to the complex as visible from where they were now as it had seemed on the hand-drawn map.

Akil pointed forward and slightly left as Suarez scanned the trees in front of them. As stupid as Akil acted sometimes, he was dead serious and accurate when it came to directions and maps.

Crocker pushed his right hand forward, which was the signal to proceed in single file. They hadn't moved more than fifty meters when Akil held up his right fist and they all stopped immediately and went into a crouch.

"Deadwood," he whispered. "Visual on vehicles to the left."

"See them. Copy."

"Pax?"

"No pax sighted."

Crocker peered through the trees and saw a circular dirt area that contained what looked to be a tractor, mounds of sand and gravel, a stack of steel construction rods, and two cement mixers. His gut told him something was wrong.

What are they building?

"Proceed slowly and stick with your swim buddy."

That meant that Crocker and Sam rose and hurried in a crouch thirty feet past Suarez and Akil with their weapons ready. Then Crocker and Sam knelt behind trees and provided cover as Suarez and Akil leapfrogged their position. They went through two rotations before Akil stopped, dropped to his knees, and whispered via comms, "Two pax a hundred feet eleven o'clock!"

Crocker slithered forward on his belly and from the ground beside Akil saw two guards standing by the entrance, which looked like a concrete ramp with trees and shrubs around it. No flags, signs, or emblems. Bland, hidden, and utilitarian. Akil pointed to a camouflage-colored armored personnel carrier (APC) parked farther left. Aside from the construction equipment and ventilation stack, it was the only sign that the underground complex was a significant target.

Among Crocker's weapons were eight canisters of a nonlethal anesthetic gas called fentanyl. According to the DARPA expert who had briefed him via video, the canisters when charged would release an opiate-based narcotic one hundred times more powerful than morphine and with a sharp astringent smell. It would quickly knock out anyone who breathed it—but could also cause them to stop breathing altogether.

Crocker had no way of calculating how many people would

be inside the complex at night, nor did he want to risk the life of the hostage. He instructed Sam to stay with Akil while he and Suarez circled around to surveil the back.

Akil whispered through comms, "It's different from the drawing. I think the complex has been expanded, or is in the process of being expanded now."

"Copy. Agree."

When he and Suarez arrived at the rear entrance, they found a wider ramp with a forklift parked nearby, two large green dumpsters, and more construction equipment parked under a camouflage-pattern canopy. No guards in sight.

Crocker took photos with his digital camera, then signaled for Suarez to wait and cover him while he hurried forward and knelt behind a concrete abutment beside the ramp. Peering through his NVGs, he saw that the ramp led to a metal gate, the kind that pulled down from above.

He scanned left and right, then ran forward to check if it was locked. Affirmative. Turning back, he heard something inside the entrance beep three times and stop. His blood froze for a second, and he backed up and tumbled left to the other side of the abutment, leveled his weapon on the concrete edge, and counted. No one emerged by the time he'd counted to ten.

Tell me I didn't trip a fucking alarm.

He signaled to Suarez and they circled back to the front, where Akil and Sam lay waiting behind some trees.

"You hear or see anything?" Crocker asked. "Movement, alarms, flashing lights?"

"Negative."

"Anyone in back?"

"Negative to that, too."

In a matter of seconds Crocker formulated a plan. He and Akil would take out the two guards. Then, while Sam watched the front entrance, he, Akil, and Suarez would enter the complex. Akil would lead them to the printing presses on the second level. While Suarez set the charges, he and Akil would search the complex for the hostage and the lab. Once outside and away from the complex, they would fire the detonators.

"Piece of cake," Sam whispered.

"Stay focused. Silent and quick."

He tapped Akil on the shoulder. They moved on their bellies to within fifty feet of the front entrance, then got up and circled around the rear of the APC. Parked alongside it was a black Russian-built ZiL limousine that resembled a Mercedes. They were now at a thirty-degree angle to and forty feet from the entrance. Crocker used hand signals to indicate that he would take the guard on the right. Akil was responsible for the other one.

Both of their AKs were equipped with suppressors. As Crocker leveled his weapon until the crosshairs found the guard's chest, something moved across his field of vision. He lowered his weapon and indicated to Akil to lower his, too. A stocky Korean officer walked alongside a thinner, older man wearing a black parka and gloves. Behind them followed three younger men in dark suits who appeared to be aides or bodyguards. The two older men stopped within twenty feet of the APC and were talking animatedly in Korean. Meanwhile, two of the younger aides climbed into the ZiL. One of them started the engine.

As Crocker watched, the officer saluted the older man in the parka, who then got into the backseat of the vehicle. The officer and the remaining aide walked back into the complex as the ZiL drove off.

Akil whispered, "What the fuck was that?"

"Looked like an officer and a senior official."

"What were they saying?"

"No idea. Stay focused."

As SEALS, they'd been trained to execute their missions without emotion. "Keep a cool head and warm feet and heart," went the Shinto saying that Crocker repeated in his head.

He waited for the officers to enter, took a deep breath, and whispered, "Engage in three."

Three Mississippis later, two quick bursts from their AKs caused the guards to jerk backward and crumple. Akil's guard opened his mouth to shout something, but before the sound could come out, they both fired at his head so the noise he made sounded like a cough. They were onto the bodies in a flash, making sure the guards were dead, then dragging them inside with them and leaving them in a dark space behind the entrance.

The dimly lit vestibule was clear. Crocker gave the signal and Suarez ran to join them, carrying the pack filled with bricks of CL-20. He and Crocker followed Akil down a flight of metal stairs and into another foyer-type area with a hallway that led right and another, wider one to the left.

"That wasn't in the diagram," Akil whispered, indicating left.

"Noted."

"One flight down."

They turned right, proceeded another twenty feet, then followed Akil down a stairway, making sure to rest their weight on the balls of their feet to make the least noise. The facility seemed empty and hollow.

The walls were made of concrete that had been covered with a coat of sealant or shellac to give it a dull yellow tint. The floors were covered with dark-blue linoleum, cracked in places. Fluorescent bulbs buzzed and flickered from the middle of the ceiling, which stood tall at roughly ten feet, made of concrete and painted gray. It felt more like a prison than a workplace. Cold, drab, and sterile. The hallway walls were bare except for the occasional warning sign in Korean, which Crocker couldn't read. Akil reached the second level and pivoted right. The second door on the second-level hallway was wider than the first. He stopped and tried the knob. Locked.

Suarez stepped forward and popped it open with the thin iron bar he kept in his pack. Inside, Crocker did a quick inspection. Two large intaglio presses. Long, tall beige-colored machines with six rows of trays and stainless-steel rollers. Check. Stacks of clothlike paper wrapped in bunches. Check. Bottles of ink. Check.

"This is Target One. Start laying charges. Akil and I are going to look for Target Two and the hostage."

"Copy," said Suarez. "Take this."

He handed him the metal bar, which Crocker tucked under his right arm.

Akil went out before him and was already inspecting the other two doors along the opposite side of the hallway. Crocker jimmied open the first on the near side. Storage, mostly—stacked with boxes. Ripped some open and found ink and paper. The second room contained a toilet, sink, mops, and cleaning supplies.

"What'd you find?" he asked Akil.

"Paper and random shit. Nothing that looked important."

Crocker pointed up.

They climbed to the next level and started checking the rooms there, one on one side, one on the other, knowing that every minute that ticked by put them in more peril. This inspection was aided by the fact that some of the doors contained windows. Through them they saw offices with desks, chairs, flags, maps, and framed photos of the Supreme Leader.

The hallway narrowed, with more rooms farther along.

Crocker whispered, "You continue. I'm going to check the other side."

"Roger."

He hurried across the central atrium with its two large elevators and down the wider corridor. Up ahead he heard the shuffling of feet; backed up and squeezed himself against the wall at the corner. Someone was coming up the stairway to his right. He heard the person stop and strike a match. Then the individual continued, humming to himself—sounded like a lament. The song echoed up the stairway, then stopped. The man seemed to be calling someone on a radio. He called again. No one answered. He continued, closer and closer, until he emerged and was standing so close that Crocker could smell him—kimchi (sweet-and-sour cabbage) and cigarette smoke mixed. Smelled like a fart.

The North Korean grunted something, then stepped past Crocker. He was a short, wide man in cheap civilian clothes and worn black shoes. Crocker considered detaining him for a second and asking about the location of the U.S. engineer, but the language barrier made that problematic. So he came up behind him, slapped his right hand over the man's mouth, the left under his jaw. Pulled his head up and twisted violently until his spine snapped and the man's body trembled and went limp.

Sorry, bud.

He dragged him by the back of his collar into the stairwell and left him there, then proceeded down the hall. The doors here were metal, with no windows. He used the metal bar to pop the lock on the first. Saw a large lab/machine shop, mechanical parts lying on tables. He saw what looked like a gyroscope on one of them.

Gotta blow all this.

In the next lab, diagrams on the wall showed stages of a rocket.

Where's the engineer?

As he approached a third door, with a nuclear symbol on it, he heard Akil's voice through the earpiece.

"Deadwood, what'd you find?"

"Target Two. Tell Suarez to get his ass up here and lay more CL-20."

"Copy, boss."

"One dead enemy in the stairway, so don't be surprised."

"The officer?" Akil asked.

"Negative. An aide or guard."

"I've seen no one."

"Help Suarez with the first floor. The first three or four rooms on the left. Labs of some sort. I'll inspect two."

"Copy. Over."

As Crocker entered the stairway and started down to level two, Naylor's voice came over the radio.

"Deadwood, Tiger One. You read me?"

"Copy, Tiger. What's up?"

"Currently got eyes on a Korean People's Navy patrol boat moving past us in the general direction west. Approximate speed fifteen knots. Approximate distance two hundred meters."

"Copy, Tiger. I assume the SDV is still fully submerged."

"Fully submerged, check."

"Keep me appraised of any changes in the PT's course, especially if it turns north to circumvent the island."

"Will do, Deadwood. What's your ETA?"

"Fifteen. Start the engines at thirteen."

"Thirteen. Copy."

"Over and out."

The last thing Crocker wanted to do was engage the KPN, which had a large base in nearby Munchon and could block their exfil.

Reaching the lower level and sweating under the smart suit, he jimmied open the first door, which opened to reveal a small kitchen with hotplates, cupboards, a sink, and an old refrigerator. The second room was crowded with two sets of bunk beds and a small TV. It led to a tiny bathroom with a shower. Both were unoccupied.

As he started to jimmy open the third, Akil's voice pulsed in his ear.

"Boss, charges set on first deck, west left. Possible presence of nuclear material."

"I saw the signs, too."

"Location?"

"Down one deck."

"Time on target eight minutes and counting. Probably don't want to detonate until we're off the island."

"I'll be there A-SAP. Wait in the atrium. Watch the front and back doors. Sam, you copy?"

"Copy, boss."

"All clear out front?"

"All clear."

"Stand by. We'll be there soon."

As he jimmied open the door on his left, an alarm went off—a high whining sound that hurt his ears.

Fuck!

"Boss! Boss! You hear that? You read me?"

"I hear it. Clear the complex and wait outside."

"Boss!"

"Go. I've got this. Over."

The room he entered was dark and cold. Through his NVGs, he saw a metal table and chairs. A dark liquid on the floor. Smelled like someone had gotten sick. A pair of men's shoes. In the corner, a mattress and someone in the fetal position with his back to him.

He took a step closer and poked the individual with the barrel of his gun.

The man had thinning brown hair. Leaning closer, Crocker whispered, "Dawkins? James Dawkins?"

The man turned and looked up. He was gaunt and middle-aged, with Western features. Crocker thought he matched the photo he'd been shown at NAB Coronado.

"Can you stand?"

"Who are you?" the man asked weakly.

"Chief Warrant Tom Crocker, U.S. Navy," he whispered back to the frightened-looking man with a missing front tooth.

"Who?"

"I've come to rescue you. Take my hand."

As he reached down, he heard the click of metal behind him, followed by a blast that lit up the room and hit him between the shoulder blades like a sledgehammer. He flew past Dawkins and smacked the side of his head against the wall.

His head spinning and sharp pains shooting up and down his

spine, he reached for his modified AK and pushed off from the wall. As he turned, the thin mattress slipped out from under him and a second shotgun blast flew past his head, almost taking off his ear. Pellets glanced off his NVGs and a few tore into the side of his neck.

Men near the doorway were shouting in Korean. Through the haze of burnt gunpowder, Crocker saw that Dawkins had squeezed himself into the corner. Six feet away a thin man in glasses and civilian clothes stood in the doorway struggling to reload a shotgun. He slipped the shells in and snapped it shut, but his finger remained above the trigger guard. This gave Crocker the split second he needed to rake him sternum to head with AK fire.

They were so close the bullets almost ripped the Korean in half. Smoke rose from the dead's man's chest. Crocker saw a larger uniformed individual in the hallway using the doorframe as cover and aiming a Russian-made Grad AR with one arm. He lunged to cover Dawkins as bullets careened off the concrete floor and tore into the walls and mattress. At least one round was stopped by the ceramic disks in the Dragon Skin armor on his chest, which had just saved him from the shotgun blast to his back.

With no time to call for help, he squinted past his shoulder through the swirling smoke and unloaded on the officer's wrist until the Grad flew into the air and the officer screamed.

Cordite burning his nostrils, he met Dawkins's terrified eyes and asked, "You okay?"

"I think so."

"Wait here!"

Ignoring his body's sharp warnings, he bounded and slipped

on the blood-smeared floor, pulled himself up at the doorway, and tore down the hallway.

Akil screamed in his ear, "Boss! Boss, we heard gunfire! You read me?"

He had no time to answer. The officer limped thirty feet ahead, the remains of his right hand dangling from his wrist. He was holding a walkie-talkie in his left and frantically speaking into it.

Seeing Crocker, he dove into the stairway. As Crocker took aim, something metal rolled toward him from behind and a volley of bullets ricocheted off the walls and floor. He turned and went prone onto the cold tile only to confront an olive-green RGD-5 grenade, the pin pulled. All he could do was kick it back with his left foot as he squeezed off a buzz of AK fire.

He covered his head and face with his arms as the explosion rocked the hallways and deafened him. Shards of the RGD-5 fragmentation cups ripped his vest and tore into his shoulders and arms.

Someone ahead was screaming like a dog on fire. He needed to finish the fucker off and get Dawkins, but wanted the officer in the stairway first. So he turned and followed the trail of blood to the steps he'd descended earlier. Heard a man grunting and cursing above. Then a round of bullets careened off the concrete walls. He pushed himself upward until he saw the uniformed legs past the metal posts to his right, and squeezed the trigger of his AK. More glancing bullets and sparks, then the officer collapsed onto his knees, and grimacing, twisted onto his back. Crocker stood over him as he reached for a Czech CZ 82 pistol at his left side.

He kicked it away.

"General Chou Jang Hee? You the Dragon?"

The general hissed through a mouthful of blood, "Fuck United...States."

"Not this time, asshole."

Crocker put two rounds between his eyes.

Blood dripping from his neck and shoulders down the inside of his smart suit, he went back down and retrieved Dawkins. The injured man at the end of hallway was still shouting, and the alarm was reverberating loudly. Halfway up the stairway, his heart pounding, Crocker remembered something and stopped.

Turning to Dawkins, he asked, "Any other hostages here?"

Dawkins looked confused.

"Scientists? Engineers? Americans?"

"No, no. There was an Indian gentleman, but he left. No one else that I know of."

They hurried up the remaining stairs past the first guard's body, into the atrium, and outside. Both of them were very happy to be out of there. A strong breeze greeted them, like some weather was blowing in.

"Boss, behind the APC to your right," he heard through comms.

Adrenaline blotting out the pain, he joined the others—Sam, Akil, and Suarez—all coiled and ready to spring.

"Good. Charges set, left side and right?" Crocker asked, trying to catch his breath.

"All set," Suarez answered. "You okay?" he asked, pointing to Crocker's bloody neck.

"Nicked a little. Fuck that."

"This the hostage?" asked Akil.

"Name's Dawkins."

"Hey, Dawkins."

"Let's get back to the boat!"

They cut through the woods in the same formation as before, with Dawkins in the middle, half in a crouch, stumbling and falling.

Crocker said into his mike as he helped him up, "Tiger One. Coming your way. Three minutes! Fire it the fuck up!"

Akil shouted, "Boss! Vehicle right!"

"Everybody down. Down!"

Through the trees he saw headlights coming around a bend two hundred meters away. He made lightning-quick calculations. The vehicle was likely on its way to the complex, probably responding to the alarm. If they let it pass, the soldiers inside it would find the bodies. It would take them a few minutes at least to discover the explosives.

They could either engage them now or let them pass.

"Stay down," he instructed. "Let the vehicle pass. Soon as it does, we cross the road and continue as quickly as possible. Suarez, the moment it goes by, I want you to start counting. When you reach three minutes, fire the detonators and let it blow."

"Copy."

CHAPTER NINETEEN

Our doubts are traitors and make us lose the good we oft
might win by fearing to attempt.
— William Shakespeare

WHEN SUAREZ raised his right hand and held up three fingers, they stopped and went down in the grass. Dawkins wheezed beside Crocker, trying to catch his breath. Even though he wore no coat or sweater and the temperature hovered around fifty, sweat poured off his forehead. "Why... why... we stopping?"

Crocker cupped a hand over Dawkins's mouth and pointed at Suarez, who flipped off the safety on the handheld radio detonator and got ready to push the button. Crocker shoved Dawkins to the ground and covered him with his body.

"Cover your ears!"

In his head he started to recite the Lord's Prayer. When he got to the word "art," white light flashed around them, and a second later a huge explosion tore through the air, shaking the ground and rupturing Dawkins's eardrum. They waited as secondary explosions went off and a sharp blast of warm air blew past. Then debris started to rain down nearby.

"Fucking epic!" Akil muttered into the comms.

"Couldn't have said it better."

Sam muttered, "If you build it, they will come."

Crocker was amused by that. It was a line from one of his favorite movies, *Field of Dreams*.

"And fucking destroy it!"

"Let's get off the X before we all turn green." He was referring to the possible nuclear material in the area. As he ran, holding Dawkins by the arm, he thought they had completed the hard part. Now all they had to do was get home.

Naylor crouched behind a tree near the shore and checked his watch. Hearing a rustling sound, he looked up and saw Crocker with the collar of his smart suit covered with blood.

"What happened?" Naylor asked.

"Get in the water."

"But…"

"Turn around. Let's go!"

Naylor and his copilot, Hutchins, had already loaded the rebreathers, so they swam out to the sub. They ended up tossing the Draegers to make room, and also quickly sank their extra equipment, backup comms, med bag, spare AKs and mags.

Vice Admiral Greene, commander of the *Carl Vinson*, had promised to send an air rescue team in an emergency, but this location wouldn't work. They had to make it to one of the outlying islands at least.

Crocker helped Dawkins into a spare wet suit, and then they squeezed in even tighter than before and took off.

Unprompted, Akil started to sing "The House of the Rising Sun." Maybe he was thinking of the female turpitude waiting for him back in Virginia, or friendly Japan, which was close. Whichever it was, Sam and Suarez joined in in a kind of celebration.

Crocker refused to let his mind wander. The mission wasn't over. He concentrated on breathing the oxygen mix and passing the mouthpiece to Dawkins, squeezed onto his lap. The edge of his pelvis tore into Crocker's thigh.

An hour or so and we'll be in position to be recovered by helos from Carl Vinson, *if we don't stop at one of the outlying islands first.*

"Tiger One, what's the opsec?" he asked through comms, "opsec" meaning operational security.

"Territorial waters extend another twelve nautical miles. That's thirteen-point-eight on land. We can't call for air rescue until we're outside the continuous zone, which extends another twelve nautical miles past that. So sit back and enjoy the ride."

As cold and uncomfortable as he was, he'd been through worse. The bleeding from the pellet wounds to his neck had stopped. The Dragon Skin body armor that now felt like a straitjacket had saved his life.

He felt the adrenaline start to drain from his system and tried to get comfortable, which was hard with Dawkins leaning into his chest. He imagined holding Cyndi, with the sun setting in front of them, and then making love. Her skin felt like magic.

Suddenly the SDV hit something. *BAM!!!*

His head jerked violently forward and back, and he braced himself for an explosion.

"Hold…!" Naylor half screamed.

A loud grinding noise blotted out all other sounds. Crocker saw the right front of the vehicle crumple like wet cardboard, crushing the copilot's legs and sending the SDV tumbling left.

Wedged between Dawkins and the metal seat behind him, he couldn't move.

"Boss! Boss!"

"Fuck!"

The pressure grew more intense and cut off his breath. What remained of the SDV spun right, causing him to hit his head against the side abutment and black out. He dreamt he was swimming with Cyndi, and she was holding on to his collar. He opened his mouth to complain that her nails were digging into the side of his neck. Then he realized that ice-cold salt water was burning his wounds and he was sinking. He started kicking, when something smacked against his right side, and a hand tried to grasp his arm but slipped off.

His lungs burned like hell, so he used a trick he'd learned in BUD/S—breathing out a little and releasing some of the carbon dioxide that had built up in his lungs. It worked, but he was struggling, disoriented, and couldn't see shit. Something slid across this chest. First he thought maybe it was a sea lion or a large fish, then realized it was a person, struggling to get to the surface. He linked his right arm under the other person's armpit and kicked upward with all his might. The night air above hit his lungs cold and hard. His eyes and skin stung from the salt.

He pulled the two of them up and remembered where they were—the North Korean bay of Hamgyong. Not his favorite location. He searched for his men, signs of the enemy, and wreckage of the SDV. His NVGs were missing, so all he saw was dark sky and ocean, and the reflection of the island complex burning to his right.

Nothing to his left. Nothing in front of him or to his immediate right. No flotsam he could make out. No one calling out.

Only us two?

He hadn't even bothered to check the identity of the man he was holding. In the light from the fire saw Dawkins's gaunt, expressionless face.

"You with me, Dawkins?" Crocker asked. "You okay?"

He moaned something unintelligible and seemed even more disoriented than Crocker was.

"Lay back alongside me and we'll kick together."

Dawkins's body provided some warmth. The current was taking them past the east end of Ung-do. If it continued like that, it would pull them out to sea.

Hearing a hissing sound, he thought for a second that maybe it was someone calling for help. He stopped kicking and listened. All he heard was the wind slapping at the whitecaps in the bay, and maybe playing tricks with his head.

The best he could do was keep them afloat and hope to steer to land. When they got within three hundred meters of the east end of the island, the current started to pull them north. Now Crocker worried that it would take them back into the bay and into the hands of the North Korean People's Army. Given a choice between drowning in the Sea of Japan or being tortured, he wasn't sure which was worse.

It wasn't really up to him, because the current was too strong to fight. The best he could manage was to use his arms and legs to try to steer north and away from the island. Dawkins remained in a state of semiconsciousness. When they passed the eastern end, he saw signs of the NKPA response. Maybe a dozen military patrol boats sat in the penumbra of the burning facility along the northern shore. What they were doing besides observing the fire was impossible to tell from a distance.

He heard engines and the faint echo of men shouting, and hoped they wouldn't be spotted. Not likely, as they were at least two hundred meters away, and the northern current was growing more robust.

Seeing the boats in the distance, Dawkins shouted, "Help! We're drowning!"

Crocker immediately clamped a hand over his mouth. "Bad idea!"

He'd rather freeze to death or drown in the bay than give himself up. No way he was putting himself, his family, and his country through that.

His body was almost numb now, and as the numbness spread so did a primordial warmth, which he understood was one of the first symptoms of hypothermia. Nothing he could do except to try to stay afloat and not lose consciousness. He heard helicopter blades beating in the distance and saw searchlights exploring the water south of Ung-do. Maybe they had spotted wreckage, bodies, or survivors.

"It's a good thing we're drifting north," he said to Dawkins's head, cradled under his right arm.

Dawkins didn't respond.

Crocker was in Alaska on a winter warfare exercise, blowing hot air into his hands. Then he was back. The sky overhead was still furry black—no moon or stars. He saw his mother knitting by the fire, glasses perched on the end of her nose. His father stood by her side, holding a ball of yarn. He thought it was his first memory, and he was going back to the beginning of his life.

Water washed over his chest and reached his mouth. He spit it out and coughed.

It happened again, and he looked left. Realized he was on land. The island of Ung-do glowed in the distance. Dawkins lay on his side like a beached fish. Crocker extended an arm in his direction, but he was out of reach.

"Dawkins. Hey, Dawkins!"

He slid over and lifted him carefully. Saw that he was breathing.

"Dawkins! You hear me?"

Dawkins blinked and looked at him with surprise. "What happened? Where are we?"

Dawkins's lips were blue, and he trembled from head to toe. Crocker wanted to start a fire or wrap a blanket around him, but realized he had nothing on him but his smart suit, boots, and belt. No body armor, no NVGs. Even the SIG Sauer was missing from its holster.

Hearing a scraping noise, he lay belly-down on the sand. About seventy meters down the shore to his right, someone was emerging from the water, pushing something flat and dark. The sight was so surreal, he wondered at first if he was imagining it, like his mother by the fire. But when he blinked and opened his eyes the dark figure was still there, so he continued to make himself small and narrowed his focus. The man seemed to match a familiar shape and size.

Crocker squeezed Dawkins's arm, held a finger to his lips to tell him to remain quiet, and scooted on his belly to the shrubs along the bank. From there he made his way closer. When he was sure it was Akil, he emerged and approached, optimism surging into his system like oxidized blood.

"Akil! What the fuck took you so long?" he whispered.

"Boss? You son of a bitch…"

They embraced like it was the happiest moment of their lives—two exhausted men in shredded smart suits on a beach in enemy territory.

Akil was pulling a plastic panel that looked like it had come from the SDV, with another man on it.

"Who's that?"

"Sam. Smashed his leg and ankle. You locate the others?"

"I've got Dawkins with me. That's all."

"Oh." Akil looked disappointed.

"He's suffering from hypothermia," Crocker said, pointing at Dawkins's silhouette on the sand. "I lost everything—comms, weapon, med kit, even my pistol."

"I found this." Akil gestured toward a backpack lying beside Sam on the plastic panel. "Don't know what's in it. Pretty sure Naylor and Hutchins died on impact. Suarez, I didn't see him."

Crocker was already digging through the backpack, which seemed to have belonged to Suarez. He concentrated on the toaster-sized metal Personal Recovery and Survival (PRS) kit at the bottom. Inside, sealed behind a watertight rubber gasket, he found a stainless-steel mini-multitool with pliers, a wire cutter, file, and awl; a 14mm AA-liquid-filled compass; a red LED squeeze light (red to protect night vision as well as not give away your position); a ferrocerium rod with tinder tabs in a resealable bag; forty water purification tabs in an amber vial; a 2x3-inch signal mirror; two thermal blankets; fifteen feet of Kevlar cord; safety pins; a can opener; duct tape; a roll of stainless-steel wire; a fresnel magnifying lens; a pack of antibiotic ointment; two water storage bags; and a small med kit.

As he catalogued everything, he said, "We'll keep an eye out for Suarez. Your comms work?"

"What fucking comms? I lost everything except for my pistol."

"What'd we hit?"

"The fuck if I know. Don't think it was a mine, because I didn't hear an explosion."

"Me neither." Crocker unfolded the blankets. "Let's get these around Sam and Dawkins. Then we've got to ditch the wreckage and find a place to hide."

"Sure, boss."

"We drifted northwest. Looks like the Koreans are searching south."

"I believe we're on the southeastern tip of the Hamgyong Peninsula. Maybe half a mile from Ung-do," added Akil.

"You're the navigator." At the bottom of the pack Crocker located an Emerson GPS distress marker, which was the size of an iPhone and usually worn in a holder on the operator's wrist.

"Good. We've got a distress marker. The batteries seem weak, but it works. Probably should wait a night or two to use it. Find a place where the guys from the *Carl Vinson* can land. Once we got that sorted out, we'll signal them and catch a ride out of here. Meanwhile, let's keep looking for Suarez, Naylor, and Hutchins."

"You make it sound easy, boss. You sure you're okay?"

"Fuck, yeah."

Dense shivers ran up Crocker's legs and arms as he and Akil carried Sam on the heavy plastic-and-Styrofoam panel. Akil, who appeared to be in the best shape of the four, led the way, with Dawkins stumbling beside them, a blanket wrapped around his shoulders, mumbling to himself. Crocker suspected that he and Dawkins were both suffering from stage two hypothermia.

But he couldn't worry about that now, or the numbness in his toes, or the pain throughout his body. They were moving inland to find a place to rest and build a fire pit, heal, and regroup. Even as he was drifting in and out of awareness, he managed to place one foot in front of the other down a slight incline, albeit slower than he would have liked.

Something rustled to his right, and he saw a flash of silver and fluorescent orange. Thought he might be having a stroke, then realized it was Dawkins rolling in the Kevlar blanket until he hit the base of a tree and stopped. Crocker had lowered the makeshift stretcher to the ground and was bending over Dawkins and offering him a hand up before he realized what he was doing. Through the dim light he saw dirt and leaves matted on Dawkins's hair and face. His eyes shone, but his voice was shredded with exhaustion.

He said, "Leave me. I'll die here. Thank you for what you did. It was…good." This came out in one continuous stream, as though he was expending his last bit of energy.

Crocker wasn't about to accept it. "No. Not happening."

"No, no, it's okay. I'll die here…Just get a message to my wife."

"Get the fuck up!"

Crocker pulled him to his feet, stood him up, leaned him against a tree, and peeled the wet leaves off his face.

Dawkins shuddered and started to weep. He said, "I told you…I can't do this."

"You have no idea what you're capable of, Dawkins. No fucking idea. We're going to get through this together."

"No…"

"Hold on to my hand."

The warmth felt good. Crocker was sitting before a fire.

Holly handed him a cup of tomato soup with big brown croutons floating in it. He leaned forward to sip it, and stumbled. He quickly caught himself before he let go of the makeshift stretcher.

"Boss!"

He thought he saw Cyndi lying on it, naked, a red hibiscus blossom behind her ear.

"Boss, this okay?"

He saw Akil looking back at him, his eyes bigger and darker than usual. They were standing in a little oval clearing in a dense stand of trees.

"Boss, you all right?"

"Yeah. Yeah, this is good. Thanks."

He let go of Dawkins and lowered the stretcher to the ground, then stood there trying to think what to do next.

"Lie next to Sam," he said to Dawkins. "Wrap the blankets around yourselves. I'm gonna build a fire."

A massive shiver ran from Crocker's feet all the way to his head, snapping his teeth together.

"I'm gonna start collecting wood," he said to Akil. "I want you to surveil the area. See if there's anyone in the vicinity."

"I'm going to look for a hotel with a pool. Take a swim, then catch a movie."

"You're funny."

"What's the plan? Stay here tonight and look for an exfil site in the a.m.?"

Crocker was finding it hard to think that far ahead. "Something like that…"

Next thing he remembered, he was searching through the pack for the med kit and locating a thermometer, which he placed in Dawkins's mouth. The little LED screen read 93.5 degrees Fahrenheit.

"I feel sick," Dawkins moaned, his skin pale and lips still blue.

"Stay under the blankets. I'll get you warmed up."

Definitely stage two hypothermia, he said to himself.

CHAPTER TWENTY

Some of you young men think that war is all glamour
and glory, but let me tell you, boys, it is all hell.
— General William T. Sherman

HE WAS on his hands and knees, using the lid of the PRS kit to dig a hole about a foot away from a modest-sized tree, which would help to disperse the smoke. A gust of wind blew up his back and he shivered. Akil sat six feet away, gently rubbing blood into Dawkins's arm. He saw Crocker staring at him and stopped.

"What's wrong?"

"Nothing."

"You hear something, boss?"

"No. Did you?"

He couldn't remember what he had determined about their present location, but he thought it must have been acceptable, because they were still there, and he was digging.

He'd constructed so many Dakota fire pits that he could make one in his sleep, which was essentially what he was doing now. He saw Jenny at two and a half, standing in a wading pool in the backyard holding her arms out to him. He tossed a beach ball, which sailed between her outstretched arms and bounced off her nose.

He started laughing.

"What's so funny, boss?" Akil asked.

"I was remembering something."

He blinked and looked down, and was surprised as how much progress he'd made. The main hole was about fourteen inches deep and eight inches wide. He'd already completed a narrower outlet hole at a slight angle on the windward side that intersected with the bottom of the pit. This would provide the fire with oxygen and keep it burning. Now all he had to do was fill the pit with the kindling he'd gathered and light it.

Which he did now, using the ferrocerium rod and rubbing his knife into it at a thirty-degree angle. The spark produced by the metal lit one of the open packets of treated cotton tinder. He tossed it into the pit and covered it with kindling, then set progressively larger sticks over the little flames.

They grew larger. The hotter the fire got, the more oxygen it sucked into the tunnel.

"You can laugh to yourself all you want, as long as you get shit done," Akil remarked.

"Thanks, douchebag."

Together they carried Sam closer and huddled around the fire. Akil cleaned the metal PRS kit holder in a nearby stream and filled it with fresh water. Crocker heated it over the fire, poured some into the lid, and passed it to Dawkins, who sipped some, then passed it to Sam.

"You're a fucking genius," Akil said as he refilled the lid and passed it to Crocker.

The water warmed Crocker's insides. "No, I'm a frogman."

"Same thing, only different."

"What the fuck does that mean?"

Akil's wide face creased into a grin. "It means you're feeling better. Later we'll go looking for some Korean babes to keep us warm."

"You're crazier than me, and always have been."

"Crazy keeps me sane."

Now that Crocker's mind was clearer, he realized that he'd forgotten to examine Sam. In the reflected light from the fire he cut away the right leg of Sam's wet suit. His ankle was completely dislocated, and the fibula and tibia had both sustained compound open-wound fractures. The pain had to be excruciating, yet as far as he knew, Sam hadn't swallowed any medicine, nor had he complained.

Most of what Crocker found in the med kit were Israeli bandages, tourniquets, tape, QuikClot, and triangular bandages— more suited to dealing with combat wounds. At the bottom of Suarez's pack he found a universal SAM splint and a vial of extra-strength Motrin.

He fed Sam two pills, cleaned the wounds, and stabilized his ankle by placing the splint around the bottom of his bare foot, wrapping it around both sides of his ankle and securing the aluminum alloy bands with a bandage and tape.

Crocker slept for thirty minutes and woke up remembering Suarez, Naylor, and Hutchins. He asked Akil, who was still awake, to watch the camp and keep the fire going while he went back to look for them.

"Is that smart, boss? You want the pistol?"

"You keep it. Guard the camp."

At the beach he looked out over the bay and saw that the Ung-do complex was no longer burning. Patrol boats and helicopters with searchlights traversed the seas south, west, and even east of the island. None of them bothered to look north.

Eventually they'll turn this way, he said to himself, trying to be realistic. Their current vulnerable state afforded no margin for error. Nor could they rely on hope.

He searched up and down the beach along the east side of the peninsula, then along the little area that jutted south, then west, making sure to walk along the water's edge so as not to leave footprints.

No sign of Suarez, Naylor, or Hutchins. No wreckage from the SDV, either. He gazed south one last time, praying that they were still alive and hadn't been captured.

Then he searched the beach again and tried not to feel sad.

He awoke stiff from his neck down and squinted into the sun shining through the leaves. The air carried the scent of burning wood. He saw Akil cleaning and drying his SIG Sauer by the fire pit. Sam lay beside him, sleeping. As Crocker stretched, he noticed that the skin around Sam's ankle was purple and swollen.

"How long did I sleep?" he whispered. "Where's Dawkins?"

"He went to the stream to wash himself."

"This isn't a fucking camping trip. You shouldn't have let him go alone."

"He insisted. I think he shit himself."

"Which way'd he go?"

Akil pointed to his left—generally east.

Crocker pushed through bushes still wearing the smart suit and Merrell boots. Past a patch of honeysuckle, he saw Dawkins naked except for a gray T-shirt, with the water midway up his thighs—pale, vulnerable, and lost in his own thoughts. He was the kind of guy Crocker had passed hundreds of times in the mall and never given a thought to. He was the quiet, smart, physically meek student he used to terrorize in school.

Crocker had never asked him about the circumstances of his captivity, but wanted to. Now, as he stepped down the embankment toward the six-foot-wide stream, he saw something move up ahead on his right. The flash of a blue shirt, and then a boy of maybe seven holding a bamboo fishing pole. The kid turned right when he reached the stream and walked away from them, disappearing around a bend.

Back in the clearing, Crocker knelt beside Akil and said, "There are people living nearby, which means of one of us has to recce this end of the peninsula. You know anything about it?"

"From what I remember reading, it's sparsely populated. Small family farms and swampland. The population centers are farther south."

"The other thing we've got to do is locate an exfil site big enough to land a helicopter," Crocker said. "If we find one that's far enough from civilization, we'll signal tonight."

"Sounds like you've been thinking."

"If we don't find one, we'll keep moving and searching, which won't be easy with Sam. But if we follow the stream and use the purification tablets, we should have plenty of water. We also need to start looking for food."

"Prime rib?"

"Fish heads and rabbit balls. I'll set some traps."

An hour later, while Crocker was boiling water, a Russian-made

Mi-14 helicopter passed overhead, then banked left back over the bay and returned. They hid under the thickest foliage they could find and waited. After a half-dozen passes it moved on.

After the sun went down, they feasted on two large trout Akil had speared in the stream, drank water, and rested by the fire. Shortly after midnight they broke camp, covered the fire pit, and hiked three-quarters of a mile northeast, picking their way through pine trees and swamp to a camping area that had been cleared near the beach with two rotting picnic tables. The over-grown narrow dirt road that fed it from the north looked like it hadn't been used in months.

While Akil, Sam, and Dawkins waited in the woods, Crocker stood in the clearing and activated the Emerson GPS distress marker for a full minute, then flashed it three times according to the prearranged emergency signal. He repeated the process three more times and waited. When an hour passed and no one came, he signaled again.

Crocker repeated the same sequence for the next three hours, while Akil sat with Sam and Dawkins. Straining his ears for the sound of an approaching helicopter, he grew frustrated. The signal from the Emerson distress marker wouldn't last forever, and they had no extra batteries.

Figuring that there was a possibility that the North Koreans had picked up the signal, he joined the others and they hiked as fast as they could two miles north along the beach, skirting several huts, until he found what he thought was a suitable clearing. They made makeshift beds of twigs and dried grass to elevate their bodies off the cold ground. Then Sam, Dawkins, and Akil slept while Crocker kept watch.

As the sun spread its fingers across the sky Crocker considered the possible reasons why the *Carl Vinson*'s rescue team hadn't responded—weather, mechanical problems, North Korean air patrols. He decided there was no reason to lose hope. They would try again tonight and every night after that until the battery wore out. Then he'd think of something else.

Three nights later, Davis sat in the Tactical Operations Center (TOC) on the *Carl Vinson*, positioned approximately eighteen nautical miles from the Hamgyong Peninsula, staring at the large digital map of North Korea in front of him, praying for a red beacon to appear. Even though the clock on the wall read 0213 hours, the dark room was still crowded with more than a dozen male and female techs sitting before screens and computer terminals, monitoring nearby ships, aircraft, and weather.

Davis had spent the past several nights and mornings right here, watching in frustration as the emergency beacon moved north up the east side of the peninsula, and the Air-sea Rescue Team (ART) failed to respond. He had volunteered to be part of the four-man team that would fly on the specially designed stealth Blackhawk helicopter—the same one used in the Bin Laden raid—that waited fully fueled and geared up on the *Vinson*'s flight deck. All he, the other three members of the team, and the 160th SOAR Night Stalker pilot and copilot needed was a go order from the carrier's commander, Vice Admiral Stanley Greene, who had been granted final authority by the commanders at SOCOM in Tampa, and they'd be aloft.

The first night the emergency beacon had showed on the screen, Greene ordered the rescue team to stand down because of the number of North Korean air patrols in the area.

The second night he used the excuse of unstable weather. Last night he'd explained that the survivors on the ground were signaling close to a populated area. Davis had pointed out that the latest satellite imagery and heat signatures indicated that it was only a collection of small farms about four miles from the site.

Now Davis willed so hard for the beacon to appear that his head hurt. Those were his teammates on the ground. All of them alive and uninjured, he hoped. Even though he had a wife and two young children waiting at home in Virginia Beach, part of him remained with his teammates, in enemy territory, looking for a way out.

The first satellite images of the destroyed Ung-do facility, received a day and a half ago, had filled him with an enormous sense of pride. That was quickly giving way to frustration and anger. Davis considered himself thoughtful and reasonable—the kind of person who saw all sides of a dispute. But now he couldn't understand why officers on the *Carl Vinson* weren't willing to take the risks and launch the rescue.

Last night he'd tried to convince the Blackhawk pilot to disobey orders. When that failed, he had unleashed his frustration on the ship's operations officer, calling him "a disgrace to his uniform" and "a fucking coward."

He apologized later, at breakfast. That wasn't like him, he explained. He was usually the mellowest guy on the team, referred to by his teammates as "surfer dude" because of his laid-back demeanor and blond hair.

Now the same operations officer looked back at him and shrugged. Davis glanced up at the clock. Another ten minutes had passed, and the beacon still hadn't appeared. His stomach roiled and he started to sweat as he realized that it was growing too late to launch a rescue tonight.

One of the technicians squeezed Davis's shoulder as he headed for the exit.

"Maybe tomorrow night," he said. "Don't give up hope."

The twenty-two men and two women who made up North Korea's military and political leadership had been stunned by the attack, which completely disabled Office 39's operation, resulted in the death of its leader, the Dragon, and set back their nuclear program five to ten years. As they waited in the plush red velvet seats in the beige marble conference room under military head-quarters in downtown Pyongyang, they knew they should expect reprisals.

They had been sitting for two hours now, waiting for their thirty-two-year-old Supreme Leader to appear and rail at them. All of them secretly wanted that. They hoped for a catharsis, a cleansing, followed by a call to action. That they could accept. It would help them map the future. What they were hearing in-stead was that the Supreme Leader had literally become sick with humiliation. So sick, in fact, that he couldn't fathom a re-sponse to the attack.

He had reputedly told an aide, "There's no point trying to cover the whole sky with the palm of your hand," a variation of a Korean proverb. What the Supreme Leader had meant by it was the subject of much speculation. Maybe he was saying they had been deluding themselves into believing that they were a strong country, and this attack had revealed that they were weak. Maybe that's why he was allowing himself to feel humiliated.

The men and women in the room—with one or two

exceptions—shared a deep sense of insecurity. They weren't ignorant people. All of them had traveled to China, Russia, and Japan. They'd seen smuggled videos and DVDs from the United States and Europe. They knew their country was essentially backward. If they had any chance of remaining in power and continuing to enjoy the special perks they had been given, they knew they needed to be ruthless, vigilant, and clever.

Still, five days after it had occurred, little was known about the attack. No bodies had been discovered, no equipment had been found, and no surveillance video had survived the devastating explosion. None of their radar installations had reported violations of North Korean airspace, and no foreign ships or submarines had been detected by sonar. The only evidence that had been found were small, unmarked pieces of some kind of underwater vehicle that had washed up near Munchon. Some speculated that the attack was a South Korean response to the sinking of its Pohang corvette two years earlier. Others suspected that there had been some inside collusion, perhaps supported by the United States and South Korea.

The red light flashed near the door above the Supreme Leader's chair, and the room grew still and silent. But in place of Kim Jong-un, it was Dak-ho Gun-san, the wizened interior minister, who descended the steps and took his place behind the podium. The skin under his right eye was swollen and blackened, and a bandage covered the side of his face. According to rumor, the night Dak-ho reported the attack and death of General Chou to the Supreme Leader, a pajama-clad Kim Jong-un had grabbed a brass figurine of his grandfather from his desk and thrown it at Dak-ho, hitting him in the face.

Now Dak-ho's voice quivered with outrage as he read a list

of the names of those present who the Supreme Leader had declared enemies of the state. As these men and woman heard their names, they slumped in their seats and wept. Soldiers in tan uniforms quickly handcuffed them and led them away. They left in unimaginable anguish, knowing that their careers were over and that their wives, husbands, and children had probably been arrested, too. All of them, including former minister Dakho Gun-san, would spend the rest of their lives in one of the country's political prisons, scavenging for food like animals.

A light rain started to fall as Dawkins watched Crocker and Akil standing outside the primitive shelter they had constructed from the two Kevlar blankets, tossing leaves over the top so they wouldn't be visible from the air. Six days had passed since his liberation. During that time, he was sure he was either going to die or be recaptured and put to death.

In the moments when he wasn't numb with exhaustion and fear, he sometimes resented what these brave men had done. Maybe, he thought, it would have been better had they left him alone in his cell to be blown up with the rest of the underground complex. That way, he wouldn't face almost certain torture, and his wife and daughter would be left alone.

Yet the more time he spent with Akil, Sam, and Crocker, the more he started to believe in them and to adopt their the-only-easy-day-was-yesterday approach. Crocker fascinated him. He was a man who never showed fear or disappointment. Even now that the batteries in the emergency beacon had died, he seemed to take it in stride and remain optimistic that they would be rescued or find their way to safety. From the way the men casually joked with one another and went about the business of hunting for food, collecting wood, finding water, and walking through enemy territory at night carrying Sam and never complaining, you would have thought they were on a camping trip in an American national park.

"I love danger," Akil had confided to him. "It turns me on."

When he first said it, Dawkins thought he was just trying to boost his spirits. Now Dawkins believed him. Today the Egyptian American had entertained them with stories of moving to the States when he was six, joining the marines, and the many women he had pursued and bedded—Dutch twins in Mexico who kept him up all night and left in the morning with all his clothes, the Jewish stripper from Boston he had run into in Dubai, the female diving champion who would make love only underwater. He talked about them all with so much enthusiasm and affection that they became real. He remembered their scents, eccentricities, the way they walked and the sounds they made in bed.

The more Akil talked about women, the closer Dawkins felt to Nan. He realized that his modesty and shame about his body had caused him to miss a lot. Life was richer than he had realized. People were filled with pathos, humor, courage, and some kind of magic.

When he asked Akil how he remained so centered and optimistic, the rough man responded by pointing to his head and said, "It all comes from here. What we achieve inwardly changes outer reality."

"Is that a Muslim belief?"

"No, I think it came from a guy named Plutarch."

"Plutarch the Roman philosopher. Did you study him in college?"

"No. Never went."

"Then where did you come across that concept?"

"I read it on the shitter door of a yoga studio. It's stuck in my head ever since."

Crocker might have appeared untroubled, but in fact he spent most of his time trying to figure out how they were going to make it to safety, given their dwindling supplies. Now that the juice had run out of the batteries in the GPS tracker, their chances of being rescued were almost zero.

What he didn't know was that the morning after the batteries ran out, an enraged Davis walked into the Vice Admiral Greene's office and punched him in the face, breaking his jaw.

A half-moon peeked through the branches of the Japanese red pines as they trudged, Crocker and Akil carrying Sam on the jerry-rigged stretcher and Dawkins walking on his own. Sam's ankle had become infected and they'd run out of Motrin, so the Korean American had to suck it up, which he did without complaint. Since they had run out of disinfectant as well, Crocker lanced the infection every day and cleansed the wound with boiled water.

After six nights of walking, Crocker and company had reached the top of Hamgyong Peninsula. The closer they drew to the mainland, the more farms and clusters of huts they saw. So far they hadn't run into barking dogs, which was odd. Akil joked that the North Koreans had eaten them all, and Crocker thought he was probably right.

They were roughly 110 miles north of the South Korean border. On a good night they managed to progress from eight to ten miles over footpaths through forests, swamps, and fields. It helped that the streams that ran down the peninsula to the bay provided a steady supply of food and water. Crocker expected both to become harder to secure now that they approached denser population centers along the southeast coast. According to the map, the terrain ahead was mountainous, and they would have to cross at least two major rivers before they could continue south to the cities of Munchon and Wonsan.

The terrain and climate reminded Crocker of woods of New Hampshire. He'd camped in them often—intimate days and nights with his mother, father, sister, and older brother dining on grilled chicken and baked beans, followed by his dad pointing out the constellations and telling jokes and stories.

Crocker recalled a story his father told about a widow who fell in love with a rich nobleman. The nobleman wouldn't marry her because he didn't want to raise another man's offspring, so the widow drowned her children in a nearby river. When she told the nobleman what she had done, he was horrified and wanted nothing more to do with her. She went to the river hoping to retrieve her children. Unable to find them, she drowned herself and was condemned to wander the waterways of the world, searching for her children and weeping until the end of time.

Akil, leading the way, entered a clearing alongside a stream and stopped. They set down the stretcher and looked for a place to cross. Crocker checked his watch—0314 hours. The stream was about twenty feet wide, and there were no bridges in sight.

"What do you think?" Akil asked.

"Let's try to cross here, and look for a place to sleep on the other side."

"Okay, boss. You wait here while I test it."

Akil handed him his web belt and holster with the SIG Sauer

with two remaining mags, waded into the ice-cold water, and came out shivering and raising his thumb.

Seconds later they entered together—Akil and Crocker carrying the stretcher with Sam, and Dawkins beside them. Crocker held the stretcher over his head and was concentrating on his footing when he heard Dawkins cry "Look!"

On their right, past a bend downstream, a brown bear was in the water, presumably looking for fish. It stopped, turned, rose up on its rear legs, and roared. The noise startled Dawkins, who slipped and fell. In the moonlight, Crocker saw that the current was hurling Dawkins back toward the shore they had come from, about twenty feet ahead, and was moving so fast that when he tried to slow himself by grabbing a boulder, he smacked into it chin first and went under.

"Wait!" Crocker said to Akil. "I'm going after him."

Akil seemed to intuit exactly what he wanted him to do, taking the stretcher and balancing it over his head.

Crocker dove into the current, which carried him past the boulder as if he were on a ride at a water park. He used it to push off, and tried to locate Dawkins by his pale shirt. Eight feet ahead he saw an arm and let the powerful current take him until he was able to reach up under Dawkins's shoulder and neck, and pull his head out of the water.

Dawkins coughed up water, and the bear roared again. But the current was strong and they had no way to stop. When Crocker glanced to the right he saw the bear watching from thirty feet away. Dawkins spotted him, too, and started to panic and pull away.

"Relax!"

He held Dawkins tightly to his chest with his right arm and

let the current carry them past the bear, to a bend in the stream where the water was shallow and they could easily walk ashore. The roaring bear was so close they could smell his rancid breath.

"Run," Dawkins whispered.

Crocker reached out and stopped him. "Unwise."

The bear rose with a fish clenched in his left paw like a trophy, spun, and ambled off into the woods.

CHAPTER TWENTY-ONE

The only mistake in life is the lesson not learned.
—Albert Einstein

CROCKER AWOKE with the sun directly above him in the sky.

"Boss?" Akil asked.

"Yeah. What's up?" His right shoulder hurt and his leg muscles were sore and tight.

"I want to show you something."

He relieved himself behind a tree and noticed that they were on a moss-covered outcropping of rock surrounded by tall pines. Sam and Dawkins slept beside each other under a blanket near the base of one of the trees.

He found the water bag and chugged purified water, then remembered that they had no food. It was something he would have to take care of soon, probably using the stainless-steel wire to fashion head-snare traps, which had been successful so far in catching squirrels and rabbits.

"What is it?"

As he followed Akil, he decided that they needed to set out earlier tonight—maybe a few hours after dark, start descending along the coast and turn south. The sky was clear, but gray clouds approaching from the north threatened rain.

Akil stopped on a rocky promontory that looked south over the bay. "Look. That's Ung-do over there," he said, pointing to the teardrop-shaped island to the southeast. It appeared peaceful in the pool of sunlight that shrank and faded.

"And that's Munchon," Akil said, moving his arm to a dark collection of structures in the southwest. A dark delta, a glowing river, and several tributaries bisected the space between where they stood now and the city in the distance.

"Yeah. Those rivers are gonna present a challenge."

Back at camp, he tried to avoid thinking too far ahead, concentrating instead on the immediate tasks before him: setting the traps, gathering kindling, building the fire pit, and boiling water. He dipped a bandage in the water and applied it to a dark red spot on Sam's ankle, then removed it and let it cool.

The sky had turned darker and the wind was whipping up the leaves around them. Crocker repeated the process three more times to draw the infection to the surface. Then he sterilized the blade of his knife by holding it over the fire, waited for it to cool, cut into the skin, and drained away the pus.

"How is it, boss?" Sam asked as Crocker rebandaged it.

He lied. "Better."

He checked Sam's forehead with the back of his hand and found it slightly hot.

"I think I've got a fever. Last night I dreamt I was attacked by a shark while surfing on Maui and lost my leg."

"Your leg is fine."

"The last thing I want is to be a burden. If I become too hard to carry, you can leave me behind."

"That's not going to happen. Keep drinking water. I'm gonna go check the traps."

Nan woke up suddenly at one a.m. in the bedroom of her temporary apartment, looked at the clock, and sighed. Today was her husband's forty-seventh birthday, and she hadn't heard anything more from the FBI, except that they had passed on the information she had received to the appropriate authorities. They hadn't specified who those authorities were and what actions they were taking to rescue her husband.

The FBI had asked her to keep the information she had received to herself, which she had. It amused her now when friends, family members, colleagues at work, and neighbors continued to relate their theories of what had happened to James—he had run off with another woman, he had taken his life because he was suffering from depression, he had been abducted by a cult.

The questions she asked herself were more pertinent and troubling: Had the government demanded James's release from North Korea? If the North Koreans refused, what action was the United States going to take? And why were FBI agents guarding her and Karen? She wanted to trust her government and decided that she would, even though she was by nature skeptical.

Now she got out of bed in her cotton nightgown and walked on bare feet to her daughter's bedroom. She sighed at the sight of Karen sleeping with a stuffed rabbit clutched to her chest and a framed picture of James on the pillow next to her.

If there's a silver lining or a blessing in all this, she said to herself, it's that in a strange way this ordeal has pulled the three of us closer together.

Crocker felt sick to his stomach as he looked over his shoulder at the tin-roofed hut on the bluff. Forty feet in front of him, Akil stood on the shore of the bay trying to push a wooden post low enough to free the metal chain around it that was attached to a small boat. The chain grated against the wood, but he couldn't manage to push the post down far enough.

Stealing the boat had been Crocker's idea, but now he wondered if it was smart.

"Try not to make so much noise," he said to Akil as he watched him struggle.

"You know a better way of doing this?"

Absent a metal saw or other tool to cut through the chain, which they didn't have, he didn't.

When Crocker cast his gaze back toward the dim light in the window of the hut, the muscles in his stomach contracted. The lion's share of the rabbit he had captured and cooked earlier had gone to Dawkins and Sam. Then he remembered how he had tried to preserve those last four water purification tablets by putting half, instead of a whole one, in the gallon bag he carried.

Bad decision!

He started to scold himself and then stopped. He needed to focus. It had taken them six hours to descend to sea level. All of them were tired and weak. Sam was running a fever.

Hearing the grate of the chain again, he turned and saw that Akil had manipulated the dock post to a forty-degree angle and was using the heel of his right boot to push the chain over the top. Crocker watched as Akil stopped, leaned over, and threw up into the water.

Fuck!

He crossed to help him, then turned to recheck the hut.

"Let's try together."

The combined power of Crocker's arm and Akil's leg pushed the chain free. Akil stepped down into the open boat, stopped, and leaned over the side like he was about to get sick again.

"I think it's the water in the bladder. Don't drink it."

"Too late."

Together they fetched Sam and Dawkins. With them loaded into the boat, they pushed off and used the lid and bottom of the PRS kit to paddle into the bay. When they were a hundred meters out, Crocker couldn't hold in the contents of his stomach any longer. Half a minute later, his stomach muscles contracted and his pharyngeal reflex activated again.

This time nothing came up except a ribbon of bile. He rinsed his mouth with a handful of salt water and continued paddling.

"When are we gonna try the engine?" Akil asked, his face appearing greenish in the moonlight.

"Let's get out farther. How are you feeling?"

"Like shit. Why?"

Another two hundred meters out, he squirmed past Dawkins and Sam, both lying on the bottom and already asleep, and pulled the cord to start the little four-horsepower Chinese Seanovo outboard. It coughed and ignited on the third try. Steering the boat south, he wondered how far the percussive pop of the engine would travel.

A feverish feeling was coming over him. Minutes later, when

Dawkins opened his eyes and reached for the water bag, Crocker stopped him.

"Wait."

He reached into the pouch on his belt, retrieved a whole purification tablet, tossed it into the bag, sloshed it around, and handed the bag to Dawkins.

"Give it another minute. Then it should be good."

He blinked into the sun that was starting to dip west, opened his eyes again, and shielded them. His body ached and felt hot, his head hurt, and his mouth and throat were dry. He drank from the two-thirds-full bag of water and looked around the boat. Dawkins sat in the middle, running a wet rag over Sam's forehead and neck. Akil slumped in the bow of the twelve-foot-long craft with his legs propped on the side.

How he could sleep or even rest in that position surprised Crocker. More importantly, the position of his body was pushing the little craft east. He corrected course south and tried to fix their position in the haze-filled bay. They appeared to be about a half mile east and three-quarters of a mile south of Ung-do. He made out the shape of the larger Ryo-do ahead, but couldn't see the mainland. Judging from the picture of the bay he held in his head, they were almost parallel to Munchon. Another twenty or thirty miles, and they'd reach the south end of Hamgyong Bay.

He lay with his back against the stern, holding the steering arm on the Seanovo to keep their course steady and let the sun draw the sickness out of his body. He dreamt he was riding his Harley down Route 29 past the town of Covesville in the Shenandoah Valley. Now he was passing some Monacan Indians, the tribe that had once mined copper from the hills nearby and tried to keep away from white settlers, who spread epidemics of smallpox and influenza.

Feeling sick himself, he awoke to the sound of the engine sputtering. Dawkins looked anxious as the engine coughed one last time and stopped.

"You want me to look at it?" Dawkins asked.

"No point. We ran out of fuel."

It took some vigorous shaking to wake Akil. When he opened his eyes, he seemed disoriented. Crocker changed positions with Dawkins and fed Akil sips of water. He was running a fever, too, so he splashed cool water from the bay over his face and chest.

"Where the fuck are we?" Akil asked.

"Same place we were last night—Hamgyong Bay, North Korea."

Hunger gnawed at Dawkins's stomach, Sam's, too. Crocker told them to take sips of water and hold it in their mouths before they swallowed. He and Akil paddled, singing in unison, descending from ten thousand bottles of beer on the wall to zero as the chop tossed the little boat from side to side.

They continued despite the wind, falling temperature, and lack of food. After the sky turned dark, Akil began humming an Egyptian lullaby over and over, and Dawkins and Sam fell asleep.

When Dawkins awoke hours later, he saw the two men still paddling with the lid and bottom of the PRS kit. He couldn't fathom how they had been able to continue this long. When he turned to ask Crocker how he felt, he saw his eyes were closed.

The SEALs paddled all through the next day and into the night before they both collapsed from exhaustion. One minute Crocker's arms and shoulders ached, and the next he was lying in bed with Cyndi, completely rested and pain-free, eating pancakes covered with butter and maple syrup from a wooden tray. Then the tray and bed shook as though the house they were in had been hit by an earthquake.

He heard the wood crack, which jarred him awake a split second before the front of the little boat shattered on a sharp rock. Bracing himself, he saw Akil struggling to hold on as the boat pitched right. The splash cooled his face, and a second later he was in the water, flailing his stiff, tired arms, trying to get them to work. Even in his weakened condition, he remembered why he was doing this—the mission, the freed hostage, their escape from North Korea. His feet touched soft silt and he relaxed. Cold surf slapped his chest. To his right, he saw Akil helping Dawkins to the shore.

As these impressions coalesced, he scanned the narrow ten-foot-long strip of beach and a cliff above it covered with foliage. A voice in his head told him to look for a structure or lights. Then he forgot.

They were lifting Sam and carrying him out of the water when Akil slipped. Crocker bent down to help him up, tasting salty water and resisting the impulse to drink it. They set Sam down on the sand. His head felt so heavy he could barely hold it up. In his mind he was reaching for something—the reason for being where they were, an idea of what to do next.

Someone asked, "Where are we?" in a weak, pleading voice.

He couldn't answer. Leaves rattled above him. Through them he made out stars.

Picturing Holly and Jenny standing over him, he awoke. The warmth of the sun felt good. An orange crab waited a few feet from his arm. He sat up and saw a man in a dirty shirt and black pajama pants squatting next to Akil and feeding him something from a ladle. He wondered if he was dreaming.

"Akil?" His throat was dry and caused his voice to crack.

The man with the ladle pivoted his head toward him. He looked old, withered, and Asian.

"Where are we?"

Crocker slapped a fly off his wrist. His body begged to sleep, but something told him not to. He fixed his eyes on the yellow bucket. The man kneeling beside it muttered something that didn't make sense.

He heard Akil moan "More."

"More what?" he asked.

Akil turned and looked at him sideways. His eyes were red, his neck and face covered with thick, dark beard, and his forehead was chalky gray.

He thought he heard Holly say, "It's okay. You can rest now." But when he blinked again, she wasn't there. Looking at his blistered bare feet, he pushed himself up.

"Akil, what's going on?"

He found his boots in the sand near where he'd been sleeping but couldn't find his belt.

"Akil, who took my weapon?"

"You didn't have one," Akil replied weakly. His lips were badly cracked. "I did. Besides, he's friendly."

"Who's friendly?"

The word didn't make sense.

He woke up in a dark place. Thin ribbons of sunlight peeked through rough boards. Someone handed him a plastic cup.

"Drink this. Drink it slowly."

He didn't recognize the man's roundish face. The liquid brought his body alive, but it didn't feel good. Pain and nausea radiated from inside him.

"Drink."

It tasted sweet. He wanted to be alert.

"Drink slowly. A little at a time."

The man looked familiar. Wisps of brown hair fell over his high forehead.

"Dawkins?"

"Yes."

He saw a gray wolf staring at him. He stared back. It licked his face.

He sat leaning against something. Someone was running a wet cloth over his forehead. He opened his eyes and tried to focus.

A man said, "See if you can get more water in him. Then feed him some rice."

"I'll try."

He sat alone in a boat on a lake. Someone was calling him from a distance. He heard his voice skip over the water. A light blinded his eyes.

A candle was burning. In the glow he saw Sam's face. He was sitting up next to an Asian boy who was holding a red plastic rectangular device that looked like a Game Boy. The boy pushed the buttons at the bottom of the screen and the device made funny noises.

A wave of information hit his brain at once, causing his head to hurt. "Sam?"

"Yeah, boss. How you feel?"

"Better, I think. Where are we?"

"We're safe for the time being." Sam pointed. "In that plastic bag in front of you is a bottle of water and a plate of food."

"Yeah?"

"We got some into you earlier, but you need more."

He untied the knot in the plastic bag, removed the bowl of rice and chopsticks, and started to shovel food into his mouth. When he took a long drink of water, his stomach felt like it was going to burst.

"Slow is better," Sam said. He crinkled his eyes and then returned them to the little screen. Crocker thought he hadn't seen him looking this happy and healthy in a long time.

"How's your ankle?"

"Hee cleaned it up and rebandaged it. She gave me some ginseng and herbs to battle the infection."

"Who's Hee?"

"Dang's wife. He's the guy who owns this little plot of land. He's away now working at a farming cooperative up the road. He and his son, Ju, found us yesterday."

Crocker shoveled more rice into his mouth. "Where are we exactly?"

"About eighteen miles south of Wonsan, still in North Korea."

It started to come back to him, the mission, the SDV, the crash. "How far are we from the border?"

"Somewhere between forty and fifty miles. We did good."

"Akil and Dawkins okay?"

"They're in the main house helping Ju's sister with something."

"How sure are you that we can trust these people?"

"About sixty percent. They're real nice, and they've been hospitable, but Dang confided to me that if we're still here when the soldiers come around, he'll have to report us. Otherwise they'll kill him and his family."

"How likely is that to happen?'

"He said patrols come through here at least once a week. Sometimes as many as three times. It depends."

"On what?"

"Rumors. Reports."

Crocker finished the bowl of rice and fish and set it aside, then took another long gulp of water.

"How long have we been here?" he asked.

"A day, more or less."

"We'd better leave soon."

"You're probably right."

The next night Crocker presented Dang with forty of the hundred dollars he kept in the sole of his boot. The four Americans thanked him and his family, and set off through a field of new wheat with the moon over their shoulders.

Dang had advised them to move farther inland and avoid the coast, which he said was more heavily patrolled. The KPN was constantly on the lookout for South Korean naval vessels and North Korean refugees escaping south. For that reason, the prospect of the Americans commandeering another boat and reaching South Korea by sea wasn't good. Furthermore, as Dang explained, the currents along this part of the coast were particularly strong and the waves high, because they were no longer in the bay.

So they walked slowly in single file, Sam for the time being hobbling on crutches Akil had made for him. Dang had also supplied them with a piece of canvas tarp that they could use as a makeshift stretcher when Sam got tired. Each man carried a plastic bag containing more plastic bags filled with rice and pickled fish, a large bottle of water, and something Dang had called *doraji*, which was bellflower root brined in vinegar.

It felt good to have a calm, full stomach and to be moving again. For these two things, Crocker was enormously grateful to Dang and his family. They were another example of a phenomenon he had experienced in war-torn parts of Iraq, Afghanistan, Somalia, Syria, and Yemen. In all of those places, he had come across generous, decent people who had no allegiance in the local conflict and whose basic humanity trumped religious, cultural, and political differences.

Now, as he walked, he asked God to bless them with abundance, happiness, and health.

CHAPTER TWENTY-TWO

And lead us not into temptation,
but deliver us from evil.
—The Lord's Prayer

THEY HAD camped in a thicket at the base of a hill and slept for several hours. As the sun started to rise, they were attacked by swarms of flies and mosquitoes, and a very foul smell that blew in from the west. Despite the discomfort, Crocker determined that it was too dangerous to move. Not until he scouted the area. So while Dawkins, Sam, and Akil covered themselves with the blankets and tarp and tried to rest, he set out alone.

It was an overcast spring day of moderate temperature with long streaks of gray in the sky—some dark, others taking on an almost lavender hue. The sweet smell of wildflowers and new leaves was blotted out by thick, disgusting rot whenever the wind blew. It caught in Crocker's throat as he peered from behind bushes to look for signs of human life. Saw no houses, roads, or farms to the south or west. His view north and east was hindered by tall trees two hundred meters away.

Using whatever he could find for cover, he picked his way west to the base of a hill covered with the same red pines they had seen on the peninsula. The hill rose several hundred meters, with a rough, rocky base and no trails or roads leading upward.

As he used a branch to pull himself up, two jets ripped through the sky. He traced their dark profiles under the layers of cloud.

MiGs of some sort, he thought. *Ridiculous fucking country.*

Dang had explained that while the government spent most of its money on its million-man army, navy, and air force, a sizable segment of the estimated twenty-million-strong population was starving. He, his wife, and son were lucky, Dang said, because not only did he earn a modest salary as assistant manager of the local government farming cooperative, but they also grew crops of their own on their little plot of land. Especially in the northern part of the country, thousands of adults and children died each year from malnutrition. Thousands of others succumbed to dehydration and dysentery, which they got from eating roots, leaves, or cobs of unripe corn.

Sick, Crocker thought as he climbed three-quarters of the way up and started to circle south. *Isn't the first responsibility of any country to take care of its people? Sure, protecting them is important, but what's the point of protecting them if they're starving to death?*

On the south side of the hill, the stench was stronger. Past the branches of some pines, he saw what looked like the tin roof of a guard tower below. He stopped, gathered himself, and, carefully proceeded west to a gap in the trees that afforded a better view.

What he saw took his breath away—a field stretching as far south as he could see, surrounded by a fifty-foot-high fence topped with barbed wire and guard towers. Scattered willy-nilly within the fences were very primitive lean-tos made from sheet metal and wood, and rusting shipping containers. Along the west fence stood a long warehouse-like structure with four large smokestacks emitting thick black smoke. Stacked at the far end were pyramids of tires.

When he looked closer, he saw that the men, women, and children carrying tires out of the plant were sticklike figures, so emaciated and gaunt that it was surprising they could even move, let alone lift or push anything.

Anger rose from the pit of his stomach. When he focused on the field of refuse that took up most of the camp, he was even more repulsed. Lying on the ground like clumps of garbage were people of all ages who appeared too weak to stand. Some had covered themselves with scraps of cardboard, paper, and wood.

Crocker was clenching his jaw so hard his teeth started to hurt. *How can people justify doing this kind of shit to one another? This is as evil as the most depraved images I've seen of the Nazi holocaust, and it exists today!*

He wanted to do something—tear the fences down, or shout to the world about the camp's existence. All he could do in the present was shake his head and ask, *What the hell is wrong with mankind?*

He had decided not to tell the others, so as not to dampen their spirits further. In fact, he wasn't sure what to do with the information as he sat on his haunches between Dawkins and Akil, eating rice and sipping water, and thinking about home, and government, and why it was important not to vest power in any one party or individual. The founding fathers had gotten that right. You couldn't trust anyone who wanted control over others.

Maybe the impulse itself was wrong. He felt a jittery uncertainty gnaw at the edges of his stomach as the sky turned dark and rain started to fall. What was a person's responsibility when confronted with unthinkable evil like the one he had just seen? The answer involved some strange moral calculus that he couldn't grasp in his current state. He had excuses—his responsibility to the men on his team, the fact that they were wanted men in an enemy country, their weakened condition and limited options. But none of them quieted his conscience, which twitched with outrage.

At least the rain diminished the smell as they packed their few belongings and continued south, across a field of knee-high corn and into the shrubbery along a ribbon of water. Frogs croaked, reminding him of summer. He and his brother loved catching fireflies. His brother had gone from precocious kid to long-haired drug dealer and user to responsible businessman and father. *What is he doing now? What would he think of the camp I saw earlier? Would he tell me that as an American it wasn't any of my business? If he said that, he'd be fucking wrong!*

A light appeared in the distance and he stopped, knelt, and pumped his arm up and down to indicate to the others to drop, too. He heard gears grinding. In a field, a truck turned so that its lights faced northwest and stopped. The echo of men shouting reached their ears.

"You think they're looking for us?" asked Dawkins at his elbow.

The rain hissed and splattered. He wiped the water from his brow and saw another truck approach and park parallel to the other one. The second truck appeared to be pulling a trailer. Both trucks left their headlights on and engines running.

"Don't know."

Men moved in front of the lights, casting shadows. He remembered Akil's SIG Sauer, which he now carried tucked into a rope around his waist, and the fact that the mag in it had only six rounds.

"What should we do?" Dawkins asked with fear creeping into his voice.

He waited a minute to see if more trucks and soldiers would arrive. They didn't. Thirty feet ahead, in the middle of the field, stood a mound of earth the size of a small car. Atop it was a dying tree, and surrounding it was dense foliage.

"Let's hide over there," Crocker whispered.

They hurried low to the ground. The trucks hadn't moved, and the figures remained clustered around them. From where Crocker and company now waited, there was no cover to the south, only a fallow field of weeds and wildflowers that stretched half a mile.

"We'll wait here until they leave," Crocker whispered to the men huddled around him. Sam's faced appeared twisted in pain. Crocker removed the last two aspirin from the vial Dang had given them.

"Take these."

"I'll be fine."

"Take one, at least."

Akil tilted the bottle of water and helped Sam wash it down.

"While we're here and it's raining, we should capture more water in the tarp and pans. You guys stay low and cover yourselves with the Kevlar. I'm gonna to try to find out what's going on with the trucks."

"Boss, maybe that's not so smart."

Akil's words glanced off Crocker's back as he hurried west. When he closed within a hundred meters of the trucks, he stopped and squatted in a row of new corn. The headlights shone almost directly in his eyes. Squinting, he saw figures standing near the front of the first truck and what looked like shorter, thinner people unloading objects from the backs of the vehicles.

What the hell are they doing?

He continued another fifty meters, then pushed south in a long, wide arc until he reached a row of bushes. Here the thick smell of human decay entered his nose and throat again, and he thought for a moment he'd be sick. It was a smell he'd experienced before but never gotten used to—like the reek of a putrefying animal, only a hundred times worse.

From this vantage, perpendicular to the trucks, he saw frail, gaunt figures—short, like teenage boys and girls—unloading naked bodies and carrying or dragging them to what appeared to be a long trench. He counted twenty teenagers in rags, and as he did, his whole body started to burn with rage. He couldn't even begin to count the number of bodies, because the trucks were large, and stacked high.

Sick, evil fucks...

From here he couldn't determine the number of guards and drivers, so he continued west, past the front of the vehicles. Now he made out several uniformed guards standing beside the farther truck—the one without the trailer—holding AK-47s. One guard was wearing a rain poncho with a hood and had a cigarette clenched in his teeth.

As one of the teenagers passed him, dragging a corpse, the guard kicked the kid in the back so that he stumbled, let go of the body, and fell into the trench. The uniformed man threw his head back and issued a shrill, high laugh that hit Crocker in the face like a Mike Tyson uppercut.

His anger sent him scurrying closer on his hands and knees. The teenagers moved past like zombies, their knees, ribs, and cheekbones sticking out at sharp angles, while the guards with the guns made comments and cracked jokes.

Outrage, disgust, fury, and the conviction that someone had to pay for this motivated him to return the way he had come until he reached the back of the trailerless truck. Waiting until the coast was clear, then scooting under the rear axle, he removed the suppressor from his belt and screwed it into the barrel of the SIG Sauer thinking that his colleagues were far enough away to escape should something happen to him.

Crocker slowly crawled forward, located the legs of the guard wearing the poncho, and came up slowly. He was so close he could hear the guard clearing this throat, then spitting at the back of one of the teenagers.

The girl turned to face the guard. That's when Crocker rose, aimed, and put a bullet in the base of the guard's skull just below the green helmet. His head exploded and he fell forward, the sound drowned out by the noise of the engines. No one seemed to notice. Not even the girl, who turned away with dead eyes and continued pushing the body toward the trench.

The kids did their grim work silently. The rain hissed. Steam rose from the headlights to Crocker's right.

Five more rounds.

He cut down the second guard with a shot between his shoulder blades that tore through his heart.

Four.

The driver of the truck saw the guard slump and leaned out of the cab to see what was going on. Crocker sprang out from under the truck and yanked the driver's leg out from under him so he

275

slipped and hit his head on the metal step. Finished him off with a swipe of his knife across his throat.

Thunder rolled in from the north like a reproach.

Two guards down, one driver.

He skirted around the front of the trailerless truck low to the ground, wet from head to toe, forgetting the smell, where he was, everything except the task in front of him. Crouched near the right front bumper, he saw the back of another guard, his AK propped on his shoulder. Crocker rose, aimed, and squeezed the trigger in one continuous motion.

The bullet entered under the guard's chin and clanged as it hit the top of his helmet. Almost immediately another uniformed man at the front of the second truck lowered his AK and fired. The first shot tore through Crocker's left shoulder and into his collarbone. The second whizzed past his chin as he dove into the man's chest, causing him to fall backward and let go of his AK, which flipped and landed on the back of Crocker's leg. Partly stunned, Crocker reached behind his back and grabbed the barrel as the guard reached for his pistol. Two kids dragging bodies stopped and stared in disbelief as Crocker drove the butt of the AK into the guard's throat.

Behind him he heard footsteps, but was blinded by the headlights. Breathing hard, he circled left around the trailerless truck, then slipped and fell so that the AK he carried slithered into the trench and disappeared in a mound of twisted limbs and torsos. Glimpsing the horror frozen on a dead's woman's face, he decided not to go in after it, and felt for the SIG Sauer in the wet grass instead.

He found it but couldn't remember if it had one round left or two. Covered with mud and blood, he spotted a driver forty feet ahead of him running in the direction of the camp. The rain had picked up, making it harder to gain traction, but Crocker pulled himself up and pushed. Got within twenty feet of the driver, and was trying to aim in the dark when the man turned and fired three shots in succession that barely missed Crocker's head.

He shot back, then slipped and hit the ground with his chin. On his belly, he heard the sound of feet running past. Thought for a second that they belonged to soldiers, then realized it was the young prisoners running away.

Noticing the dark splotch of blood that had traveled all the way down his chest to the top of his pants, he limped back to the trucks. In the glove compartment of the first one he found a Type 54 Chinese military pistol and two egg-shaped Soviet F1 hand grenades. He ripped a web belt from one of the dead guards and tightened it under his arm as a makeshift tourniquet.

Then he hobbled away, hoping the teenagers would find sympathetic countrymen who would take them in and nourish them back to life. It was the best he could manage, he thought, but hardly enough.

Across the field where his colleagues were waiting, Crocker watched Akil smear QuikClot into the wound, then climbed back to his feet and led them south. He refused to answer Akil's questions about what had happened. "No time to talk about that now," was his reply.

Despite his loss of blood, the encounter seemed to fill him with determination. When the sun came up, the four men consumed the last of the rice, rested twenty minutes, and continued past farms and around hills, avoiding roads and any kind of structure, Akil and Crocker carrying the tarp containing Sam, and Dawkins following.

Crocker urged them on. "Faster. As fast as you can." A grim, resolute aspect had come over his face, and his eyes seemed focused on a single objective. The rain proved equally relentless, resulting in slick paths and difficult mud.

Dawkins had no idea how Crocker was able to continue, carrying Sam with his injured right arm and shoulder, but somehow he did. When they stopped, which they did every two hours, he noticed that Crocker had difficulty raising either of his arms above his waist.

They had ample water but no food. Akil suggested that they wait in a forest stretching up a hill while he circled around it and recced.

Crocker refused. "No, no," he said. "We can't stop!"

"Why?"

He offered no reason. He seemed pushed by a relentless will to get to the border and safety, and to report on what he'd seen.

Sometimes he couldn't remember if he was awake or asleep, especially when the sky turned dark and the rain fell in a steady whisper.

In a state of semiconsciousness, he heard Akil call, "Boss! Boss!"

"What now?"

When he opened his eyes and focused, he wondered how much time had passed, because Akil and Dawkins looked older and thinner, and both men's faces were covered with beards.

"Boss, look."

It hurt to even turn his head.

"Where?"

He saw headlights approaching through mist and rain, and was mindful enough to know that this wasn't good. They were in a field with nowhere to hide. Instinctively, he felt for the grenades in his pocket and the pistol in his belt.

Fifty feet ahead was a little brook with a bridge over it. He lifted the tarp and continued walking.

"Boss!"

"Let's go!" Somehow his legs responded and he broke into a sprint. In his right periphery, the headlights rounded the bend and reached the straightaway. The vehicle or vehicles were maybe sixty feet away and closing quickly.

Realizing that if the people in them were paying attention, they could be spotted, he lunged for the embankment and felt his feet slip out from under him. His legs hit water and the tarp holding Sam crashed into his right shoulder. He bit down hard on the urge to scream. In the background he heard an engine idling and music: "Like a Virgin" by Madonna, sung in Korean. When he opened his mouth to comment, Akil slapped a hand over it.

Next thing he remembered, he was on his feet again, walking up an incline. He saw a glowing yellow line in the distance. Wasn't sure whether it was a mirage or not.

"What's that?" It hurt to move his mouth.

"A fence, I think," Akil answered. "Maybe it's the border."

"South Korea?"

"Fucking better be, or..."

"What?"

They left Dawkins and Sam in the bushes behind them and crossed the mist-covered field where rabbits scattered. Helped each other over a patch of gravel and railroad tracks, and stood before a twenty-foot-high fence. Crocker touched it to make sure it was real.

"Nicest thing I've seen in months," Crocker said, emotion building in his chest.

They had no wire shears to cut through the links, only one eight-foot-long thin metal blade that Akil found in the PRS kit and started using.

Crocker asked, "You're kidding, right?"

"You got something better?"

Crocker felt strangely giddy as he looked up at the fencing covered with curls of razor wire. Given his weakened condition, it seemed as challenging as summiting Mount Everest. But somehow he knew there had to be a way to reach the other side and the lighted two-lane strip of concrete road in South Korea.

"Get the tarp and blankets," he said weakly.

He blinked and found himself halfway up the fence, holding on and reaching down for the covers, then tossing them over the razor wire one at a time. Next thing he knew, he was pushing the tarps and blankets down and watching Akil climb over like it was a dream.

But it wasn't. Because when Akil was halfway down the opposite side of the fence and asked, "Now what?" he saw that his smart suit was a shredded rag.

"Wait there," Crocker said.

He hobbled back with Dawkins, who muttered to himself as Crocker and Akil held down the razor wire as best they could and he clambered up and crossed over.

Despite minor cuts to his right thigh and arm, Dawkins didn't complain. He just looked back at Crocker through the fence with tears in his eyes and asked, "Am I really standing in South Korea? Are you sure about that?"

"Sure as I'm standing here," Akil remarked. "You're a free man now."

Crocker tried climbing the fence with Sam on his back, but when he reached the top, the pain in his shoulder was so intense his arms started giving out. They weren't high enough for Akil to reach over.

Seconds after Crocker and Sam returned to the ground, sirens started to wail on their left and right.

"Let me try!" Akil shouted over the sirens, starting up the South Korean side of the fence.

"Fuck that," Crocker replied. "Sam, get on top of my shoulders and we'll pull up together."

"We tried that already…You can't."

"Don't tell me what I can't do!"

Crocker took a deep breath and reminded himself of one of his favorite SEAL mottos: Pain was weakness leaving the body. He didn't care if his body completely gave out. He was going to get Sam over the fence whatever it took, inch by excruciating inch.

All he felt was pain—not his hands on the metal fence, or his legs moving, or Sam atop his shoulders. The only way he could tell he was making progress were the encouraging words from Akil and Dawkins. The siren grew louder, until it sounded like mocking laughter.

"You're getting there!"

"More, boss! Another four feet!"

He felt himself losing consciousness. Pain hammering his head, he willed himself a few links higher. It was just enough for Akil to grab hold of Sam, and help him down.

Still clinging to the fence, Crocker smiled at them on the other side. When he tried to move his arms and legs, however, they wouldn't respond.

"Wait there, boss!" Akil shouted. "I'm coming to get you!"

Crocker knew he couldn't last much longer. Out of his right periphery he saw a vehicle approaching behind him. Swinging his right arm over, he felt a strand of razor wire slice into his forearm. The new pain seemed to cancel out the old. He pushed off on his left leg.

With a reserve of energy he didn't think he had, he swung his weight over and let go, scraping his face along the fence and hitting Akil, who helped break his fall.

Their eyes met and they smiled for a second—a moment he knew he'd never forget.

"We did it, boss," Akil muttered.

"Fuck, yeah."

Warm blood dripping down his wrist and thigh, he stumbled with Akil, Sam, and Dawkins across the road, up an embankment and into a cover of sweet-smelling eucalyptus.

He felt hands reaching under him and sliding his body onto a stretcher. He sat up and reached for the pistol. It wasn't in his belt.

"Hey!"

"Easy. Easy, big guy." A wide grin beamed down at him from the face of an Asian man in military garb. "You can relax now, sir. You're in South Korea."

He wasn't sure whether he was seeing reality or dreaming. "Where's Akil?"

"Sir, my name is Sergeant Minjoon Kim."

"Sergeant Kim, where are my men?"

"Two have already been taken away in the first ambulance. The other is waiting for you."

"Where?"

"Close by. You'll see him soon."

When they slid the stretcher into the ambulance, he saw Akil's heavily bearded face ahead and thought he looked like a terrorist. Didn't realize that he resembled one too, until he saw his reflection in the stainless-steel strip along the side panel.

"We look like shit," he groaned.

"Where are the dancing girls to greet us?"

It hurt to laugh, but he knew exactly how Akil felt.

He still had a duty. He said, "Sergeant Kim, you said my men are okay. I need visual confirmation."

"Sir, you'll see them soon. You can relax now. You're in safe hands."

CHAPTER TWENTY-THREE

Nobody who ever gave his best regretted it.
—George Halas

FOUR DAYS later the smile on James Dawkins's face seemed to permeate his entire being as he walked hand in hand with Nan and Karen down Waikiki Beach in Honolulu, from the Ala Wai Canal to Diamond Head. He didn't want the moment to end. So when they neared the zoo and Nan offered to hail a cab to take them back to the hotel, James declined.

"I think I'd rather walk together."

"Whatever you want, sweetheart."

"Yeah, whatever you want, Daddy," smiling Karen echoed.

"You sure you're not tired?" Nan asked.

He shook his head. "I'm fine."

As they passed the Marriott, Dawkins started to hum the lullaby Sung had taught him.

"What's that?" Nan asked, squinting into the sun.

"When I was on the island, in my deepest despair, the Korean woman who looked after me and made me breakfast sang this song to me. It's about a mother who has to leave her infant alone in their hut so she can go out and search for food."

"It's lovely," Nan said. "Will you teach it to me?"

"Of course. Her name is Sung. She's the one who smuggled out the message to you. I never got a chance to thank her. I hope she's okay."

"Me, too, darling. If there's a way, I think we should try to help her."

"We should try to do that. Yes."

Dawkins didn't know that a week before his escape from Ung-do, Sung had been dismissed from her job and sent back to her family. She was with them now in the farming cooperative of Genjo near the Chinese border. She, too, was happy to be back with her family, her husband and two young sons, but she was apprehensive. Any day State Security Department officers could arrive to take them to one of the country's prison camps. She'd heard rumors about a fire near Munchon but nothing about the attack. Neighbors whispered about large-scale shakeups in the government and arrests.

Now, as Sung sat in the primitive kitchen of their three-room house, she debated whether or not to try to pass a message to her nephew, who had a friend in the North Korean Strategy Center who might be able to smuggle her and her family across the Chinese border. She knew it was a huge risk to take.

The same night Sung was considering her choice, Crocker stepped off the American Airlines flight from Los Angeles. He'd spent so much time in close proximity with Dawkins and his teammates that it felt strange to walk alone from the gate to the baggage area. He carried the few things he'd packed in his duffel—mainly presents for Jenny, Cyndi, and his nieces and nephews. Sam continued to recuperate at U.S. Naval Hospital in Okinawa, and Akil had gone to visit his family in Detroit.

As Crocker approached the terminal exit, he realized that he'd parked his pickup at ST-6 headquarters and would have to hire a cab to take him to his apartment. He walked with a slight limp from the frostbite and a hunched left shoulder that was still bandaged and would take weeks to heal. None of the people around him seemed to notice him, the bandages on his forearm and shoulder, or the scabs on his neck.

Crossing to the automatic doors that led outside, Crocker realized that he hadn't given a thought about what he would do during his month of medical leave. All he could think about was the pleasure of sleeping in his own bed.

After the door slid open, he heard someone call his name. Turning left, he saw a young woman's smiling face and a bouquet of yellow flowers.

He didn't realize they were for him until Jenny threw her hands around his neck and hugged him. "Welcome home, Dad!"

The unexpected greeting brought tears to his eyes. He squeezed her back and remembered how lucky he was to be alive. "Thank you, sweetheart. It's so wonderful to see you. How did you know I was on this flight?"

"Dad, I have ways. I'm your daughter."

"I'm glad."

Standing behind her was another beautiful woman who it took him a few seconds to recognize.

"Cyndi! Wow. I never expected this." He opened his right arm to include her in the embrace and found her lips.

She whispered, "I've been waiting a long time for this, Crocker. We never got to finish our date."

He smiled and said, "Tonight. I promise. I've been waiting a long time, too."

The following afternoon, a Thursday, ten days after he crossed the border to South Korea, Crocker exited the navy clinic with a bounce in his step. A navy doctor had just cleared him to drive up to Fairfax with Cyndi and Jenny to visit his ailing father. As he entered the parking lot, his cell phone rang.

"Where are you, Crocker?" Captain Sutter asked.

He had a shitload of things to take care of—bills to pay, e-mails to answer, people to call, things to take care of around the apartment. But all that could wait. Cyndi had until Saturday before she had to get back to Vegas, which meant two more glorious days and nights together.

"Leaving the clinic and about to get in my truck and head north," he answered.

"You sure you're up to it?"

"Absolutely, sir. A couple of pains and bruises, but I've been through worse." No way he was going to lie in bed recuperating when he could be out hanging with Jenny and Cyndi.

"If you say so, Tarzan. If you're ambulatory, how about you stop by HQ for a minute?"

"Happy to, sir, on Tuesday, when I return."

"It's important, Crocker. You'll find out why when you get here. All it'll take is fifteen minutes tops."

He put the truck in reverse, backed out of the parking spot, and drove a short distance to the ST-6 compound. A couple of SEAL colleagues spotted him in the hallway and welcomed him back. Life was strange. Two weeks ago he was sleeping on the ground, curled up next to a group of foul-smelling men. Last night he'd fallen asleep in the arms of a beautiful woman. The rescue of Dawkins and the escape from North Korea had restored some of his faith. Good did triumph over evil when applied with confidence and intelligence.

Captain Sutter stood to greet him with a big smile on his face. "Damn, Crocker, you look better then I imagined. I hear you really pushed the envelope this time."

Sutter seemed thinner than before. "I did what I had to, sir. Couldn't be avoided."

He'd already heard the sad news that Naylor, Hutchins, and Suarez hadn't made it—which cast a pall over an otherwise successful mission and hostage rescue. Dawkins had invited him over to dinner Sunday night so he could meet his wife and daughter. Sometime after that, he'd stop by Suarez's house in Virginia Beach and visit with his widow and family.

He wasn't looking forward to it, nor had it really sunk in that he'd lost another teammate. For the next couple of days he wanted to focus on the good, including the news that Davis wasn't facing a court-martial for assaulting Vice Admiral Greene. Crocker got a kick out of that, and would thank Davis when he had a chance.

"Sit down, Crocker," Sutter said. "Someone important wants to thank you."

At some point he'd call his brother and sister and try to explain where he'd been.

"Who's that?" he asked.

He recognized the president's warm, deep voice as soon as it came through the speakerphone but thought that maybe it was a prank.

"Chief Warrant Crocker, I can't tell you how proud I am of you and your men, and humbled by the courage you showed in North Korea and the sacrifices you made for your country. I just got off the phone with James Dawkins, and I can tell you that he and his family are extremely grateful, too."

He sure sounded like the real thing. "Thank you, Mr. President." Crocker flashed back to the teenagers in rags dragging dead bodies.

"I hear from your commander that you're not a man who goes in much for fanfare or awards, and I respect the need to protect your identity from the public. But I don't feel that thanking you this way does you justice. So I'm wondering if you would accept an invitation to visit me at the White House tomorrow morning shortly after eleven so I can thank you in person."

"I'd be honored, sir. I want to tell you about some of the things I saw there. But there's a problem. I won't be able to make it until after one, because I want to spend some time with my father first. He's recovering from open-heart surgery. "

"Oh. How's he progressing?" the president asked.

"Very well, sir, from what I hear. Thank you for asking."

"Please send him my regards and let me know if there's anything I can do for him."

"I appreciate that, Mr. President. I will, sir."

"So I'll see you tomorrow, sometime after one p.m., here at the White House?"

"You will, Mr. President. Thank you for the invitation, and I look forward to meeting you."

"Me too, Chief Warrant Crocker. And if your family is with you, feel free to bring them, too."

"Thank you, Mr. President."

The president hung up, and Crocker turned to Captain Sutter, who was standing and looking at him with a wry smile on his face.

"Did I just hear you tell the president, who is arguably the most powerful man on the planet, that you had to postpone your visit with him because you're going to see your father first?" Sutter asked.

"I suppose you did, sir."

"Jesus, Crocker, you're something else."

ACKNOWLEDGMENTS

You can't keep a series like this alive and vital without the help of a number of hard-working and very talented individuals. They start with our agents, Heather Mitchell at Gelfman Schneider and Eric Lupfer at William Morris Endeavor, and include a whole team of people at Mulholland Books / Little, Brown— Wes Miller, Pamela Brown, Ben Allen, Chris Jerome, Katharine Myers, Nicole Dewey, and others. In terms of day-to-day support, we're supremely grateful to our families. Don wants to thank his father, who quit high school on December 7, 1941, the day Pearl Harbor was attacked, enlisted in the U.S. Navy, and served throughout the war. After retiring, he devoted his time toward helping veterans through the DAV and the VFW organizations. And Ralph wants to acknowledge his lovely wife, Jessica, and children, John, Michael, Francesca, and Alessandra. As for inspiration, we get that from the men and women in the SEAL teams and other agencies of government who do the kind of work we describe in these books. Thank you for your service!

ABOUT THE AUTHORS

DON MANN (CWO3, USN) has for the past thirty years been associated with the U.S. Navy SEALs as a platoon member, assault team member, boat crew leader, and advanced training officer, and more recently as program director preparing civilians to go to BUD/S (SEAL Training). Until 1998 he was on active duty with SEAL Team Six. Since then, he has deployed to the Middle East on numerous occasions in support of the war against terrorism. Many of today's active-duty SEALs on Team Six are the same men he taught how to shoot, conduct ship and aircraft takedowns, and operate in urban, arctic, desert, river, and jungle warfare, as well as close-quarters battle and military operations in urban terrain. He has suffered two cases of high-altitude pulmonary edema, frostbite, a broken back, and multiple other broken bones in training or service. He has been captured twice during operations and lived to talk about it.

RALPH PEZZULLO is a *New York Times* bestselling author and an award-winning playwright and screenwriter. His books include *Jawbreaker* and *The Walk-In* (with former CIA operative Gary Berntsen), *At the Fall of Somoza, Plunging into Haiti* (winner of the Douglas Dillon Award for Distinguished Writing on American Diplomacy), *Most Evil* (with Steve Hodel), *Eve Missing,* and *Blood of My Blood.* His nonfiction book about the shadowy world of private military contracting with former British Special Forces commando Simon Chase, *Zero Footprint,* was published by Little, Brown earlier this year.

If you have enjoyed *Hunt the Fox*, why not catch up on Thomas Crocker and SEAL Team Six's earlier adventures?

SEAL Team Six: Hunt the Wolf

WWhen the team learn that young girls are going missing all over Europe, they are determined to track down the ruthless men behind the kidnappings. But as they follow the trail they uncover a web of terrorist cells with more terrifying ambitions than they could ever have imagined.

SEAL Team Six: Hunt the Scorpion

A series of attacks all over the globe are linked by a single, deadly intent: someone is gathering everything they need to make a dirty bomb. The terrorists behind it are shadows; their targets unknown. Thomas Crocker and his team need answers.

SEAL Team Six: Hunt the Falcon

The team's number one enemy, Iranian terrorist Farhed Alizadeh, codename 'the Falcon', resurfaces as the mastermind behind a series of attacks on American diplomats across the globe. Crocker and his men are ordered to bring him to justice.

SEAL Team Six: Hunt the Jackal

When a Senator's wife and teenage daughter are kidnapped, Crocker and SEAL Team Six are sent to the cities of Mexico and the jungles of South America.

SEAL Team Six: Hunt the Fox

After a training exercise in Las Vegas is interrupted, Crocker and SEAL Team Six find themselves drawn into a North Korean plot that combines cyber warfare and the theft of black market nuclear weapons.

All available in print and e from Mulholland Books

MULHOLLAND
BOOKS
HODDER